MW00614403

ALSO BY JAMES L. PETERS

Turntable

SHRUGGING

James L. Peters

Six by 9 Publishing

Second Edition

LIBRARY OF CONGRESS
CATALOGING-IN-PUBLICATION DATA:

Peters, James L.

Shrugging / James L. Peters

ISBN 978-1-7366098-3-5

Printed in Wisconsin, United States of America

Set in Aldine 401 BT Type

To Sharon ~

Your friendship, wisdom and talent was my guiding
hand down the path of this story—around the edge of
the abyss and into the light.

Part One
THE THREAD

-29

Twenty-nine years, eleven months, three days, and Jack still can't think of one good reason why he should end the world.

But he does know for sure that this morning is a corn flake morning, not oatmeal.

Pretty sure.

Because he remembers having to open up a new box of oatmeal yesterday, and he had torn open the wrong end so he couldn't close it back up. It had to go in the cupboard with those flaps sticking straight up.

Or was that two days ago?

Odd-numbered weeks are hell on an alternating routine. Who does he blame for the seven-day week, anyway? It doesn't allow for a consistent oatmeal Monday and corn flake Tuesday. Come the following week, he's standing on the beige, speckled linoleum of his narrow kitchen trying to remember if he had corn flakes or oatmeal yesterday.

It's not like the world would come to an end if he had corn flakes two days in a row, though, would it?

Well, only if he wants it to.

But he's not a kid anymore. Nothing is a world-ender as an adult. Terrible things happen, people die, and the world doesn't end. As a kid, everything was catastrophic; the inevitable mortification at bat in gym class, the frantic scrub and futile buff of the scratched back quarter panel of his parents' Chrysler after he caught it with the lawnmower, the third day without a call from Christina Regitz as he laid on his bed hitching a ride with Floyd to the *Dark Side of the Moon*.

Existence hung in the balance then. Every single day.

Jack tears open the new box of corn flakes and realizes all at once that, one, he *had* eaten corn flakes yesterday because he remembers finishing off the box, which is why he's opening the new one now, and two, that he is, absurdly, opening the damn box from the wrong end.

He's committed to the cereal now. His paradigm is wired for lightly toasted, crispy flakes of corn.

To hell with the routine. He pours a Corningware bowl full of flakes and dowses them in still-fresh-for-two-days skim milk. Four steps to the living room and the TV is on. He eats his cereal, drinks his coffee, watches the news. His chewing annoys him; he can't hear the droning of the anchorwoman. Should have had the oatmeal.

Clatter and clink of bowl and spoon against the stainless steel sink. Water runs like hissing static from the tap. Jacket snatched from the back of the chair, he drinks his last swallow of coffee too fast and leaves the apartment for the outside stoop to have his first smoke of the morning.

The match flares after the second strike and he draws deep on the cigarette, sucking in his failure to quit this goddamn habit. Until six months ago, he had managed to extract it from his routine for three years. He exhales to the sky, and the question, *that* question, still lingers like the monoxide cloud around him. He's thinking about it too much, and there's no point. It never solved anything, and it won't now. But it's part of him, the order of the day. Get up, make coffee, brush teeth, shower, eat, smoke, and wonder if today should be the day he ends the world.

On this morning, this corn flake-amended Friday oatmeal morning, the question sounds like a goad, and Jack zips up his coat to the neck against the early morning October chill and recalls the First Rule, established long ago.

Never end the world based on a personal condition or emotion.

Jack watches the cars pass by on this old, tired street and thinks that, maybe, tomorrow he should have eggs for breakfast.

"Jack, I need that layout for the trade show ad by three o'clock." Rick doesn't bother to enter Jack's cubicle; he leans in, keeping those office outback boots that sprout from his pressed jeans behind the invisible border of the open doorway.

Jack swivels his chair to meet Rick's split-rock face. "That ad has been on your desk for two days. All I need is for you to look it over and fill in the blanks."

Rick's jaw slackens, eyes drift. "I don't have anything on my desk."

Jack spins back to his monitor. "I'll print out another copy."

"I don't have anything on my desk."

"You will in two minutes."

"Thanks, Jack." Amicable condescension, implying all blame is and ever will be shifted to Jack and that Jack should just accept this. Rick walks away.

The smell of sour cologne and old ashtray lingers in Jack's partitioned space and he has to remind himself of The Second Rule: *Never end the world based on the actions of, or the personal feelings for, an individual.*

Jack minimizes his current project on the screen and finds the trade ad file—a seven-piece dark cherry Mission-style dining room over the subtle watermark of the Templeton Furniture logo. Blocks of color in random placement to salvage the dead layout.

His eyes narrow to the headline he was forced to use. "Let Templeton warehouse your product, and you can reap the profit." Straight from the asshole of Rick's mouth. He clicks 'Print.'

He has to wonder if Rick's job is really as vital as he seems to think it is, as if lives are at stake. One paycheck. One life. That's what is at stake. Rick's own. Jack used to design marketing materials to sell furniture. Now, he and Greg and Samantha lay out schemes to placate vice presidents so Rick can save his own ass.

His vision narrows to the screen and the image breaks down; the solid maple of table into individual pixels, the pixels into red and green and blue points of light. Between these points, emptiness. Within those spaces between the points, his career.

What's he really doing here? Creating things that don't exist. Artists work with charcoal, oils, watercolor. They apply substance to canvas. Creativity transferred into a tangible, textured medium. He only instructs electricity to emit light to form an illusion of substance. And the illusion created is a con within a con, the promise of instant profits to some mom and pop furniture store if they carry the Templeton product line. All this will lead to a transaction, likely digital, of tiny bits of data representing a monetary concept.

Christ. What a big, expensive sweater life is, knitted knots of intricate patterns. But roll it up, look underneath, and it's all loose, dangling threads. Sometimes, the temptation to yank a thread is so bad his leg twitches.

The inkjet printer sputters one last pass and spits out the trade show ad. Viola. The modern age of impersonal art—without ever touching brush or pen to page, without any intimate stroke upon the canvas, he holds his completed work like a parent who has passed his children to nurse maids and nannies and boarding schools only to say, "I'm so proud," when his progeny return as adults.

Jack snaps up, swipes the ad from the printer, and leaves his cubicle, walking down the hall past sales offices to Rick's corner office. The marketing director's desk is strewn with leather and cloth swatches over and under umpteen different trade magazines and printouts of Power Point presentations. Jack places the ad precisely over the copy of the ad he had put on the desk two days before, then leaves.

It's one minute to five. The computer screen has been a blurry blob of light for the last hour. He's calling it.

"Hey." Sam peeks her head in, meaty hands wrapped around the edge of his partition wall, black Harley jacket a continual creak of leather. "You're stopping by Snappy's, right?" The flare of eyes from wind-worn skin threatening to crack her youth with its first motherly wrinkle tells him not to mistake her inflection at the end—this is *not* a question, mister.

There's nothing appealing tonight about Snappy's ambience of treated lumber and sour lager odor, the crunch of peanut shells underfoot that season the plywood floor. Small town Carrington digging its elbows in at the bar. He suffers the place because Greg and Sam go there.

Beer went down a little too good last Friday. It mixed with some quiet discontent, roiled into a rant, and within an hour two sets of annoyed eyes were a mute response to his comments about "selling crappy furniture to crappy stores who sell it to customers to decorate their crappy lives" and condemnations of all their work being "pointless." Some ineffective backpedaling only dug a deeper hole and it was made extremely clear to him that putting food on the table and a roof over the head of family was anything but pointless. He drove the hour-long trip home to Terrapin still wearing the wince of apology.

He powers down his computer and rolls back his chair. "I don't think I'm going to be able to make it."

She lets go of the partition, comes into full view, bulk of coat not quite hiding her stout build. Bottom lip peels down in a pout.

Jack stands up and slips into his jacket, looking all around Sam and not at all at her. "Oh, please. Not the pout."

Greg's head of gray hair pokes up well over the cubicle walls, each one of the deep creases kneading his forty-something face likely a Templeton service award. "Oh, Christ. She pouting?"

"Jack's ditching us. He doesn't like us anymore. Bastard."

Greg rests his chin on the molding cap of the six-foot half-wall and peers down. "Jack. Get your ass to Snappy's."

Jack zips up his windbreaker. "Sorry, guys. This ass is heading home." He stops in front of Sam, who doesn't budge.

"You have to listen to Greg," she says. "He's your supervisor."

"It's one minute past five. I'm free of Greg's oppression until eight o'clock Monday morning. So, do I climb over you or are you going to let me pass?"

Greg laughs. "Stay there, Sam. I gotta see this."

Sam gives up her ground. "You're a big bummer, Jack."

"Listen, I'd love to join you guys, really. I'm just tired. It's been a rough week with High Point Market. Next time for sure, okay?"

"Yeah, yeah," Sam says. "Guess I'll just pick on Greg all night instead."

Greg snorts and pulls away from the wall. "Son of a... Thanks, Jack."

"My pleasure."

The two of them head down the hall, Sam calling out from the door, "Have a better one, Jack."

Silence pushes against his ears, and he's sluggish leaving the empty office.

-28

He's a bastard to himself as he drives the fifty miles home down the bland rural highway. He keeps calling himself crazy. One crazy son of a bitch.

What a relief if that could be true. Lie on a stupid couch twice a week babbling on about his bizarre ability to the cool empathy of a psychiatrist. A pill three times a day to keep the emptiness away. He certainly could be crazy; he has to allow himself that.

The best he had ever done for himself was when he simply discarded the Shrug. Don't acknowledge it, don't deliberate it. He managed to do that for the better part of a decade. He never actually doubted it or denied it. That was the big mistake of trying to dismiss it. No, if anything, he had convinced himself even more of its existence, to the degree that he wouldn't allow argument over it. By accepting it, he could then move on and ask the real question—what did it matter?

A good question. When he had locked down on the basic truth that, even if the Shrug was real, he had absolutely no need or desire to use it, he was able to dismiss the entire concept out of logic. Real or not, he simply wasn't interested, therefore he wouldn't allow it to be a factor in his life.

He had focused on college, then on work, and shaped a respectable life. When the Shrug did slink up and nuzzle him like a lonely cat, he would give it an absent scratch behind the ears and set it aside.

Why can't he do that anymore?

Sometimes, the harder he tries to avoid it, the more it surprises him, like that step down he forgets about when he leaves the apartment building—a sudden, unexpected drop, and it's there, like he's swallowing himself in a free fall.

There is one very simple way to find out if he's crazy. He could do it. He could let himself fall into that thick black thought and let it take him.

The bitter irony is that he would still never *know* if he was crazy or not, because he would cease to exist, along with everyone and everything else, before he could witness the irrefutable proof that would follow.

Unless nothing happened.

Unless the world remained.

Then he would know. Irrefutably.

More than anything else, it has been this one reason that has tempted him. It could be the only way to finally forget this whole business and remove the Shrug from his life forever.

Rule Number Three: *Never end the world only to prove that you can.*

It didn't matter, anyway. For him to actually do that, he would have to believe that it isn't real. He wouldn't risk it otherwise.

And so, the world remains. But so does the question: Regardless of his feelings, is he supposed to use it? Is that why he has it?

Now there is a question he really doesn't like at all.

Produce is depressing. He hates being around the fruits and vegetables, the melons and leaf lettuce. No other aspect of shopping makes him so conscious of being a singular shopper. One box of mac and cheese is just like another. Rice-a-Roni and Hamburger Helper may offer variety, but always with absolute consistency. No husband and wife, boyfriend and girlfriend, or pair of roommates will ever deliberate over the best-looking, ripest Hungry Man dinner box.

Apples and melons, onions and peppers—they beg for scrutiny and opinion and discussion. They're intended to be selected only after an intense, paneled discussion. Right over there, an old wispy-haired woman is holding up a Yukon Gold potato to her hunched and pinch-eyed husband looking for tuberose approval. As it is, Jack only has himself to blame when his honeydew isn't soft and sweet or his oranges are tart.

Yet, he forces himself to the produce isles because a single man normally bypasses it. He doesn't want to be that way. He can't. Maybe the average guy can withstand a frozen, packaged life, but for Jack, that's dangerous. That's one step closer to the Shrug.

Recipes—the creation of a new, unique whole from pre-selected component parts. The entire act of cooking is contrary to the Shrug. If only he was any good at it.

He brushes aside inordinately large green peppers for one of modest proportions and bags it. On to red onions, shuffling through sad brown skins and soft gray spots, until finally his hand wraps around one of decent reddish hue that is firm but not hard. Bag it. Cart it. Roll on.

Passing the liquor department, his eyes wander, but only briefly, and he passes it without incident. Alcohol must be social only. No beer, no spirits, ever keep a place in his cupboard or on his counter. Solitary inebriation is the very essence of the Shrug. Even this—the deliberate thoughts that follow his actions and restate his motives is part of the routine denial of the Shrug. It's not a matter of trying to convince himself, but continual reinforcement and moral support. The conscious mind with its inner monologue is a 'Yes' man to the self, affirming everything he does regardless of the need to do so.

Shopping is fast, efficient and without complication. Never a thought wasted when the routine—rigid and foolproof—dictates such precise ingredients. Waiting in line to check out, he scans the periodicals, learns about some starlet's struggle with cellulite and a silver screen royalty's battle with pancreatic cancer. Eyes scan lower, to the bottom racks, to doomsday cries of plague and famine and the latest scheduled return of Jesus and the Millennium. He'll be a no-show. Again. He always is. If only the millions of *Globe* readers realized that, twenty-nine years ago, Christ subsidized the Apocalypse. Jack Cross is on the job—less fuss. No muss.

And if his milk spoils yet again before the expiration date, it just might happen.

There's no disappointment as he turns away from the periodicals without finding what he looks for. Disappointment cannot be so regularly expected and planned. Disappointment involves some degree of hope. Jack has none. Yet, he always looks for that one headline, the bold sans-serif type that would tell him perhaps he is not crazy, that he isn't alone. But just as Christ is not walking the canned goods aisle cracking seals and unleashing plagues, so is there no headline declaring, "Utah Man Claims Ability to End Existence with a Thought!"

The worst part of it is, would he really feel any satisfaction if he did read that?

Absolutely not. His one cold comfort has always been, if someone must have the Shrug, better it be him.

Often he thinks this. He thinks it always only after asking himself countless times why it couldn't be anyone but him.

The world of Taledrial. A land rent in two ages ago when the dwarven king Cyggthul Ragdall, tired of the rampages by humans and elves against his people, met the armies of his enemies on the Hystarian Wastes with his own forces and brought the Staff of Vyst'tel down upon the line of battle. The Chasm of Krak-rath'ruun was formed, dividing the dwarven lands from the other races by a treacherous sea. He tore his world asunder to save his people. On this world Jack walks, not as himself, but as Orson the Sorcerer.

An entirely different reality teeming with life in bits and bytes of data on some cycling hard drive somewhere in the UK. Through the monitor glass, the vistas of another world radiate, entered by whim and exited with the simple click of a button.

He likes Orson, even if the sorcerer's apprentice is maybe too much like himself. Jack has never been able to role-play extravagant characters. But Orson is disciplined and skilled in the arts of his magic, and Jack likes the confidence and certainty that Orson can exude in this alternate world.

He maneuvers Orson into the Four Corners, a tavern at the crossroads of main highways in the north, a starting point for many great adventures. Often, the Four Corners teems with players chattering about adventures taken or still to come. Tonight, the tavern is empty save for a lone figure sitting at a corner booth. Silver-haired and almond-eyed, the elven warrior is stoic.

He types at the keyboard. "Ca'drannia, greetings. Any luck on the quest for Vyst'tel's Staff?"

"None. The bastard god's foul stick stays out of reach. But, Xaneth and Dunidun are to meet me here shortly with news I hope to be enlightening. We shall see."

"Perhaps," he types, "the staff is beyond us now. Perhaps it does not want to be found."

"If that cursed Asterrak is looking for it, then for certain it is somewhere. I would sooner be flayed open upon the altars of Ghuul-Drae than to allow that abominable dark elf to get his hands upon it. All of Teladrial would fall to his darkness then."

He switches to a private channel and types quick words to her. "Where u been hiding?"

Another monologue of noble indignation spills across the screen from Ca'drannia, then an answer in the green text of private messaging. "Snagged me a hot rock star. Gettin down like a slutty groupie. Fun. ;)"

"Who???"

"His name's Frig."

"???"

":)"

Ca'drannia—noble elf warrior, defender of the weak and downtrodden, enforcer of righteousness and purity. By day, Liz—a crass, brazen vixen.

He can expect no less from his sister.

He also expects that Len, if he doesn't already know about this, will have a hard time with the news should he find out. The poor dope has been toking on the nicotine of Liz for eight years and still hasn't figured out where his nagging hack of frustration has come from.

Liz and Len. He stopped trying to figure those two out long ago. Their tumultuous two-year relationship ended eight years ago. As far as Jack could tell, the cement of that relationship had been their mutual enjoyment of sitting around drinking—or smoking weed when they had it—while listening to new wave and post-punk eighties bands like The Cure and Depeche Mode and role-playing fantasy games. Which of them came up with the crazy idea of traveling all around North America in Liz's '78 Impala Jack didn't know, but it only took a few weeks of rough living on the road before they turned the Impala around in Nevada and drove straight home.

Len moved out as soon as they got back and Liz needed a roommate. Jack had been two weeks from graduation and aching to get out from under the parental roof, so he tossed everything he owned—well, mostly his parent's furniture—into and on top of his station wagon and moved in with her. After a few months of cooling off, Liz and Len somehow managed to remain friends, as long as they could avoid being themselves to each other as much as possible.

Another message burns bright green. "Time for another Lollapalooza."

"Count me in."

"Sun nite?"

"I'll be there."

-27

He's worried about his mother. He looks at the house from the driveway, where once a family of five filled rooms and filed down the hallways in line for the bathroom and for bag lunches before school. He recalls none of that, of course. He was the late-comer; the mid-life surprise to his parents when they had patted a six-year-old Liz off to first grade for what they thought was a last time duty as parents. Then Jack had killed the proverbial rabbit.

That house is empty now, save for his mother. No more children, and as of less than a year ago, no husband. Only memories framed and hung upon the walls of her children moving on, living their own lives. The reminders of once having a husband by what remains of his life—the deck above the garage, the bay window of the living room, the front porch and the brick walkway, the terraced front yard. All those things he sweated and muscled into existence that now outlive him. They are reminders that she had someone to think for her and solve daily problems.

That's what she had wanted, and why she seems to resent each new day, or at least be exhausted by them. Had his father stripped the independence from his mother by being the perpetual decision-maker? Or had she forced that role upon him? Probably a bit of both. That's why they came together with the sharp snap of tightly-fitting pieces. They filled each other's gaps and found comfortable niches for their prominent personalities.

She's alone now, accompanied by failing health and failing hopes. By all appearances, she only bides her time—for a visit from one of her kids, for Sunday mass, for the next meal, the next errand, the next problem.

Or is this just what Jack sees because he can't imagine it being any other way?

Lately, a visit to his mom is like doing laundry or cleaning the apartment—get it done right away, then kick back for the rest of the weekend. He doesn't plan to stay long—he'll mow the lawn and fix yet another computer problem. Forty-five minutes feels right tonight; a three-quarter cupful of obligation, leveled off by a straight-edged scrape of tolerance. He needs to be in the right mindset for her. Right now, he definitely isn't.

Jack shuts off his station wagon, steps out of the car and walks up to the door beside the garage. It bothers him that he feels the need to knock, but he does it because to do otherwise feels wrong.

"Hello?" He steps inside and climbs the half-flight of stairs that lead to the kitchen.

"In here." Two simple words, spoken with an inflection that could just as effectively be applied to, "I surrender."

Jack follows her voice to the living room where Dorothy Cross sits in her recliner wearing that eternal, red floral muumuu, watching TV and playing solitaire on a folding tray stand. Her round face scrutinizes a card pinched between fingers, looking for where to play it. Some Hallmark movie grapples for heartstrings on the television set. She doesn't pay any attention to the screen.

"How's it going?" Jack sits on the couch facing the bay window.

"Oh, fine. That new medication they gave me is finally helping the emphysema a bit."

"That's good."

"'Course, it's making me awfully constipated."

"Oh, no." He knows far too much about his mother's biologics.

"It sucks getting old," She says this all the time—old lady hip talk tied in a bow with self pity. She sets a nine of hearts down on a column.

"Yeah. Seems to."

"Have you talked to your sister lately?" She's casting her line, letting her baited hook dance and dangle.

"I haven't seen Liz for a bit, but we've messaged each other."

"She has a new boyfriend." The edged lilt is a clear expression of her feelings.

"So I've heard."

"He's a guitar player in a rock band."

"At least he has a skill."

"If you can call anything related to that type of music a *skill*." A queen is reunited with her king. "He has a tattoo."

"So?"

"I'm just saying…"

He's an avid student of his mother, knows where this is going, and deflects the subject. "So, are Tony, Christine and Ben still planning to come?"

"Oh yeah." Her response is tired, surely anticipating the toil of playing host to a houseful of people. "And the kids. They'll just sit around the whole weekend watching that horrible MTV."

He had almost been hoping they wouldn't make it. By the time he was eight, there was only him and Liz. His brothers and oldest sister were more like distant uncles and aunt than siblings. Ben is in Illinois, Tony in Minneapolis. They visit once or twice a year. Christine's in Oregon. Jack sees her maybe three times a decade. He's a single guy in an apartment and, other than Liz, his siblings all have homes and families. He can't claim the rank of full adult around them. When they visit, after the initial "hello" and "what's new," the conversation inevitably dies. He hates the particularly itchy silences of family.

It's different with Liz. Six years older than him, and too many times he feels like the older brother. They haven't always been close—Liz hadn't been close to anybody when she rampaged through her teens—but after that disastrous North American romp with Len when Jack moved in with her, they found that somehow, at the extremes of their differences, they tempered each other, kind of like sand paper to soft wood.

"Is Liz bringing this new boyfriend of hers?" he asks.

Her eyes roll. "Oh, I'm sure she'll bring Frig."

"Frig." He says it because it because he hasn't had a chance to speak it out loud yet. Frig. It sounds like a vulgar fruit.

"That's his name. Frig. It's a nickname, I guess. Something to do with that music. I don't *know* his real name." She crumples her face and leans in. "It's probably sexual."

Jack exhales. "I don't think so, Mom."

She reclines back again, returning to the cards with a petulant energy. "Oh, everything with that music is *sexual*."

She's on a tangent now, in her zone, and ruminates about this new generation's music, about politics, family, and religion. Jack lets her roll and grabs a photo album from under the coffee table. As his mother rambles, he flips through it with distraction. He turns to the pictures of his father from before Jack was born. An image of his father courting Jack's then young, slim mother with her long black hair that decades ago had been chopped down to a close, masculine cut; a snapshot of his dad holding a one year old Ben, radiating fatherly pride; a group shot of his father, Ben, Tony, Christine, and Liz just a newborn on his mother's lap, all posing on the couch. His father, right there, at a point in time before Jack existed when now his father doesn't exist.

And that's what really troubles him. His father isn't dead. His father *died*. It was a singular event. In a jagged splinter of time less than a year ago, Jack watched his father exhale his last rattling breath. 'Is' no longer applies to Walter Cross. No condition can be assigned him. He cannot *be* dead. He can only *have* died. His father simply doesn't exist now, and that thought pushes up against his throat.

"Father Karrigan asked about you." His mother has cycled through the deck and now runs through it again, one card at a time.

"Oh?" He closes the photo album and returns it to the coffee table.

"He said he hasn't seen you in church since Walt died. I said, 'That can't *be*. That would be…a *year!*'" She pauses, staring at Jack. "But you know, I think he may be right."

"Mom—"

"Are you ever going to come with me to mass again?"

"I've been busy. It's hard."

"So you just don't believe anymore, is that it?" She has set her cards down.

Jack looks out the window. The station wagon beckons with those wide-eyed headlights. "I don't know if I really want to talk about this."

"Well, why not? We're just talking. Can't you talk to your mother?"

Not about this. He takes a deep breath. "It's complicated, okay? I really don't know what I believe anymore."

"Oh, you always make things complicated. What's complicated?"

He'll take it too far, he's sure of it, and then he won't find his way back. But his mom will keep badgering him, as she's done every time he's been over. "It was a lot easier when I was a kid. It made sense then. My God, in my world."

"Well, nothing's changed but you."

Sure. He grew up, found out that the world wasn't his, and neither was God. All these wonderful sentiments about having a creator love and care for him was what he wanted to believe, because then everything would make sense and everything could be all right.

He would see all those people in church, watch them pray for their sick grandparents and sick friends, praying for their jobs, their safety, their prosperity, and all he saw were people who never grew up. Still thinking God was theirs and He drops whatever

He's doing to take their hand and lead them through every problem. As long as they're good, and do what they're told, they'll get the big double-scoop ice cream cone of divine blessing and a pat on the head.

What would they think if they knew their God had given him the power to end everything?

"I outgrew it. I can't believe what I don't feel, Mom."

His mom is quiet and still other than a slight, persistent nod of her head. She starts to pick up her cards again, but leaves them be. "So religion is childish."

"I'm not saying that. I'm just saying how I feel."

"Fine. Then you're saying that you personally feel that religion is childish."

"I'm just trying to tell you that when I try to believe, I only feel...empty."

"Oh my." TV tray cast aside, she hefts herself up with a small tremor of short legs and shuffles to the kitchen. "It's just a shame you have nothing to help you through the tough times. They'll come, don't you doubt it. I wouldn't have gotten through losing your father without my faith to hold me up." She opens the refrigerator.

Jack follows her, taking a position safely behind the island. "That's good. I'm not saying there's anything wrong with that."

She takes out an all-too-familiar lime-green ceramic bowl from the fridge, plastic wrap flapping off its lip. Her tuna salad. He honestly cannot remember anything other than her tuna salad being in it. "Do you want some lunch?" She sets it on the island, then grabs two bowls from the cupboard.

"No. Thanks, but I should get that lawn mowed."

"Oh, garsh, yes. It's supposed to rain later today, you know." She holds out a bowl to Jack. "You sure you don't want any?"

He nods, shifts in place. "Mom, you're not...disappointed with me, are you?"

She draws the bowl to her chest and cradles it tight. "No, Jack. Goodness, no. I'm just sad. For you. You make me think about your father, what he must have gone through…in the end. I always thought somehow I could turn him around. Enough times at church, with the family, and he'd see the truth. Silly, I suppose. Egotistical. I don't know. But, the last thing I'd ever believe is that he's damned for not believing. If anyone deserves Heaven, it's Walt." Her eyes shimmer and widen. "But, to think of what he must have faced in the end—no comfort, no hope. No expectations." His mother's eyes shut, and Jack's vision blurs. "Just…fear. Loss. I can't bear it sometimes. *That* must have been the closest thing to hell your father *ever* experienced."

Images threaten that he never wanted in his head, and he locks on to the first thought he can, anything to keep that particular memory dark and vague. And the old thought is there, right where he's always left it, where it's always been. Just as dark, but so much more comfortable—numbing. He can't go there, no, can't let it take him, but he can nuzzle against it, rest on it, float on its surface.

Her breath hitches and she coughs, thin and dry. A few deep breaths bring back her composure. "It might be silly, but I really do believe that the fear he must have faced at the end is sort of a price to pay for someone without faith to get into Heaven. Maybe it's God's way of demonstrating what it's like without Him so those without faith will accept Him gladly." He's pierced by her look; a serrated edge of motherly love.

Jack can't think of anything to say, and settles on the fact that saying nothing could be the smartest thing he's done for a while, so instead he just adds a soft smile to his stupid nod and leaves to mow the lawn before the rain.

God can't exist because he exists. He and God are mutually exclusive. It's an elementary equation. Were God to exist, why would He give Jack the ability to end existence? To annihilate God Himself with a thought?

Can't explain that to his mom, though, can he?

It was so easy, when he was young, to play the secret identity of a comic book hero. Wear the colored cape of a special power under his clothing and hold a secret tight. He didn't know any better then. Now, he finds only meaninglessness in it. Every aspect of his life is a numerical value being multiplied by this thing, which has a value of zero.

In one month, he'll be thirty. How's that for a numerical value? It has a zero in it, that hole of a number—an unblinking eye of appraisal. One year older, but he doesn't feel it. Everything around him just seems more weathered and worn.

And he's tired of listening to himself think.

Part Two
THE BUTTON

-26

He'd sleep in if he could, but his body is calibrated for the weekday eight-to-five. With his hour commute, that means up at 5:45am so he can be out the door just before seven. He always has every intention of staying up until midnight on Fridays and Saturdays, watch old movies and sleep in the next morning. By 11pm, though, he's drifting in and out, groggy head playing deranged editor, wondering if Ilsa has left Casablanca yet, if the young couple in the cemetery have transit papers, and where the hell did all the zombies come from?

So, Sunday morning and 5:45am.

Wake up, make coffee, brush teeth, shower.

Definitely a cornflake Sunday.

He kicks back on the couch, a calm and casual coast into Sunday, to watch whatever recycled entertainment is playing on the tube. He flicks past some infomercials and, lacking any ambition for good entertainment, stops on the first non-advertisement he finds—Bond weekend on the Superstation.

He's seen this one, many times, but he has no clue which Bond movie it is. Could be any one of them, really. Q is talking Bond through the gadgets he's installed in the Aston Martin and being really petulant about it. But it's Roger Moore in the double-O tuxedo, so that narrows it down. Jack starts to feel contempt watching Q be petulant to Bond's smugness. Fact is, Jack always thinks he likes these movies until he watches them.

It was Mark Bennings who had been so enamored by the gentleman spy. He owned all the movies and too often Jack would be on the sofa with him, drinking Busch light and delivering running commentaries with Mark through each quip and stunt of the British agent.

He hasn't thought about his old roommate for a while. Mark had been just what Jack needed after finally fleeing Liz's excessive lifestyle that had become too comfortable and easy for Jack. Mark was high-strung but low-key, organized, head always angled up to the next rung on his ladder. Jack would have never passed his physics classes without Mark's help. Unwittingly, he had also become Jack's sounding board for playing out theories on the Shrug. An offhand statement about the Heisenberg Uncertainty Principle, or on the natures of dimensional space and subatomic forces, and Mark would whirl with a tornado of refutations against Jack's 'implausible theories based more on sci-fi than sci-fact.' In the end, Jack gave up devising a definitive theory of the Shrug.

A letter of acceptance from Texas A & M sent Mark packing and moving out a year later, onward to a future of supercharged particle collisions and cracking open the universal cookie to find an equational fortune to grand unification. And so Jack began his solitary life.

He was sad to see Mark go, yet quickly lost touch with him. Liz, on the other hand, said good riddance. Mark annoyed the hell out of her. An elementary conclusion, though not to Mark He brimmed over with achievement, sloshed success that spattered her like spilt coffee. He had also been racked with infatuation for Liz, and for all his quantum knowledge, he was maimed and crippled by social adolescence around her. Mark never had a chance.

Bond gives one final smarmy comment to Q, and Q emphatically reminds bond that, whatever he does, do not push the red button on the shift stick.

The Button.

It always boils down to the Button.

Why build a button just to *not* push it? There must be some occasion or situation when it must be pushed. But *when?* And by *who?*

One thing is for sure. Bond is going to push that button. No doubt about it. It's in the script.

He won't be going to Liz's place for another ten hours. Right now, she's just slipping into bed to sleep off a night shift at The Copy Place. He needs to do something, but can't commit to anything. He paces from the kitchen to the living room to his bedroom, then back into the living room where he drops himself in front of his computer. He surfs the web in an aimless malaise. Soon, self-obsessed personal sites litter his screen spouting their opinions about movies, politics, and religion. Why would he even care what some thirteen-year-old cyber-junky thinks about Star Wars and how it relates to the current administration?

He ponders his overstuffed brown couch and the wasteland of cable TV, but opens up his design software instead.

He creates a severe-looking red button surrounded by a yellow and black sign declaring "DON'T PUSH!" This is placed in the upper right-hand corner of the screen. He drops an image of the Earth in the opposite corner. In the middle, he lays out a header in monolithic letters: "SHOULD I END THE WORLD?"

Down the left side of the screen, he designs a navigational bar. HOME, ABOUT THIS SITE, CONTACT ME.

He exports the graphics in a web-ready format and pieces the site together in his web-editing software. Time is lost to him. After some minor coding and adjustments, he has a working site.

The home page features two columns, one headed by alarming yellow text against black declaring, "PRESS THE BUTTON," the other stating, "DON'T PRESS THE BUTTON." Comments can be posted to either column expressing reasons why or why not to Shrug existence.

Just below the top banner, he writes a small introduction to the site:

> Welcome. My name is Jack. I have the power to erase existence with a thought. So, in true democratic fashion, I have decided to put it to a world vote. Submit your reasons here why I should or should not expunge existence.

In the "ABOUT THIS SITE" page, Jack writes the following:

THE SHRUG

Is this for real? Am I crazy? It doesn't matter. I believe that I can undo existence with a thought. I call it the Shrug. You would probably like some proof. Sorry. This performance is a one-time-only show, with no refunds available.

THE PURPOSE OF THIS SITE

Let's not get sidetracked. This website is not about IF I can negate all existence. This website pertains to whether or not I SHOULD. So, treat this as a hypothetical if you'd like, or just take what I say for fact. Regardless, what I want from you is your thoughts on why I should or should not end the world.

THE END

I want to make something very clear: If I can do what I claim, I am almost positive it would not mean creating some kind of universal apocalypse—planets crashing into each other, suns going supernova, and any other kind of wrath of God imagery you can imagine. This will UNDO existence. Not only will the universe no longer be, but for all practical purposes, it WILL NEVER HAVE BEEN. The guiding forces which create for us past, present, and future (what we sum up in a general term called time) will be obliterated. Try to imagine an existence without any time—no linear path of progress. In that condition, things cannot be, will not be, and WILL HAVE NEVER BEEN because the way these states of being can exist is no more.

So, with all this understood, think it over and let me know:
Do I "End the world," or do I keep it going?

It's up to you.

Jack saves his work, goes online, and registers the URL www. shouldiendtheworld.com. He finds a hosting service, runs his credit card number and selects 'transfer' to publish the site.

His head is buzzing and his awareness hangs off kilter from his body. The files transfer, progress bar crossing his screen. He doesn't move, won't move, can't move. A virgin, naked with a woman, the dreadful and arousing anticipation when breath can be forgotten—all that from the click of one button.

The bar reaches one hundred percent. Transfer complete. He draws the breath that has long been waiting for him.

And jolts to the ring of the phone. The clock on the kitchen wall over the table says 6pm.

It's Liz.

-25

"So, boyo, what's new with you?" Liz sits by her computer system, the tinny din of Bauhaus blaring from her crappy boom box as Jack hauls his computer into her living room. Len, his spiky peroxide-blonde hair more at attention than he could ever be, drapes across the couch like stretched taffy.

"Not much." He nearly trips over a stacked upright pile of empty beer cans heaped over with cigarette butts and ashes. A grease-stained cardboard pizza circle lies curled on the coffee table balanced on a beer can, fossilized crusts of chewed pizza remnants scattered across it like gnawed bones. With his foot, he pushes a cracked CD case closer to the debris of discs and tapes around her boom box and waits for his nose to acclimate to the odor, almost tangible, occupying the apartment in such a manner that it should be forced to pay rent.

When he had lived with Liz just out of high school after her and Len broke up, he felt charged by the clutter and disarray of her lifestyle. Every dirty dish left on a counter or chip bag spilling out bright orange triangles of tortilla onto the coffee table looked like freedom, the chaotic potential of unpredictability. There was momentum to living in the mess and clutter of a life never sealed up or scrubbed clean or folded neatly away in a drawer. As long as the trash overflowed and CDs lay discarded and uncased, anything could happen. Those memories are a twinge in him now, like two rusty parts of himself grinding together. So very different from his place, where everything is ordered and filed, alphabetized and sorted. There, he finds something exactly where he expects it to be, with nothing in the way of getting to it, and the act is motionless.

Liz swivels slow on her chair, following him with those dark-lined eyes that contrast her pasty skin, scratching at her frazzled black hair cut short to the nape, as he carries his CPU to the kitchen table. She's a snug fit in this decimated scene with her combat green cargo pants and tight black tee shirt ending at her midriff. His sister clamps her world like a cigarette between thin lips bleeding lipstick in a perpetual grinning sneer.

The irony confounds him. She'd appreciate it, too, maybe laugh out loud, if she knew anything about it. But she doesn't. She has no idea that the responsible, orderly, anal younger brother can, quite possibly, think the entire universe away rather than the tough older sister, two steps removed from Goth, who often enough acts as though she wouldn't care if he did.

Len salutes with a gangling arm. "Evenin', Cap'n." Deep, mellow monotone. "Hey, score me a deal on a couch, huh?"

"You want a couch?"

"Yeah. I wanna start fixing up my place."

"How are you going to afford that?" Liz asks.

Len drops his legs over the side and sits up, digs into his pocket and pulls out his wallet. "Check this out." He draws out a Mastercard. "How about that?"

Liz leans in, studies the card. "Holy shit. It's even got your name on it."

"Oh yeah."

Liz shakes her head, dismissively or with pity, and jabs a

black-polished finger at the plastic. "Bad move. That's like loading your pocket with stones and jumping in the lake."

"I can get you twenty percent off a sofa," Jack says.

"Cool." A long, loose smile grows on his face. "I'm gonna get me a couch. Leather, maybe. With studs. And a kick-ass home entertainment system. Bachelor pad." He sings that last part, guttural and bovine.

"No thanks." Liz swings back to her computer. "Just what fits into my car, that's all I want. Everything else can just be the crap I leave behind."

Jack's heard this before. Liz on the go—no attachments, no obligations, no burden. Up and out at a moment's notice. He knows better than to argue the point, but that mantra has always seemed an excuse for lack of ambition and commitment. Their father had a word for that kind of philosophy—laziness.

He's daydreamed of it, though, of riding off with just the clothes he's wearing and a trunk-load of necessities. Redefine himself within the context of the unknown. The Frostian road not taken.

For all Liz's talk, she's never done it. Not really. She's evacuated from jobs, relationships, leases. But only down the block and across the street. To the next job or boyfriend, but always in Terrapin and familiar surroundings. Still the same Liz in the same place, late to pay the rent to a different landlord.

Jack looks to Liz. "Give me a hand? I still have to grab the rest of my system from the car."

"Oh, please?" A begrudging push off her chair and she joins him outside in the cooling evening.

He looks behind him, making sure Len doesn't follow. "So, where's this 'Frig'?"

"He's practicing with his band tonight."

Jack opens up his passenger car door. "And how's Len handling it?"

A classic Liz eye roll. "Being a complete baby about it. That's what this apartment makeover shit is all about, I know it."

Jack grabs his keyboard and mouse and hands them to Liz, then reaches back in and hefts the 21" monitor up with a grunt. "Not everyone is blessed with an emotional on/off switch like you." He begins the trudge back to the house, back arched to adjust for the off-balance weight, arms gripped tight and already starting to throb.

"He's just pissed that he's not going to be getting any for a long time."

Jack stops. "Tell me you're not still sleeping with Len."

She smirks. "Well, you know. Just every now and again. Kind of a...mercy screw."

"Jesus." He's feeding her the disapproval that always makes her grin with pride.

"Poor, innocent Jacky. Listen. We both get something out of it, and..." A hesitation that, from anyone else, would immediately suggest the onset of sincerity. "...It's really the only time Len and I are in-synch."

Jack waits on the stoop, the plastic monitor base digging into his fingers. He wonders why he hasn't bought a flat screen yet. "What the hell kind of name is 'Frig' anyway?"

"I dunno. Something to do with his guitar solos, I guess." Liz pulls open the door and holds it wide for him. "You'll have to come and see Sewage play sometime. They kinda suck, but Frig is hot."

"Sewage?"

"Trust me. It's a pretty apt designation."

It doesn't take long for Jack to set up his system. Operating from the kitchen table isn't the most comfortable setup, but it's functional, and it beats Len's layout, which is on the couch, keyboard in his lap, monitor on the coffee table between his propped-up legs. Jack follows the network cables that coil and curl about the disrupted living room to the router hub at Liz's desk.

Liz's gaming system is the only possession she cherishes. She had it custom-made a few years back with top-of-the-line components. The CPU casing is red-fronted with oscillating black light and red smoldering LED's illuminating a chromatic dragon rising from flames airbrushed on the clear plastic sides of the massive tower. The screen is a flat 25" plasma and the speakers put out ten stories of sound from six inch woofers. The monstrosity of a computer is flashy and loud, capable of tremendous feats, and completely dedicated to performing frivolous, empty tasks, just like Liz.

"Hey, Jacky, there any openings at Templeton?" Len keeps his attention to his screen as his system whirs and clicks through its boot up.

"You mean like on the factory line?"

"Yeah."

"All the time. Why? Still having trouble with Carl?"

"He still won't make me a manager. And the tips suck, man. I'm getting out of there pronto." Len's been saying this forever. Ten years and six vehicles at Italy on Wheels and the poor guy still can't make night manager.

Liz turns around. "Len, plug your nose, shut your mouth, and blow really hard."

Len looks up. "What?"

"Maybe that'll force a pair of balls to pop out of you. You'll need them before you ever quit that job or stand up to Carl." Liz sucks on her cigarette, winks, and flicks the ash to the floor.

Len flushes and scowls, looking back at his screen. If he were liquid, he would seep into the couch. "Eat me." His fingers jab at keys.

"Baby, we already had that discussion, and that request cannot be accommodated." Liz connects to the game server and chooses her character. "All right, boys and girls. Enough chatter. Are we ready?" She clicks the play button. "Goin' in. See you on the flip side."

He is Orson the Sorcerer. He has magic, the power to destroy with a word. He travels with Ca'drannia, the silver-haired elven warrior, and Lillith, a spry halfling rogue. They are on a mission, a quest, that will decide the fate of an entire world. There is no question, there is no hesitation. Everything is good or evil, right or wrong, and he knows his place. He knows what he has to do.

"We're going to die," Jack says as he types "((BRB))" into the TALK box. They've been playing for two hours, met up with two other players on the server, and are about to explore the dangerous cavern home to Asterrak, the dark elf wizard who has stolen the Staff of Vyst'tel from the dwarves.

Jack is always nervous partying up with others. It's a difficult game, hard to advance in levels, and if a character dies, the penalties are severe. It may be a game, but players take it very seriously when they lose hundreds of hours worth of experience points to a careless death. He walks into the kitchen and grabs a beer.

Liz is sending a message to Xaneth. Jack hasn't played with the paladin for a while. He's from Australia and usually logged on when Jack works and sleeps. Ca'drannia and Xaneth often travel together, since Liz plays the game like a 7-Eleven—all hours. When she's with Xaneth, it's epic level adventuring.

"Maybe," she says. "But what a way to go, huh?"

"If Liz doesn't go rushing in and lets me lay some traps in the lair, we'll get through this no problem," Len says.

Jack returns to his seat and types "((Back))." "Listen. When we get to Asterrak, keep back. I want to use a fireball on him."

Liz eyes the beer in his hand. "What the hell is this? You snag my brew and you don't grab one for me?"

"Uh…sorry?"

Liz leaves her system and walks off to the kitchen. Fridge door squeals, beer can pops, and she's back. "Let's just hope the DM's are feeling merciful tonight. Ca'drannia is only 1200 points from level 24."

"All right, show time," Len says. Their characters stand before the entrance to the Lair of Asterrak.

A dark cavern. Flickering torchlight. Shadows dance.

A scurry of legs ahead. The scratch of claw against rock.

Suddenly, from every direction, Arachnids falling upon them, gigantic and vicious. Crossbow bolts fly. Swords clank against bony armor. Too many. Too much. Overcome.

Say the words. Speak the spell.

Fire.

"Fuck, Jack! What the hell were you doing?" Liz throws herself away from her computer and stomps to the refrigerator for another beer. "Jesus!"

"Sorry, sorry, sorry. I saw that thing coming and thought it was far enough away. It would have killed us anyway." Weak defense. He made a mistake and he knows it. He knew it the second he did it.

"No way, Jacky," Len says. "We had them all. My traps worked perfectly. It was a done deal, man. Until that fireball."

"I told you I was planning on using it. You should have fallen back."

Liz storms back to her computer desk. "Fallen back *where?* Christ, we were surrounded. Besides, you said you were going to use it on Asterrak, not on the fucking spiders."

"That queen came out of nowhere. I thought I could hit it before it got to you guys." He killed two characters, both who have gone out of their way to help Orson in the past. What a goddamn mess.

"Tell that to Xaneth and Dunidun." She's clicking away on the keyboard, sending messages to the other two players. Probably talking about him.

"Well, I fucked up. We can either keep yakking about it, or find a cleric for Xaneth and Dunidun."

"Just think a bit, huh? Last thing we need is one of our own guys taking us down."

Jack's cheeks are hot and stiff. "Enough already. I get it."

"*Area* spell, Jack." She's needling him, digging in. "It means it has an area of effect. Spells don't distinguish between friend and foe."

One too many times being on the receiving end of Liz's overbearing ego. He's had enough. "You know, if an apology made for a mistake in a fucking *game* isn't enough for you, then too bad." Jack is slamming keys and slapping the mouse on the table as he exits the game.

"Come on, Jacky. Cool down. Get back in the game." Len's words flame like condescension and simmer Jack's boil.

Jack powers down his system. "Hey, I was cool. I'm not the one who can't get over a goddamn mistake." The CPU sighs and winks out, and Jack unhooks his cables.

Len stares. "Jack—"

That natural sneer, so comfortable on Liz's face, is a bitter sieve for her words. "Let him go, Len. He gets off on these little tantrums."

Jack doesn't want to look at her anymore. Just get out. Get to the door. He hoists up the monitor and starts walking.

"You know, Jack, this is the same shit Dad pulled on us all the time, but at least he had his drinking as an excuse."

He muscles the monitor out the door, down the porch, and to his car, cursing the fact that he has to go back in there for his CPU. A rough toss of the big screen onto his passenger seat and he stands there, looking back at the shabby old house. What the hell? He knows better than to take Liz's bait. At work, he and Sam joke about life needing a "control-Z" so mistakes could be undone like in a computer application. He could really use that about now.

Of course, he *does* have an undo button. Just not one he'd ever use.

Shit. Now he'll stand here, be cold on a dark street. He'll wait pathetically for Liz to come out and make the first move. But she'll never step foot out that door. Liz never concedes, never apologizes.

Len, however, does come out, beer in one hand, cigarette in the other, bemusement knotting his brow and curling his lips. "What the hell, Jacko? What's going on?"

"Forget it, Len. Just forget about it, okay? Everything's fine. Great."

Len sputters. "Really. *This* is fine? Peachy-keen? Wow, that's…" A scratch to the side of his head while he squints, "…sad, man."

Jack takes in a breath and looks to the clear black sky, lightly speckled with the few stars that overpower the city lights, and just wants to go home.

"Jack, I don't wanna, like, make a situation worse here. You know me. Going for that smooth, fluffy normal I can back float on. But, you do get that, three minutes ago, you had an off-the-scale overreaction. Right? Tell me you get this. 'Cause I gotta know whether to talk level with you, or like I do my weird old grandma. 'No, Gram, I did *not* let the purple aliens into your room. I swear I told them your brain isn't for sale.'" He slinks a smile on his face.

Good old Len. Nothing ever sticks to him. Jack smiles back, an unspoken "thank you" for being exactly what he needs. "Yeah. I think I have a basic grasp on that." He gives Len a thumbs-up.

Len slaps his back. "Cool. Piece of cake, man. Grab your shit, come back inside, and realize we're not pissed at you. Just the heat of a moment already gone." Len turns sideways, gesturing Jack to the door.

"Be a bud for me, will you Len? Grab my CPU."

Len's face slides. "Oh, man."

"Len, we're cool. Okay? And I'll be cool. But right now, I'm just not in the mood to be around Liz anymore tonight."

Len takes a drag from his cigarette, chases it with a swig of beer, and blows a loud blast of air. "Yeah, that's the problem, huh? Man, don't let her get under your skin. Liz is like Mexican food: Tastes great, burns like hell, and wants out fast. Either you don't eat it, or enjoy the burn and gear up for a nasty ride on the toilet."

"Yeah, well, tonight I'm not liking the taste, and I never asked for the extra hot sauce."

Len pokes his cigarette into his beer can and crushes it. "Alright, Cap'n. I'll get your gear and you can skidaddle so the both of you can mellow. But you're comin' back next week. No way you're missin' out on hunting down Asterrak."

"Deal. For now, just play it that Orson the Sorcerer has taken leave to reflect on his tragic error. Oh, and tell Xaneth and Dunidun I'm sorry."

Len nods. Long strides send him back inside and leave Jack leaning against the car. He smokes and waits. When Len returns with Jack's computer and keyboard, they're stashed on the floor of the back seat.

"Len." Jack speaks suddenly, before he can think it through. "You know Liz will never be yours. She'll never be anybody's but her own."

Len glances back at the house. His whole body seems to lean toward it, a drooping stem to light. "Yeah. I know that." He gives a stupid smile that waxes wise as he looks down at his shuffling foot. "Isn't there a song somewhere about false hope being the only thing worth hoping for?"

"If there's not, there should be."

Len raises his head again and those small dark eyes are squeezed with an intensity that could be determination or just raw frustration. "Well, until something better comes along, I'll just keep ridin' this one out."

There's no argument for this, just the mutual understanding of the consequences. Jack climbs into his car. As he pulls away, he looks into the rearview, sees Len standing solitary beside the road in the shadow of the evening, and Jack resents the long, narrow mirror.

-24

Jack rolls his chair into Rick's office Wednesday morning for the midweek meeting. Rick is reclined in his leather chair, turned away from his desk, sideways-facing Greg, Sam and Jack.

"First things first," Rick says, glancing back at his list of meeting items on his desk. "High Point Market. How's the new bedding division P.O.S. coming?" His eyes target Sam.

She slips several designs out from her pile and hands them over. "This is as far as I can take it until Bruce gets me the pocketed spring coil specs and the new 700 series info."

Rick frowns. "When is he supposed to get that to you?"

"Last week Thursday."

"Did you get on his ass about it?"

"That's not my job, it's yours."

"Well you gotta tell me, then."

"You mean more than the three times I already did?"

Rick chuffs and spins to his phone, dialing an extension and hitting "speaker."

After two rings, Bruce's voice responds. "Rick."

"Hey, Sam needs that info for your bedding signs."

"I'm working on it. I should be able to get it to her by Friday."

"Friday? Bruce, those need to ship *out* on Friday! Listen, you don't get us what we need by the end of today and you'll have empty P.O.S. frames at Market."

Exasperation. "Rick, you'll get it when I get it."

"I'm not hard-balling, Bruce. I'm just telling you the way it is. Don't blame us if they don't get done."

A long pause. "I'll do what I can."

"Good boy." Rick hangs up. "Dickhead."

"You're such a charmer, Rick." Sam smirks.

Rick turns back to his list. "Okay, next up. The *Furniture/Today* spread. What've you got?" And he looks at Jack.

He looks down at his ad. On the verso page, small black text over clean white declares: "In Furniture Retail, there is no 'Get Rich Quick' scheme." On the recto page, a Templeton semi going down the road past a speed limit sign. The words above the image state: "But that's only because Templeton truck drivers obey the speed limit." In smaller letters, just above the Templeton logo, he added, "When Templeton arrives, your business thrives." He showed the finished piece to Greg last Friday afternoon, wondering if he should even waste his time submitting it, and Greg, who seemed to really like the ad, gave Jack an enthusiastic "Go for it!"

He hands the ad to Rick. "Well, I thought I'd go a different route. See what you think."

Rick scrutinizes the ad with an intensity that lasts approximately five seconds—two if discounting the time it takes for Rick to pick his ear with his pinky finger. "There's no mention of Gross Margin Return On Inventory. And you need to call out all sixteen of our product categories."

The familiar squirm in his gut warns him he's about to say something he shouldn't. "Rick, the idea was to kind of be simple and immediate. An ad that gets right to the point for once without spelling it all out. It says 'We're going to make you lots of money.'

Short and sweet."

Greg and Sam are quiet. Greg looks at his printouts. Sam looks from Jack back to Rick.

"I know what it says, and I like it. It's a winner. But you know that Chuck is going to be looking for GMROI and the categories. They're Templeton's signature. So get those on here." He looks at the ad again. "Hey, I know. It would be cool to see the truck filled with furniture. You know?"

Jack *doesn't* know. "How?"

"Maybe have the back open. Show it overflowing with product."

Jack stares blankly. Sam just continues to smirk. Greg lets out the cross between a heavy exhale and a laugh and says, "Yeah, that would be cool." It a puking sincerity that Rick either misses or ignores. Greg isn't going to be any help.

"The truck is *driving* down the highway. You want furniture *spilling out of it?*"

The skin on Rick's rugged face bunches around his eyes. "Don't have it moving, then. Have it delivering."

"But the point of the ad is…"

"*Whatever.*" Rick's voice is a grating guillotine. He prods a finger at the verso page as if poking road kill. "And get some product on this first page. We're not spending eight thousand dollars for a white page." Rick tosses the ad back at Jack.

The best course of action is to drop the subject and move on, smiling and nodding and agreeing to everything. Rick will forget about it and they'll be tossing half-joking insults at each other in no time.

Asking his next question absolutely does not adhere to that particular strategy. "Can't you just show this one to Chuck and see what he thinks?"

Rick's face glows deep crimson. "I'm done with this!" He shoots a commanding glare at Greg, and Greg shifts in his chair.

"They're easy changes, Jack" Greg speaks with uncomfortable authority. "And necessary."

Heat and constriction. His chair is like a vise. "Yup. First thing." His lips feel funny, like clay.

The meeting drags on. Deadlines are shifted, priorities made, and tasks assigned. Jack writes everything down with a trembling hand.

Wednesday meetings conclude with the Rite of Nicotine and Ranting outside the office building on the concrete stoop. Greg, Sam and Jack usually laugh over Rickisms, complain about projects, and scratch their heads over the general mess of the Templeton hierarchy. Today, all is a cautious quiet until Greg finally speaks.

"Well, I don't think Ricky-boy's going to be asking you out for a beer any time soon."

Jack sits in a sagging slump on the stoop. "Seems my luck is changing for the better."

Sam chortles. "Keep it up, Jack. You're doing a great job keeping Rick off my back for once."

Jack doesn't look back at her. "That's what I'm here for—at your service." He can't figure it out. Sam can turn the simplest request from Rick into a verbal swordplay. For some reason, though, she never pisses Rick off. If he tries to speak his mind, Rick is all over him. And it just seems to be getting worse.

Greg keeps behind him. "You've gotta pull back, Jack. Be a little more accommodating. You know what Rick's going through with Chuck on his ass. You get him hot now, you'll only light his fuse."

He doesn't want to hear what he already knows. He just wants someone on his side. That's how it used to be, wasn't it? "It's so fucking stupid. He ruined the whole concept."

"It's not *ruined*." Annoyance frosts Greg's words. "Just play around with it, for Christ's sake. You can make it work. It'll still be a better ad than any of the garbage they usually make us run."

Jack sighs. "I was kind of expecting you to back me up, Greg. You told me to go for it." He's been saying that a lot lately. 'Kind of.' What's wrong with him? He seems unable to be definitive, even when his emotions are absolute. He's been coming in at angles, with a blunted edge, and it bothers him.

"Yeah? Well, what could I have said? If I had told you to for-get about it, you'd have given me the same shit you just gave to Rick." His chuckle is dry and humorless. "I mean, Jesus. Every-thing with you lately is some kind of…ordeal. You sulk around, whining about shit that ain't gonna change no matter how much you want it to. So I said 'Go for it.' Just to keep you happy. But it's getting pretty obvious that nothing's going to make you happy." He throws his cigarette butt to the ground and walks back inside, leaving Jack with Sam behind him against the wall.

"You want some advice?" Sam examines the long-ashed stub of her cigarette.

He's sure to get it no matter how he answers. "Why not?"

She flicks her butt into the distance with thumb and middle finger. "You used to be fun, Jack. Used to be cool to be around. But you got some kind of bug up your ass, and you're not gonna find any kind of cure here. Do whatever you want, but don't be shoving your shit in our faces and asking what stinks."

Sam goes back inside, leaving Jack alone on the concrete stoop.

-23

Night is a window to emptiness. He can make out the blotchy streak of the Milky Way across the blackness of sky above him if he takes his attention just off of it. Lying on the hood of his car, staring up from the old county road outside the city, hearing the frog song and the occasional guttural groan of some far-off cow in the spread of farmland around him, he swears he can feel the pull of the galaxy as it spins.

Space. There couldn't be a better name for it. Say it slowly and the word exudes the nothingness that surrounds the horizons he gazes upon. He lays prone to eternity, and he is adrift.

He's come here before, but not for a while. After his last few days at work though, he needed to get away from those walls of his apartment. He last came here a year ago with Liz, after the funeral. They had lain against the windshield of her Impala and stared at the gray-blue backlit clouds that billowed in the moonglow of the midnight sky. She had been drunk and belligerent; Jack had been numb.

"You think he's up there somewhere now?" Liz had cupped

her hands like a telescope and peered into the sky. "Dad? That you, big guy?" She gave a half-wave with her fingertips.

"Something really looked funny about him. Did you see that?" Jack had hated having the coffin at the front of the chapel. He had no choice but to look at it, the body of his father packed up like freight ready to be shipped.

"Course he looked funny. They made him look happy and content. Fucking peaceful even." She shot out a dismissive snort.

Liz had been more coarse than usual that entire day, and Jack had received the indirect brunt of it; how the funeral home was raking mom with the price, how Ben was being a total control freak over funeral details, what an asshole Tony was for cracking jokes about the will. Everything that afternoon had been seething little comments from the background.

Maybe if he drank faster she wouldn't bother him so much. He turned over, hung himself down the side of the car, and stretched for a beer in the passenger seat. He came back up with two and handed one to Liz. "So you don't think Dad was ever content? Not even a little?"

Liz drank deep, eyes to the sky. "Hell no. Dad lived for the battle. Conflict. When he couldn't find it anywhere else, he'd throw it on us." She rolled her head to his side. "Well, maybe not you, but sure as hell on me."

Jack twisted to that. "Oh come on, he laid into me heavy, too."

"Not in the end, he didn't. You couldn't do anything wrong, could you?" She rolled away again. "But that doesn't matter. That's not the point. The *point* is, Dad died all wrong. He should have gone out kicking and screaming. A fiery car crash would've beat that cancer shit." She belched and set her beer down beside her. "That's how they should have set up his body. Should of given him a good, mean sneer, you know? And hands reaching out in a clutch of death." She mimicked this, clawed hands outstretched to the sky, grappling against a spectral foe.

Jack stared at her, swallowed hard. "Jesus."

Liz's arms dropped back to her sides and she nodded.

"Uh-huh. No doubt about it." She picked up her beer, polished it off, and shot the can under her into the open driver side window. It clanked against a case-full of empties.

A soft breeze ran over them; the exhale of a long day. Jack lit a cigarette. "Hey, you remember that time when Dad was working on the toilet in the basement, and he was trying to get that flange off, so he—"

Liz bolted up, looking at him hard. "You can just stop right there. No way. I'm not doing this."

"What?"

"This 'remember when' crap. I won't play that game. Not after having to sit through three days of it." She dropped back down hard on her back and glared at the stars. "Coffin's closed." She held up her beer can. "See ya later, Daddy." She drank, and the conversation ended.

Jack had wanted to be angry at her then, to be shocked, but the truth was, he hadn't wanted to call up old memories. It just seemed like the thing to do. Maybe it was the beer, maybe it was wading three days deep in death, but that night, on that car, those memories just hadn't tasted right anyway.

A year later, in the same spot, looking up once again at the night sky, those same memories have become distant like the old twinkle of some dead sun.

Had his father ever held his hand? Had there ever been contact? He wants to remember the feel of him, the smell, but all he can see is the black between the stars, and that's just fine, too. That's his father now. The absence. The hole.

He lets himself slip between everything, and he's there.

-22

On Friday evening, he opts out of drinks at Snappy's. Sam and Greg give little protest. Sam's words from Wednesday are still an abrasion on the skin of his thoughts. He thinks about taking some time off of work—he still has two weeks of vacation coming—but what would he do during the time off?

He throws his keys onto the stand by the door, glances at the answering machine showing a big red zero on the display, then heads to his computer. Checking emails, he finds nothing but a few spams and a reminder from his Mom that Tony, Chris and Ben are coming up next weekend.

He logs on to the administrative pages of www.shouldi-endtheworld.com. There's been no traffic to his site. He hasn't expected any. It's an obscure URL hiding in the massive realm of cyberspace. It was a silly thing to do, really, creating the website. He should erase it from the server. Publishing it was just one more desperate flaying of his arms in a pathetic attempt to…what? What the hell *was* he trying to do by creating this website anyway?

He loads the stats page. Worthless, really. It'll still show zero visitors. Wipe it out. Expunge it. Like it never existed.

When the statistical data loads, however, his breath catches. His brain tells his eyes to blink, but his eyelids are defiant.

In the table of information, where it calls out visits, the number reads '1,244.'

What the hell? That can't be.

He studies the information carefully; he has to be misunderstanding something. But no matter how he reads it, there's only one conclusion. Two hundred forty-four visitors today.

His heartbeat is hasty and forceful, his mouth dry. He goes to the site.

And there are posts. There are many posts.

The counters on the column headers show "76 new posts" in the "Don't Push the Button!" column and "8 new posts" in the "Push the Button!" column.

Jack falls back in his chair, his jaw slack. "Holy shit," he mutters. His clammy hand grasps the mouse slowly, scrolls down the page, and he reads.

DON'T PUSH THE BUTTON!

Submitted by: *rthompson@xtr.com*

How can you even toy with the idea of killing billions of innocent people? All life has a right to exist, no matter what their actions in the world. Shame on you!

Submitted by: *2hot2trot@yahoo.com*

you cant do it!!! at least not til tuesday my girlfriend promised me a blow job!!!!!111

Submitted by: *oneofthesaved@zeronet.net*

Only God has the ability and capacity to pass judgment on others. For you to do so would be blasphemous sacrilege. Seek judgment at www.theonetruelight.org and pray for forgiveness and guidance.

Submitted by: *Georgette111769@msn.com*

It's this kind of irresponsible garbage that is confusing our children and ruining the internet.

Submitted by: *anonymous*

who the hell do u think u r anyway?

Submitted by: *teddybearmania@aol.com*

The univserse should not be destroyed because of luv. Luv is the binding force. It conquers all and it is indistructable.

Submitted by: *ilovebritneyspears@hotmail.com*

If you did it you'd kill Britney Spears, and she's a Fox!!! Don't kill my babe!

Submitted by: *anonymous*

Hope is worth holding out for. Don't despair.

It goes on and on. He's dumbfounded by how many people will take time to post on a website presenting what should be a ludicrous proposition—and of those, the percentage of them that have done so with apparent serious-mindedness. Welcome to the twenty-first century, where people have become so conditioned to the ridiculous number of inane surveys forwarded to them from friends and family ("Take this survey to find out what cartoon character you are most like!" "Answer these questions and discover your animal spirit!") that they will compulsively dive into any fill-in-the-blank, desperately check off any multiple-choice answer they can, to bask in the fleeting euphoria of results that group them into some meaningless category based on pop culture, trendy religion, or popular psychology.

Jack scrolls quickly down the remaining posts—they're all similar—then zips back up to the top and reads the column that intrigues his morbid curiosity far more.

PUSH THE BUTTON!

Submitted by: *anonymous*

pleez if this is real pleez do it and end the nightmare stop this insanity push the button

---

Submitted by: *666feast4thebeast@z-net.net*

Kaos rules!!! Fuckin A baby, wipe the slate! Show these fuckers what a meaningless empty worthless cesspool this is!!!!

Submitted by: *anonymous*

Why not just kill all the fucking niggers you goddam niggerlover NIGGERLOVER FAGGOT!!!!

Submitted by: *anonymous*

Life sucks.

Submitted by: *midwestmumford1567@hotmail.com*

Wow. A universal reboot. What a novel idea.

Submitted by: *readyfortherapture@metro-cable.com*

God has imbibed you with a power to become the initiate of the apocalypse. You must obey the will of God and break the seal as the Revelations of John declare. The earthly reign of the Devil shall finally be at an end, and the Messiah will now return to bring his final message to us as we ascend to our heavenly reward.

Submitted by: *atrophy@eternaldarkness.com*

Is there

nothing to love for, nothing to hope for, nothing to lead me by the hand?

I ask the question, and nothing answers.

So will I Nothing love, and for Nothing hope, and follow Nothing to the end.

Submitted by: *anonymous*

you really need a reason?

"Oh boy," Jack says with a forceful exhale after he reads these responses existing on *his* website because *he* solicited them. And yet, what did he expect? Did he think perfectly sane individuals would submit rational essays on why he should or shouldn't end the world?

This is stupid and irresponsible. The site needs to come down. But, how and why did his obscure little site become so popular so fast?

Before he can think of a solution, he realizes he forgot to connect his website email to his Outlook. He hasn't retrieved any mail sent to his *jack@shouldIendtheworld.com* account. He goes to the "Retrieve Mail" section of his hosting service and isn't surprised to discover thirty-two emails waiting for him. The first email is an automatic message from the hosting service confirming his account. He skips it. The second email is dated three days ago.

FROM: *AStriber@weirdweb.com*
TO: *jack@shouldIendtheworld.com*
SUBJECT: Congratulations!

Dear owner/operator of www.shouldiendtheworld.com:

Weirdweb.com has selected your site to be featured on our internet publication. Congratulations!

WeirdWeb is a small, relatively new website that is growing in popularity every day. We provide the service of finding interesting, quirky or just plain bizarre websites and feature one per day for our readers to visit. Subscribers can opt to receive daily emails with links to the latest website being featured on WeirdWeb.com. Anyone visiting our site may vote on that day's selection. We poll viewers based on two categories: Weirdness and Revisitablity.

You will find that, by WeirdWeb.com featuring your site, your web traffic should significantly increase. Although WeirdWeb requires no reciprocation on your part, we would greatly appreciate it if you could find a way to call us out on your site and provide a return link to us.

Your site will be featured in three day's time, on Friday, October 13th.

Once again, congratulations, and if you have any questions or concerns, please feel free to contact me.

Sincerely,
Abe Striber
President, WeirdWeb, llc.
www.weirdweb.com

And that clearly solves the mystery. But he never wanted actual publicity, and witnessing now what a little bit is doing for the site, he is filled with trepidation.

The emails that follow are all from people who visited the site and, though perhaps not posting publicly, felt compelled to let him know how they felt. Most are derogatory, telling him that he needs help, that he is crazy. A few just think the website is stupid and pointless. There are several, however, that are complimentary.

Again, Jack skips through the emails. Toward the end of them, he holds on a short message. He reads it three, four, five times, and he can't seem to get away from it. He is stuck on it.

FROM: *Iamsurfacing@illinoiscable.com*
TO: *jack@shouldIendtheworld.com*
SUBJECT: None

Dear Jack,
You must be terribly lonely. Perhaps we should talk.
Pauline Swanson

It's that first line that staggers him, reverberates in his mind, growing in volume. *You must be terribly lonely. You must be terribly lonely.*

He moves the cursor up to the "Reply" button.

Forty-five minutes later, Jack looks at the response he has written, rereading it several times as he hovers over the "send" button. *What am I doing? Am I actually going to reply to this person? She's probably a wacked out cultist or fanatic or lunatic. Smart, Jack.* He looks over his response one more time.

FROM: *jack@shouldiendtheworld.com*
TO: *Iamsurfacing@illinoiscable.com*
SUBJECT: RE: None

Dear Pauline,

I've sat here for some time now trying to figure out if I should reply to you, and what I should say. All I can admit is that I feel a strange compulsion to do it.

Lonely? I guess you could say that. I think everyone in this strange universe is lonely in some way. We tend to live in a very detached and isolated state from one another. How often is it that we can actually be truthful to another without risk of further separating ourselves from them? Instead of being ourselves, we try to conform to a compatible version of whomever we are with. I wonder now as I write this, are you lonely too?

You want to talk. What do you want to talk about? The website? Life? Me? You? By replying to you, I guess I have to say that I am open to the idea. I just want to make sure that you don't judge me by this website. Despite its crazy nature, I am a normal, average person who—I think, I hope—is stable and rational. I don't have fanatical beliefs, I don't hear voices, I don't think I've been given any kind of mission by God.

I work in the creative department of a large furniture company doing graphic design. In my off times, I read, watch movies, and get together with friends. Ordinary as can be.

If you still want to write back after reading this, you are more than welcome. I have to confess that I am still not clear why you would want to, but maybe that doesn't matter.

So, perhaps I will hear back from you.

Jack

He has reworded the email four times, and it still sounds odd and rambling, but before he can waste more thought on it, he clicks "Send."

In the kitchen, he warms up dinner. He has been home for three hours now and hasn't stepped away from the computer. He throws leftover meatloaf into the oven, grabs a beer from the refrigerator, and drinks down the irrepressible feeling that, for better or for worse, he has just stepped off that well-trodden path and into the long grass and shadowy foliage of obscurity.

Part Three
THE BALANCE

-21

At 9pm, Liz calls, easy-going and amnesic to last Sunday's argument. "Hey, boyo. Come on out to a show tonight."

It's as close to an apology as she'll give. Jack plays along. "Let me guess. Sewage?"

"Yeah, baby. At the Quartermaster's."

He knows the place, at least by reputation, but he's never been there. The Quartermaster's is on Water Street, the college bar strip of Terrapin's small downtown. Wild weekend nights of rambunctious students enjoying the tug and snap of the parental leash. The Quartermaster's is the favorite backyard for the mangier academic strays to find a tree to piss on, or to bury their bone. He's never wanted to go there, but tonight the idea goes down like a shot of whiskey tossed back with eyes clamped shut. "Yeah, all right. When?"

"Meet you there in a half-hour."

In his bedroom, pulls open drawers and stares at stale clothes. What to wear? Instinct makes a grab for a nice pair of jeans and his favorite green sweater, but he overrules it. He needs something a bit less conspicuous than an outfit that cries out "I don't belong here, please kick my ass." He throws on his old, worn and torn jeans and a tee shirt.

Before he walks out, he checks his email one last time.

Nothing.

Why are a few words from an unknown woman sending his insides on a lurching elevator ride? What does he really expect could come from this?

But it does intrigue him—not the mystery of this stranger who has contacted him, but the honesty of it. She knows something about him that no one else in his life is aware of, and the idea of sharing his secrets with someone else is virtually erotic.

There's something about this particular evening, a quality he can't express. The night has substance to it—the halogen lights from cars and streetlamps shimmer and deflect off its surface. As Jack drives down Water Street, a vague, puckering pensiveness nudges him and he mentally slides over to make room for it. He circles the packed streets around The Quartermaster's bar.

On this fall Friday night, Water Street is awash with the soft luminescence of neon bar signs and street lamps. It's an amber glow that softens the scene and emotes a cozy warmth and welcome that absolutely does not exist on this street. He finally settles for a parking spot two blocks down a side road and steps into the settling chill that reeks of fish from the Terrapin River.

Pedestrians flow down the main drag in clumping herds. Their distant laughter and shouts linger with hollow echoes. Foot traffic spills to the road as much as it flows down the sidewalks. A car honks at maundering crossers who return singular gestures and verbal attention. Jack rounds the corner and approaches The Quartermaster's entrance.

The massive dark wood double doors of the rustic facade

impose upon the street corner, two long, weathered oars crossing themselves from above. Over a large window glowing with beer lights, paint flakes and curls on the sign of a nineteenth century sailor raising a foaming mug in silent, perpetual toast as he leans with cocky confidence against the "Q" of "Quartermaster's."

Between Jack and the doors is the obligatory gathering of people that seem to accessorize any raucous bar, at least the few he's been to. This group is complete with a very drunk girl casually passed between the others to keep her upright while she laughs uncontrollably at some joke the others have gotten over, or just don't get. Jack slinks past them and steps into a wall of noise against a mass of flesh.

Thumping jukebox bass pounds against him when he opens the door. Not two steps in and an arm bars his path. Jack turns to a sheared head and braided goatee perched on a tall stool, wad of dollar bills in a tight fist held close to a flannel-covered chest. "Four bucks."

Jack digs for his wallet, hands over a five, and takes his damp dollar change.

It's hard to move in the place. A pack of patrons shift and flow before him in the muddling light and agitates his lack of motion. Ahead, past the large oval bar, a wide archway leads to an adjacent room, and he shoulders past people toward it. Each blink burns from thick smoke, and his throat clenches to the light beer vomit air as he passes the bathrooms. There's a stage at the back with a band setting up their gear. A voice carries thin but prominent over the din. "Jack!"

Liz is at the front of the stage, standing below a tall, wiry guy about twenty-five years old with mean, angular features cinched tight by a grin and poking through a mop head of black hair. Slithering down and around his right arm is the black tattoo of a snake. The splay of Liz's stance and the line of her shoulders strike a line of demarcation—the stage hers and this band's performance for her benefit.

Frig turns away from her, picks up a guitar, and Liz waves Jack over.

"You made it," she yells above the noise. She's in tight, hip-hugging black jeans with horizontal rips running down the left thigh and a small black tank top with "Sewage" emblazed in glowing green across her chest. Dressed to the nines tonight.

"Busy place." Jack can barely hear himself.

"What?" Liz leans into him.

"Busy place!"

She gives a dangerous smile and pulls him closer to the edge of the stage. "Come on and meet Frig."

The stage is laden with huge amps and speakers, guitars, and drums. The rest of the band—three sets of dirty denim, wrinkled cotton and hair—hop around the mess of wires to check connections, plug this into that, turn knobs. Frig steps on a floor pedal and rips out a quick guitar lick, then leans into the microphone. "Bring up the guitar in the monitor, and cut back the fucking high end, would ya?"

"Frig!" Liz shouts.

Frig looks down. "Yeah, babe?"

Liz's hand on his back, pushing Jack forward. "This is Jack. My brother."

Jack waves an awkward hand, craning his head to the shaggy guitarist.

"Hey man. How's it hangin'? Glad ya made it."

"I've heard a lot about you from Liz." Such a stupid thing to say.

"Yeah." Frig turns back to the rest of the band. "Mick! Don't forget to watch for my signal on 'Wasteland.'"

Liz tugs on Jack's sleeve. "Let's grab a table."

They wander to a table against the wall, close to the stage. Liz's small leather purse, just a utility case for her money, smokes, keys and lipstick, drops to the table top. She splits it open and gropes for smokes and bills. "Wanna drink?"

Jack exaggerates his nod, as if the noise might drown it out, and Liz disappears into the crowd.

No Len tonight. He's not in the plans. No visual confirmation of Liz being with someone else. This is the way it's been ever since they broke up. Chum around for a while, then Liz's attitude or some new guy sends Len running. Sooner or later, he's back again, like he was never gone. Jack is frustrated by the whole situation; Len's inability to let Liz go, and Liz's ability to keep leading Len on.

Movement ahead makes him look up, expecting Liz, but instead a large guy with a buzz-cut, looking like the front line of the college football team, steps up to the table and grabs Liz's stool.

It takes a second to register what he's seeing. "Um, that's taken."

The six-foot-two wedge of meat looks at Jack for the first time with a quick flash of surprise. He flexes a grin. "Fuckin'-A right, buddy." He walks two tables down with stool in hand to rejoin his three friends who shed their jackets and take a seated huddle around the table. He waggles a thumb at Jack and laughs as he drops down onto Liz's stool. All Jack can do is glower at the table-top in front of him and call it an asshole.

When Liz returns with two beers in hand, she cocks her head at him. "What's wrong?" She sets the beers on the table and looks down. "Hey. Where's my stool?"

Jack stands and slides his stool over to her. "Right here." His eyes bounce off the Hulk twelve feet away.

Liz follows his glance and stares hard at the big man's table. Hulk catches her gaze and deflects it with a smile that's all teeth. Eyes thin, she drags on her cigarette and says, "Be right back."

"Liz—!" But she's gone. "Shit."

This must be why she comes to these places. She's looking for the chance to face off against a challenge, an adversary. It's Ca'drannia striding to the big guy's table, deficient of epic adventures, reduced to petty squabbles with some half-orc in a rowdy tavern. Hulk is playing his role admirably, and by the light of intensity in Liz's expression as she moved to engage her target, she's probably even appreciative of Hulk's efforts. Liz needs a supporting cast to make her star shine.

Len is only useful to her as the archetype of the bumbling sidekick. The contrasting fool to her competence, the frail spirit to compare her strength. That's how the relationship makes sense.

It must be this. Otherwise, that role defaults to Jack.

He follows behind her, he has to, but every acidic surge of his gut pleads against it.

"Hey, Stud," Liz says, a touch of coy and a splash of menace. Even seated on that stool, his cinderblock of a head still looks down at her. "Your ass and my ass seem to have a disagreement."

The table of friends laugh and Hulk swivels on Liz's stool to face her head-on. "What's that?"

"Speaking too fast for you, fuck-wit? I'll slow down. You. Are. On. My. Stool." Jack knows that smile flaring out her cheeks and he wants to grab her, get her out of here, but he'd rather face this linebacker than Liz's wrath if he did.

Hulk stands up, a full half-foot over her. Stupid grin becomes astonished grin. "*Fuck*-wit?"

Liz sidles around him with slow, small steps in the choreography of hostile encounter. "Oh, man. I'm still being too cryptic for you? I'd draw you a picture, but I don't have a crayon."

Hulk turns with her, keeps the intimidation of his girth full on her. "Just go sit down and shut up." The smile on his face flattens to a sneer as Liz's slow dance puts the contested stool beside them. The blood that had rushed so fast to Jack's face moments ago turns icy cold, acquires panicked mass, and drops to his stomach.

"Sit down? Thanks, I think I will." Liz swipes the stool away and moves with long-stride determination back to their table.

Jack follows her while Hulk is slow to react.

"Hey!" His friends clutch the table sides and double over with laughter as he trails three steps behind Liz.

Jack sits down fast and stiff. Liz wiggles her butt into the seat of her stool, sighs with pleasure and bats her eyes at the looming stereotype when he arrives. "Listen, Stud. No hard feelings, but the score's even and this round's done." She tosses him a dismissive wave. "Move along."

That must have been annoyed amusement dumbing up the large man's face back there. Jack realizes it only by witnessing the absence of that humor now. "Get off the fucking stool."

Liz sighs and takes another draw from her cigarette. "I've got some advice for you, big guy. Take it or leave it. See your chums over there? They're laughing at you. Now, you can either continue to look like a dumb-ass, or you can shake this off, let rip a nice big laugh, and save face." Liz looks away and swigs her beer.

Jack watches Hulk as he strains to process Liz's speech, but he can't keep eye contact and focuses instead on Hulk's broad chest. This view offers no better comfort. From the other table, one of Hulk's friends shout out, "Give it up, Ox!"

Ox, Jack thinks. Perfect.

After an uncomfortably long stare-down, the big man's face softens. Then, Ox *does* laugh. "All right. You win...*this* time."

"Ox, honey. I win every time." Liz winks at him. "What're you drinking? Next round's on me."*

Ox laughs again, lets her know his drink, and withdraws to his friends and their jibes.

The throbbing of Jack's heart subsides, and he takes a moment to appreciate that. Fucking Liz. "You are unbelievable."

"And you look like you need to charge your shorts. God you are a push-over."

"What? Liz, you got away with that because you're a woman. That guy would've ripped my head off."

"It's all about being in control. See, that's your problem, Jack. You don't take control of a situation. You let the situation control you."

He takes a long swig from his bottle. "Thanks for the beer-slogan psychoanalysis."

"I'm just calling it as I see it."

Jack wants to say more, but Frig steps behind Liz and wraps her up in his arms. "Hey, babe. Got five minutes for ya, then we're on."

Liz turns her head and gives him a deep, forceful kiss. "You going to play my song tonight, sweetie?"

"Oh yeah."

"That's good, "she says, "or you won't be getting any tonight."

He snatches the dwindling cigarette from her mouth and takes a puff, looking over to Jack. "So, you're Liz's brother, huh?"

"For some time now." No reaction to that. Just the flaccid stare. "And you're Liz's boyfriend."

Frig puts the cigarette back in her mouth. "Nah. More like she swiped a piece of my soul when I wasn't looking. I follow her around 'til I get it back."

Liz reaches behind and grabs his crotch. "Baby, I chewed up that little piece like an appetizer—I'm after the main course." She gets up and takes cash from her purse. "I'm getting another beer. You need another, Jack?"

Jack waves her off. "I'm good."

Frig pulls a ticket from his back pocket. "Get me one, will you? Give them this. The house is buying for the band tonight."

Liz strides off, intention and determination leaving no alternative to the mulling clutter of crowd to make room for her. Just Frig and him now. Alone.

Too many quiet seconds makes it clear that Liz's new beau isn't a conversation-starter. Jack is forced to speak, just to take the spotlight of silence off him.

"So, is this a full-time thing for you?"

"I wish. I'm on the assembly line at Ryklin Tractor. Pays the bills. Sewage plays a couple times a month. This town's a shitty scene for original music."

"Really? I'd think a college town would have more to offer."

Frig snorts. "These college assholes are 'bout as fickle as they come. And they don't care about anything original. College brats stick to their own. If you're not a college band, forget it." He turns and spits on the floor, which introduces a renewed silence. Frig looks back at the stage and Jack stares at his beer.

Liz returns, two bottles in hand and one tucked under her arm. She hands a beer to Frig, sets hers on the table, and drops the third off with Ox, who barks out a loud, appreciative hoot and shows it off with pride to his friends.

Frig raises a brow. "What's that about?"

Jack shakes his head. "Don't ask."

Liz makes a place for herself between Frig's legs, takes his arms and wraps them around her waist, wears him like a trendy jacket. Jack imagines their father's reaction to Frig, how automatic his dislike would have been. As such, their mother carries that disapproval in his stead.

They tease and fondle their words, apply slippery innuendo over each other. Nothing significant passes between their lips, only the mutual pleasure of two egos stroked and privacy kept. Jack shifts in his seat, wonders what it must be like to be his sister, to suck the juice and leave the pulp of a relationship clinging to the rind. Wonders. Wishes. Is he not making a distinction, or admitting that, at least in this moment, there isn't one?

When the jukebox cuts out and a drum roll rips through the PA, Frig downs his beer and pushes Liz away to stand up. "That's my cue."

"Knock 'em dead." Liz grabs him by a wad of shirt and draws him to her, devours him with a hungry kiss.

Frig jumps to the stage and straps on his guitar as the band makes last-second adjustments. The houselights go dark. The drummer raises his hands and brings his sticks together quick— one two three four—then sound and light explode into a bulldozing, breakneck thrumming of metal. Four heads of hair thump up and down in rigorous time to the thashing beat, and Frig leaps and lands with every power chord he strikes. Liz hops to her feet and begins screaming, and others in the audience, Ox included— he's already standing—join in. Jack resists the urge to plug his ears against the sheer pressure of volume. This night has overtaken him, a disorientating wander into tribal ritual—rites of passage and dominance, rapturous displays to primal music—with him an outsider to their revelations.

After five distortion-growling, drum-pounding songs of screaming vocals, Frig steps up to his microphone as the audience howls and claps. "Hey! You guys are a fucking great audience! All right, all right. This next song we're gonna slow down a bit—let's see the ladies take the floor. This one goes out to Liz…" Frig points to her with barroom rock star drama, "…my sweet, dark angel."

Liz screams again, all her attention on Frig as he plays a snarling melodic intro on the guitar that the accompanying instruments fall into eight beats later. A straightforward metal ballad that swells to an eruptive chorus of chords and thundering drums backing the blonde-haired vocalist who shoots straight for the screaming falsetto while Frig provides a bed of harmony:

"Dark angel, you…
Cut me down,
tear me in two,
raise me up,
to soar with you.
Dark angel, my sweet dark angel."

It's words like these the quiet kid in the camouflaged pants might have scrawled onto a notebook cover as he hunched over his desk in the back row of homeroom. Jack and Liz have cursed this kind of music so many times, but here and now, she absorbs every word sung and sways to the music as Frig aims his guitar solo right at her.

The song is winding down, the lead singer sitting at a keyboard and hammering out a pseudo-classical piano motif. Liz looks to Jack, smiling. He shrugs at her for lack of a better response, then Liz's face goes taut, looking somewhere behind him, and though he can't hear her, he sees her lips clearly form the word *Fuck*. Jack turns around to see Len walking a staggered line toward them. This, perhaps, is not good.

"Hey, guys, here you are, how's it goin'?" Len slaps his hands upon the tabletop, grinning widely first at Jack, then at Liz for a long, lingering moment. The mellow passivity of his usually drooping eyes and pale face flushes and broils with steaming intoxication.

"Len," Liz says with an even tone and a cold stare. "What are you doing here?"

He huffs. "Well, that's a warm welcome, hey Jacky?"

"Hi, Len." Jack is cautious. "Did we miss a party?"

"Party?" Len stretches out his arms to the stage. "The party's right here. No way I'd miss the musical stylings of Sewage, featuring the great Frig." Within the loud bar, Len is too loud.

Liz says nothing, grabs a cigarette and lights it.

"Is that our wonder boy right there?" Len waves to the stage. "Hey, Frig! You're the man!"

Liz breathes smoke with stony lividity. "Len. Don't do this."

Frig and the rest of Sewage disarm instruments as the lead singer shouts into the mike. "All right, we're going to take a quick break and we'll right back!" The crowd screams and claps, cries for more. Len breaks out into spastic applause, bumping into the table and tipping over Liz's beer bottle. Liz jumps back and Len makes a failed attempt to upright the bottle spewing foam, instead knocking it to the floor where it shatters against the metal base of the table.

"Whoa, all right, their music shatters glass, man. Fucking fantastic." He moves toward the mess.

Jack stands up and grabs Len's arm. "Hey, leave it. Don't worry about it."

Frig hops off the stage and walks over to them, appraising Len. He sends Liz a questioning look and she gives a slight nod and roll of eyes. "Hey, buddy, how's it hangin'?" He puts out a hand to Len.

Len laughs a high, strained laugh. "Frig! You're Frig! Hey, man, this...this is an *honor,* man." He pumps Frig's hand violently. "I'm Len...Lenny...just a friend, just a friend..." His voice trails as his smile fades, attention back on Liz. "Just a friend."

Liz stands. "Len, I swear to God—"

Frig interrupts her with an intense silence, raising his chin in a request to let him handle this. Stifled, she returns a sweltering stare, then pushes her upturned palms at him—a bitter handover—and about-faces.

Frig pulls his hand free from Len's grip with some effort. "Well, thanks for comin', man. Glad to see ya."

"Oh, yeah, wouldn't miss it." Len looks back at Frig, but his plastic joviality has foamed over. His features slide into a scowl.

"So, you and Liz, huh? A duet? A pair? That's…that's *awesome*, man. Really."

Jack moves in closer to Len and lays a hand on his shoulder. "Len, you need a beer? Let's get you a beer."

Len bucks his knob of shoulder away. "Hold on, Jacky, I'm talkin' to Frig, man." He leans in a bit closer, as if ready to share a secret. "She's nice, isn't she? She's so fucking nice and sweet and fun and shit, isn't she?"

Frig's face is hard, his eyes pinched together, and he pushes Len back. "Dude, don't start anything, all right? I got a show to do here."

"Yeah, a show. You know, Liz knows all about show business, man. Puttin' on an act, playin' to the crowd. Gettin' what she needs. But man, don't fool yourself. You can't play her like you play your, your, your *guitar* over there. She'll just play right along, 'til she decides the song's over." Len moves in again. "Then you're old news, and she'll find a new tune to hum."

Liz whips back around. "Len, you fucking tool."

"Dude, back the fuck off." Frig pushes Len back harder.

Jack tries to draw Len away again with a firmer grip on his shoulder. "Come on, Len. Let's step outside so we can—"

Len flails an arm back and all Jack sees is the blur of a hand, then a *thud* and the fat pain of a fast-swelling lip. The taste of blood on his tongue. "Damn it!" Hand goes to his mouth, hope goes south, and this night has gone completely to hell.

Len looks back, dull shock stupifying his face. "Oh Jacky, man, I'm sorry, I—"

Frig grabs Len by the collar and swings him around. "Dude, you gotta get the *fuck* outta here NOW."

Liz shouts out, "Frig, don't! Just let him be. Lenny, just GO."

"You got trouble here?" a baritone voice rumbles and Ox moves in behind Frig, facing Liz with itchy eagerness. Always when it seems like it can't get any worse.

Liz, flustered, glances at Ox briefly and waves him off. "Thanks, we're fine."

"Get your goddamn hands offa me!" Len yells, grabbing Frig's shirt with both hands. Frig shakes Len hard back and forth twice, growling "Son of a bitch," from locked jaws. Len frees a hand, draws back, and swings wild, side of his fist connecting with Frig's ear. Frig stumbles beside the table, legs skitter for control, and he sits hard on the floor. Liz cries out "Christ!" and moves toward Frig.

With a crooked grin, Ox takes a step forward. Jack screams "No!" and reaches to move Len away as the massive man draws back the brick of a fist and drives it straight into Len's jaw with a *smack-pop*. Len careens back, Jack tries to brace himself but Len is just six feet of fast-falling flesh and they both go sailing back, fast, too fast, and Jack tries to bring his head up, or put his hands down, but it's all a blur, and Len is an insurmountable force against him, and he is falling, falling...

...into the black void.

-20

"Make sure you're laying enough sand for the base," his father has always said on the dirt-churned steep slope of the hill in the front yard. "And take care that it's level."

Jack digs the trench that curls gently around the property, the stone retaining wall that will always be there, cupping the ground and holding back the soil that would shift and flow down but for the repelling force of stone that blocks it.

His dad has poured the sand in the trench, the sand that Jack packs down with the heavy tamping tool, and the cement blocks of the retaining wall have been laid carefully, checked with a level, and stacked up.

"We are unwelcome guests, Jack," His father has always said. "There's no balance with nature, there's only the battle against it. All we can do is dig in, build up, and push back." His father's hand is on Jack's shoulder. "That's how we exist, Jack."

The hillside is a severe drop, and at the bottom, the soil is ragged and cut by the runoff of rain that gouged the ground in clumps. His father points out the eroding earth to Jack. "We have to defend ourselves, Jack. We have *to take a stand. The forces of nature don't want us here. Nothing has been granted to us. We are defined by our defiance, and we grow through our resistance." His father bends down and grabs a clump of grassy skin in his massive hand, tearing it away, the humus flesh bleeding loose soil. Brushing away the sprinkles of dirt from the divot, he reveals a red button. "Gotta be careful where you dig, Jack. Understand?" And those firm, forceful eyes have been staring at him desperately since the beginning, and Jack squeezes his eyes shut and says, "It's not level, Dad. I'm sorry."*

And Jack has laid the final blocks on the wall, and the east end slopes down slightly because Jack isn't careful as he tamps the sand in the trench that he will dig with his father. And his father has touched the wall and said, "It's good, Jack. The wall can't be perfect."

"But, will it hold, Dad?" he asks his father, and turns from the wall to face his father's coffin, and the priest sets a level to the ledge of the coffin, watching the colored bubble come to a rest at the center line, and he solemnly makes a sign of the cross. "Balance," Father Karrington declares, and steps away, and Jack looks around him, and he is all alone as the rain begins.

A white, noisy fuzz as his eyes half-open. Vague figures move around him, over him, saying things that he can't grab hold of because he can't cut through the gelatinous pain.

"…stopped the bleeding…"

"…IV is in…."

"…want a CT scan stat…"

And he sinks into blackness again.

The rain seems eternal as he struggles against the current of raging run-off that flows savagely against the retaining wall, digging at the soil, tearing at the foundation, loosening the cement blocks. Jack is drenched by the sheet of unending water pummeling him and he grabs at the shifting blocks of the

wall to hold them in place.

And then light like a million strikes of lightning and everything is oblit-erated by white and he is falling or floating or rising and the white dissi-pates to gray and the gray swells to black and he feels himself breaking apart breaking down expanding in every direction by every geometric point of his being spreading into the void into the eternity of black and he is nothing and everything and empty and whole like the infinite opposition of duality and he aches for balance for perfection for nothingness and he is strangled and squeezed by oppressive weight and mass and seared by infernos and battered by the chaotic rending forces of motion and now he just wants it to end to be done to be undone to draw into himself to pull himself back into a single point into nothingness into

Balance. That word floats in his throbbing mind and even now the meaning drains from his consciousness. He seems to be awake; beyond that, there's only jumbled fragments—broken pieces he can't fit together.

Everything is stiff with light. He wants to shut his eyes again. A sound, or sounds, soft and quiet; the long exhale of a heat regis-ter, a light and steady beeping somewhere near him.

His head is hazed by pain, and he smells a sour clean odor, like an old body bathed too many times. When he swallows, his eyes squeeze shut again to a throat of steel wool.

When is it, Thursday? No, that's wrong. It can't be. What is the last thing he remembers

Balance

before this? The meeting at work. Arguing with Rick. But that was Wednesday. Think. Something about the computer, about the website. Sure, when he discovered all the responses to it on Fri-day. The email from Pauline, and replying to her. Friday night. And then he got the call from Liz, and she invited him out to The Quartermaster's—

He has it. Len, drunk and out of control. Len, who began

fighting with Frig, and then the Hulk stepping up, punching Len, and

nothing is granted to us, Jack

then just blackness.

No, there is more. Something extremely important happened between Ox's punch and his current befuddlement in this white, quiet, smelly room. Something, something about

I'm sorry, Dad

about his father. Yes. He was with his father, building the retaining wall. That was, what? Nine years ago? Ten? Why is he thinking about that now?

It was a dream, just a weird, bizarre dream, but

balance

it seems like so much more. He tries to reform the images, but he can't. He can't think because there's a force, a low raging hum of pain pulsing through his head, and he just wants to fall back into darkness, into

nothingness

the womb of sleep.

"Jack?"

A voice, distant. He could drift away from it, succumb to the weight of exhaustion, but he fights for clarity, for coherence, and struggles to open his eyes again. Liz looks down at him. She's in the same clothes from last night, still smells like last night, but against the sterile hospital room, she looks overexposed, her color bleeding beyond her borders. "Hey, boyo. Welcome back."

Jack struggles to speak, knows what he wants to say, but the wrong words come out. He tries again, his voice a raspy breath. "Where'd I go?"

"La-La land, little brother." She's incomplete. Some part of her is missing. A portrait without its frame. "You had us worried."

His mother leans over him, small and folded by worry. "Oh, Jack. Jack, it's good to see you awake. How do you feel? Are you in pain? The nurse went to get the doctor. He should be here soon." He feels the warmth of her hand cover his as she leans down to kiss his forehead.

"Hurts." He tries to give her hand a squeeze, but isn't sure if he does.

She purses her lips and her head shakes, more a palsy than of disapproval. "Oh, those damnedable *bars*. They just aren't safe. You should have never been there."

Liz glares. "Mom, *definitely* not the time."

"Not the time? Jack is lying in a hospital with his head cracked open. And you tell me that it's 'not the time?'"

Liz repels to the corner of the room and throws herself into a chair. "I'm not going through this with you again."

Jack draws his elbows up and in, tries to sit up, and the entire world collapses onto his head as his insides are yanked like elastic. His limbs are lead. Good enough reason not to try that again. He groans and lies still, which is a far more workable plan for him—he'll stick to it.

"Don't try to move. Just take it easy. Do you want the bed raised a little?"

Jack can only blink at his mother, hope she understands he means 'yes.' She takes the bulky plastic control and elevates his head, then brings a glass to his lips. With every weak sip comes cool, liquid life. Sparkles of light from the water's surface drawn from the straw to crackle against the roof of his mouth and his cheeks.

Questions, too many of them, knot his thoughts. When he can untangle one, he seizes it. "How long have I been out?" His lips don't move right, and his slug tongue worms around his mouth.

"You've been in and out all night," his mother replies, returning her hand to his. "It's Saturday morning."

"How bad?" Maybe better not to ask. He has no idea what is missing or maimed or no longer working. His hand searches for his head and touches a heavy wrap of gauze circling his forehead. He follows it around to the back of his skull and feels a thicker wad of gauze padding and a piercing pain that darkens his vision.

"You have nothing to worry about." The accent is smooth and delicate. A short, stocky man steps toward his bed, innocuously official in ceil scrubs and white coat. Asian, tan-skinned with thinning black hair slightly tussled, a smile on his round face that seems permanent. "I am Dr. Haizuki, Mr. Cross. It's good to see you alert."

Jack chuckles and his throat grinds. "This how alert feels? Alert sucks." His speech still comes out inebriated.

Dr. Haizuki's smile widens. "And a sense of humor. All good signs." He stops beside Jack's mom. "Mrs. Cross. Good to see you again." The doctor leans over Jack, slips a penlight out of his pocket, and shines it into each of his eyes. The light is like a thumb pressing into each of his sockets.

"Thank you for taking such good care of my son, doctor."

"Oh, please. No gratitude is necessary." He turns to Liz. "And you will be happy to know your friend, Mr. Cantrell, is recovering just fine and is ready to be taken home."

"Great." Liz smolders. "And I suppose I'll be the one doing that."

Jack has forgotten about Len, has no idea what happened. "He all right?"

"Broken jaw." Liz says and savors bitter satisfaction. "At least that'll shut him up for a few weeks."

"Liz!" The name snaps like a whip from his mother's lips. "That's horrible."

"No, it's horrible what he did last night. All this is his fault."

Dr. Haizuki lifts his clipboard and scans Jack's chart. "Please, that is not here nor there. My concern this moment is making sure that Mr. Cross will be leaving us soon in fitness and health."

"What's the verdict, doc?" Jack asks.

"What do you recall before your loss of consciousness?"

"I remember...the bar. The fight. Len...falling into me. Then..." Blackness.

Haizuki nods. "Good. That is good. By your sister's account, you fell against the metal base of a table, giving yourself a nasty cut to the back of the head. You lost a considerable amount of blood and required fourteen stitches. More to our concern, however, is the concussion you sustained. We need to make sure there is no skull fracturing. We haven't found anything to cause immediate concern, though our tests aren't conclusive yet. I will have a CT scan scheduled shortly."

His mother looks confused, concerned. "Again? So soon? He was being scanned when I first came here."

"Another is required."

"But is that normal?" his mother asks.

"Not necessarily. But in this case, it was simply equipment failure, not any complications with your son. The scanner is being recalibrated and then we shall try again."

Jack's first instinct is to nod, accept, and desert this frustrating and cumbersome consciousness . Something important was just said, though. Something he should pay attention to. "Equipment failure. Like a malfunction? While scanning me?"

"Hey, maybe you have weird mutant powers now," Liz says.

Haizuki's smile opens wide, a halting hand raised. "No, no. No harm to you. Not a malfunction. Just an error. A…glitch. The scan was incomplete, that is it. No danger to you."

Equipment failure…while scanning his head. There's a hum in his ears, an agitation in the air. "What kind of error?" Jack is looking at him, hard and long, from one eye to the other and back.

"Nothing to bother your head about," the doctor says, head tilted to the side, quizzical. "That is the technician's problem."

"I'd like to know. Please." A little desperate, that 'please.' Hard not to sound that way while his heart races.

Dr. Haizuki is quiet, like he's calculating a risk or motive. "Just an error, Mr. Cross. Flash of screen…data overrun error… call in the technicians. Yes? No harm to you, I promise. Simply inconvenient."

All the pain is there, but as a huge lump, and he is beside it now, removed from it. He remembers. Not all of it, but some. Of falling, tumbling into infinity. He's experienced it before, felt that tug of force when his thoughts have skimmed the Shrug, but never so vivid, so powerful, so insistent. My God, is that what happened?

Had the scanning equipment found the Shrug? Could the scan have almost triggered it?

His mother draws close to Jack, hand grazing his cheek. "Jack? Are you okay?"

He tries to be calm and applies a vinyl smile. "Fine, Mom. No worries." It doesn't sound convincing at all, and the dishonesty maroons him on that bed.

The doctor continues. "But rest assured, there are no early warnings of sustained trauma. We'll be running tests on you to gauge your verbal and motor responses, perform another scan to confirm no fracture or hematoma has occurred, and if all is well, send you home for rest and recuperation."

"Doctor," his mother says. "How long should he be off his feet?"

"That will be for the tests and continued observation to decide. In the best-case scenario, he may return to light activity in a week. We shall see." Dr. Haizuki pats Jack's shoulder. "But maybe keep away from the bars for a while, Mr. Cross."

"Thank you." Very self-satisfied, his mother's gratitude. She delivers a victorious glare to Liz. "Hear that?"

"Yeah, whatever." Liz gets up and heads for the door. "I need a smoke." Hand plunges into her pocket for cigarettes as she leaves.

Jack can't get out of that moment in time when the doctor explained the equipment failure. *Data overrun error.*

Just a coincidence. He's not thinking clearly, jumping to bizarre conclusions. But, bashed brains or not, it's impossible to discount the fact that a highly advanced machine shot particles into his head, collected the data, and then shut down because it received some overload of incomputable information. He needs to be logical, rational, and it's too hard. Too tired. Too much pain.

"Get some rest, Mr. Cross. We'll check on you regularly." Doctor Haizuki exits the room, and Jack is left alone with his mother.

"You heard the doctor, Jack. Just relax and sleep. You're going to be fine."

Jack shuts his eyes and blots the world out, but the worry and questions stay, partners to the pain. And the dark nothingness nesting behind his eyelids—once a swift comfort—now makes him hold fast to the chill steel of the bedrail.

-19

Jack surfaces from sleep, a gentle bob of consciousness, with Liz's hand squeezing his arm. "Sorry to wake you, Jack. Just wanted to say goodbye and let you know that Mom went home. She said she'll be back later. And I've brought you a visitor." Her eyes roll and angle left to a figure hanging back from his bed. It's a face Jack barely recognizes. The way his head leans and his shoulders set low make the injuries more a load he carries than an injury he sustained.

His cheeks swelling out from his narrow face turn his head into a pear. And, as fruits go, this one has sat far too long on the counter. Dark blue runs along his jaw line, ringed by purple and yellow blotches. His lips are split and puffy, dark stitches running vertically just off of center, making his mouth appear sewn shut.

"Len, you look like I feel." Jack gives him a groggy smile.

"I'm sorry, Jack." His words are a garbled mumble through that wired jaw and ruined mouth.

The apology just makes him want to roll over back to sleep. Jack doesn't have the mental energy to lay blame. Besides, Liz is taking care of that just fine.

"Forget about it, Len. You and I have enough things to feel bad about without adding this to the heap." He throws Len a limp salute of raw meat, barely the sense of that arm being his.

"Aye, Cap'n," Len murmurs and salutes back.

"All right," Liz says. "You rest up. I'm going to drive this pathetic body—" she motions to Len, "—home." She leans over and surprises Jack with a quick, awkward kiss on his cheek. "Glad you're okay, little brother." She and Len leave.

That's a new one. Jack closes his eyes, the anomoly of sisterly affection still a figment on his skin. He wonders what exactly happened at The Quartermaster's after he fell, how it must have been for Liz and Len, and he draws the covers more tightly over him.

Fragments of his dream return, the residual images and sensations exhibiting so much more substance than dream. What had been spoken, what he had seen, was like some bizarre communication with…well, he has no idea. The last he can remember—the mind-bending, incomprehensible state of being everywhere and everything at once—is a widening cavity inside him. He tries to make sense of it, but his thoughts merely skip and stick, and he gives in to sleep.

Nurses come and go like intermittent bumps and dips on a long road to nowhere. They hardly interrupt his dreamless slumber. Dawn arrives with eggs, toast, and juice, but a persistent nausea limits him to merely nibbling at the plate of food. He pushes the tray away thinking he'll be adventurous and attempt a walk to the bathroom. He doesn't relish the particularly awkward act of urinating into a bottle in his bed. Some things just shouldn't happen where you sleep and eat. He raises the head of the motorized bed to an upright position, feels pretty good about that, then swings his legs over the side. Not bad, not bad. He stands up.

Bad idea. His head rings and his stomach lurches with a fairly uncomfortable squidginess that sends him right back down onto the bed. That urinary container is silently laughing at him with its oblong mouth. He swings his legs back into bed, takes the container from the stand and surrenders with abject humiliation to the mocking bottle.

Any time now, they'll be coming to cart him off for another CT Scan. He's willing to bet that the same data overrun error will occur. The scan must have somehow found his "little gift," and the information overloaded the system. He could talk more with Dr. Haizuki about it, but no matter what angle he approaches the conversation, it will invariably lead to him mentioning the Shrug, or else create unwanted curiosity in the doctor that Jack doesn't want to deal with. Best not to tread the line of that subject.

Of greater concern is what will happen to him should he be subjected to another scan. It could have any number of potentially hazardous effects, even trigger the Shrug itself.

So, does he simply refuse the procedure? And, if so, for what reason? It better be damn good for it to sound rational to the doctor.

And then there is the fairly convincing proof that the Shrug is real, that this ability truly exists inside of him. Until now, he has side-stepped the issue after a lifetime of being unable to disprove or discount it. Now, he's compelled to some action or decision. But, other than a cryptic series of baffling images in a half-remembered dream, he has no clue what in the world he is supposed to do.

He watches TV and wavers in and out of consciousness. He awakes to his mother's return. It's good to see her, just to be able to talk. Well, at least *listen* to someone, as she handles the lion's share of the conversation. He doesn't feel like talking anyway, and listening to her eases him away from the dull but still persistent pain in his head. His mom pulls out a deck of cards, he swings the small table over his bed and they play Hearts.

Dr. Haizuki returns. "How is our guest?"

"Better," Jack says. "Though I don't think I'll be running any marathons soon."

"One step at a time. But, if the scan shows nothing to concern us, we will keep you overnight for observation and prepare for your release tomorrow."

"Oh, that is wonderful." She pats his hand. "You can stay with me until you're well enough to be on your own." Material instincts swell her compact frame.

"I don't think that's really necessary, Mom—"

"That would actually be prudent," Dr. Haizuki says. "You will likely realize the wisdom of it as soon as you try to stand up."

He's managed to already prove himself wrong with his failed bathroom escapade. "Tried that. Okay, I suppose that's the way to go." She will fret and fuss, check on him with greater frequency than the nurses coming into his room every couple of hours, inject heavy doses of guilt into her ministrations.

"So," the doctor continues, "I will send an attendant in to deliver you to imaging, then we will see what we see."

So, this is it. He hates having his mom here to further complicate the situation. He has no clue what he should say, so he decides that the best course of action is to keep it simple, and be absolutely obstinate.

"Doctor, I'm opting to go without the CT scan." The statement hangs in the air like a discordant tone. Both Dr. Haizuki and his mother stare.

"I'm sorry?" The doctor's soft grin turns rigid.

"Jack, what are you talking about?" He could have slapped his mother and received no more wounded and shocked a response.

Jack siphons all emotion from his delivery. "I do not wish you to scan me. You can do whatever else you need to, but I won't submit to any kind of scanning equipment."

For the first time since meeting him, the smile on Dr. Haizuki's face wavers and falls. "I don't understand. It is the only way we can be certain there are no complications resulting from the accident. Potentially *severe* complications."

Jack looks at him evenly. "I understand, doctor. I'll sign whatever waivers I need to, but there will be no scans."

Dr. Haizuki's shoulders straighten and roll back as his arms drop to his side. He looks uncomfortable, as if he resents having to strap on the constricting suit of professional authority. "Mr. Cross. Although I admit I have been casual in my discourse with you, I cannot emphasize enough that a concussion is a serious injury, and without the standard CT scan, we are unable to be certain that any number of disastrous conditions such as subdural hematoma or cerebral oedema, both conditions which are *fatal* without immediate treatment, have not occurred."

Just nod and agree. Don't reveal that the warnings terrify him. He doesn't want to die, didn't realize the decision he now makes could mean life or death. But the catastrophic effects of the scans that could happen can't be dismissed. "I understand the severity, doctor, but my mind is set. I'm sorry. No scans. I forbid it."

His mother's voice rises and face pulls long with dismay, that look he has seen countless times in his youth. He feels sixteen again and caught smoking in the garage. "Jack, stop this. You don't have a choice. You have to let them run the scan. Why in the world *wouldn't* you want them to?"

How easy it would be to answer her—and how damning that response would be. Especially now, having sustained a traumatic head injury, he would most certainly be declared mentally unfit and stripped of any right to make decisions for himself. It would be equally easy to throw out a fabricated reason. *I'm claustrophobic. I'm terrified of radiation. It's against my religion.* But these weak excuses would only paint him into a corner. As desperately difficult as it is for him, he remains stolid. "My decision is made. Discussing it is a waste of time."

"A waste of time?" she sputters. "Is your *life* a waste of time?"

"Mom, you're just going to have to accept my decision and trust me."

Her hands grapple and search herself for some solution. This is what she has avoided. She doesn't want to deliberate predicaments, to be forced into decisions. He expects her to make reference to his father, something like, "If your father were here…" and then she would be absolved of duty, written off from the responsibility of the situation.

She doesn't, instead indulging in the hysterics his father would never tolerate. "You're not making any sense, Jack!"

Dr. Haizuki crosses his arms and shifts in place. "Mr. Cross. I cannot disagree with your decision more. It is reckless and hazardous." He exhales and his brow rumples. "However, I also cannot force you into a procedure you do not wish."

His mother looks betrayed. "What? Are you telling me you are letting a patient with a *head* injury make a dangerous medical decision on his own?"

"Mr. Cross has responded well to all cognitive and reflexive tests and shows no symptoms that would suggest a more serious head injury. Unfortunately, I have no choice but to declare him competent."

"Oh, this is madness," she hisses, and her eyes plead one last time. "Please, *please*, Jack. Don't do this."

He hates what he is doing to his mother, and all he can tell himself over and over is that he has no choice.

Dr. Haizuki glances back at Jack's chart and hashes out notes with abrupt strokes. His manner is fragmented, half-started, a man with the right procedures in his hands, but in the wrong place and without a viable solution. "Well, all that is left for us to do is continue observing you, Mr. Cross. We will monitor pupil response, blood pressure, heart rate, and respiration. Meanwhile, it is imperative that you be completely open with us as to your ongoing condition. Have you lost olfactory senses? Is your vision blurred? Are you dizzy? Are you involuntarily losing consciousness? These are all signs of any number of complications that could be life-threatening to you."

"Thank you doctor," Jack says. "I appreciate your understanding."

Dr. Haizuki's eyes widen, and the smile returns, but bitter and unpleasant. "Understanding? I don't understand this at all, Mr. Cross. And furthermore, I resent the position you are putting me in. I have a sworn duty to do whatever is in the best interest of my patients, and you are making me compromise that." He gives Jack one last hard stare, swivels on his heels and with controlled, measured strides is out the door.

-18

They run tests on him throughout the day—verbal, visual and motor response. His mother just sits, swapping worry for frustration, anger for resignation. When she leaves, Jack avoids worry and guilt with more sleep.

When he's discharged from the hospital the next day, he does indeed sign a waiver acknowledging his refusal for urgent medical treatment, and that refusing such treatment could be harmful to himself. Dr. Haizuki writes out a prescription for pain pills, tells him to take only as needed and no more than three a day. Jack is to schedule an appointment for another examination in two days. He's wheeled out of the hospital forty hours after arriving, at 3pm Sunday afternoon.

His mother, never one to submit to silent acceptance, berates him for the reckless abandonment of his well being as she drives. He retreats to semiconscious oblivion, his only defense. When he wakes at the foot of the driveway, she is blaring silence.

His vision comes to slow focus on the retaining wall of the front yard as the car turns onto the driveway. The tiered concrete rows stretch out, holding back not the weight of tons of earth, but the surging force of some terrible truth flowing against him—pulling him under.

There's no balance with nature, there's only the battle against it. All we can do is dig in, build up, and push back. That is how we exist, Jack.

Just what the hell is that supposed to mean?

Nothing. Just a dream, no more.

In the garage, she shuts off the car. "I have your old room all ready for you. I put the little portable TV in there."

"You were all prepared, weren't you?"

"Well, someone has to look after you. You're certainly not."

Jack reverts to silence again and opens up his door. Standing is not the challenge. Remaining on his feet however is a chore without everything around and inside of him swirling and twisting. He grabs the frame of the car for support and his mom rushes over. "Careful. Here, put your arm around me."

He does, and walks clumsily with her into the basement. "Just when you thought you didn't have to take care of me anymore, huh?"

"A mother's duty is never done. Besides, it'll be nice having someone else in this house for a change."

They lean and half-step against each other from the family room into Jack's old bedroom. Just the bed, a corner desk, and a dresser. His mom hung some family pictures in the room, including several of his father. Jack can barely recall the room as it once was, with all his posters and books, his stereo and computer. He had spent so much time here, struggling through the throes of his teenage years, keeping out of Liz's way, pining over Christine Regitz who never wanted to be anything more than a late night phone friend as Jack regaled her with his obsessive attention. It's an odd mix of nostalgic comfort and unease to plop down onto his old bed again. His mom draws back the covers and he lies down.

"All I need is for you to come in here and yell at me to clean up this pigsty and I'll be back in time."

"Do you want soup? Let me fix you some soup."

"Not now. I'm pretty tired. Thanks, though." He pulls the covers up to his chin.

She hovers, not saying anything, but obviously wanting to. He can't stand that piercing stare.

"Mom, I really don't want to talk about it, okay?"

She purses her lips and, after a moment, turns, saying only "I sure hope you know what you're doing, Jack."

And as he lies in these familiar surroundings of his past, he slips back into sleep, hoping the same thing.

That evening, Jack watches TV and eats his mother's thick, meaty version of soup, the only way his father would tolerate it, then drifts off into an uninterrupted slumber. He wakes early Monday morning and his body is not so much refreshed as it is anxious and restless to do anything other than lay in bed and sleep. He has, after all, been sleeping for most of the last two-and-a-half days, and it seems like much longer. His legs twitch with volts of eager energy.

He needs to go to the bathroom, bad. Such a mundane action, and he has to fret and bother over it as a major undertaking. He takes it slow, peeling back the covers and dangling his legs over the side. Head thuds as he eases himself up, but the queasiness of his stomach is all but a faint memory. He walks through the downstairs family room to the bathroom, fighting some light-headedness, but confident and determined.

Urination. Upright and full stream. Reveling in the regained dignity of not having to piss into a container in a prone position. Some of the sweetest moments in life are for relishing in the solitude of a bathroom.

He's up and about now, and wants to stay that way for as long as his body can manage it. He walks to the stairs and gazes up at this next challenge. It's not even six in the morning yet; his mother will still be asleep for several hours. He can avoid any reprimands for trying this stunt, and there is a particular goal in mind that compels him forward.

He pulls himself up with the railing. Near the top, the throb of his head, especially at the back of his skull, is seismic. Legs are weak and wobbly. He sits on the top step and waits, doesn't move, breathes. Exists within a few fragments of endless pain.

The pounding subsides to a low rumble and he moves on, through the dark, quiet house to the computer on the desk just off the kitchen. He boots it up, connects to the Internet, and logs onto his website account. Sixty-seven new messages await him. This makes his head hurt in the few remaining places where pain has not yet emigrated. He scrolls past them, searching for one particular sender. Toward the bottom, he finds it, sent late Friday night from Iamsurfacing@illinoiscable.com.

FROM: *Iamsurfacing@illinoiscable.com*
TO: *jack@shouldIendtheworld.com*
SUBJECT: Re: Re: None

Dear Jack,

Well! I have to say I was happy to get a reply from you. Well done in following the compulsive whims of fate! In getting it, I was curious to read just what an email from someone who has a site called "Should I End the World" would be like. I have to say, I'm disappointed—you sound far too normal for my tastes!

You asked if I was lonely. How dare you turn the tables on me when I hardly know you! Well, I will never the less oblige you honestly. I am only lonely, Jack, when I want to be. There is a time and place for everything. Just prior to contacting you, I had been embracing a blissful state of loneliness. When I wrote to you it was because I decided I no longer wanted to be lonely at that particular moment. So I reached out. I find you can waste far too much time looking for things when you don't know what you are searching for and don't know where to look; meanwhile, you become distracted to all the things that life is throwing your way to discover. I, therefore, was very purposefully not looking for something, and as a result, I found you! Unfortunately, if I have understood your letter, it seems you may still be looking for yourself. Maybe that's why I found you. Wouldn't that be fun?

You told me about yourself (and I am having a terribly difficult time imagining you toiling away in the corporate world, by the way), so I imagine you are expecting the same from me. But I don't think I'm going to extend to you the same courtesy. I am a complete sucker for mystery. So, I will give you clues to the mystery that is me. If you can solve my mystery, you are worthy of knowing me. And if you prove yourself worthy, I can reward you by returning to you the you that I have found.

So, here is your first clue to the enigma of Pauline:

> I guard those bindings that liberate
> and tend to spines—no bodies to support.
> Though I may seek cover, I do not hide.
> Truth and fiction are what I sort.

I hope to hear from you soon, Mr. Jack.

-P

Jack sinks further back into his chair. His chest strains against the fervor of a heart that does not question the absurdity of the order it receives to beat hard and fast. He rereads the email, feels the pull of a grin. And there is a lightness to him, like gravity has relaxed its draw—a precarious, exhilarating loss of control.

Miss Swanson, you are a very peculiar person.

Is this self-proclaimed enigma really someone he would be wise to keep contact with? After all, he has no idea who she is. Jack is certainly familiar with the more disastrous stories regarding computer-based relationships. So, perhaps the best thing to consider is what facts can be discerned.

Her Internet service makes it clear that she is from Illinois. Not too far away. Her email address, though, is an oddity. *I am surfacing.* It makes him think of someone slightly skewed in perspective. Perhaps Pauline Swanson has gone through intense trauma in her life and now sees herself returning from the dark depths of her soul.

Or maybe she just installs driveways for a blacktop company.

Then there's this puzzle—the bizarre little poem of cryptic background into this odd woman. Gut instinct says she is an adult woman and not some sheltered teen looking for fantasy, or some forty-three-year-old hairy-backed guy named Paul exploring his feminine side—but maybe this is just a desperate hope. He reads the poem twice, a third time, and the puzzle solution is obvious. Bindings. Spines. Covers. Truth. Fiction.

Pauline Swanson works in a bookstore. No, a library. It must be a library.

Well, that's…. stable, right?

Sure. Just your stereotypical asocial, repressed loner searching for the ideal man she has read in Shakespeare and Austen and Bronte. When her search inevitably fails, she'll draw a butcher knife in a psychopathic rage and lash out on the last man to refuse her, finally taking her own life after she underscores significant passages from Act IV of *Romeo and Juliet*.

The tug of gravity draws down. He struggles against it, defies it. He clicks the 'Reply' button.

FROM: *jack@shouldlendtheworld.com*
TO: *Iamsurfacing@illinoiscable.com*
SUBJECT: Solving the riddle

Pauline,

It's good to hear from you again, and with a few more words than your first email! Sorry I couldn't reply sooner, but I have just returned from the hospital after hitting my head on Friday night. It was pretty nasty, but I'm fine and recovering. I'll also be enjoying some time off of work until I'm back on my feet. In the meantime, if my words don't come out just right, I can blame it on the head wound.

You have an interesting outlook on life. I could probably learn some things from you, though I'd be fighting years of conditioning to get there.

You mentioned that I might be searching for myself. I hope you don't mind me saying, that is an expression that really gets under my skin, but maybe that's because it's closer to the truth than I'd like to admit. But I would tend to say that I'm trying to find my space within the world. A comfort zone. Right now I kind of feel like I'm leasing it, and it's a one-room kitchenette.

So you're going to keep yourself a mystery, huh? As if an email-based encounter isn't mysterious enough? Well, I'll play along. I'm not a master at word games or anything, but I think you went a little easy on me with the first one. I'm going to say you work in a library. Do I win this round?

All right. I suppose I should get myself back to bed rest. I'm looking forward to hearing from you again. You still haven't actually commented on the website, by the way, and I'd be curious to know your take on it. Looking forward to hearing from you again.

-Jack

He clicks 'send' and makes his way back downstairs.

-17

Jack's on the phone with Greg by eight a.m.

"Holy shit, Jack. Are you okay?"

"I'm fine, considering. But I'll have to take it easy. I have another appointment with my doctor tomorrow, and hopefully I'll be back to work in about a week."

"Well, not to make light of the accident, but maybe it's a good thing."

"Heh. You saying I had a knock to the head coming?"

"Well, maybe not such a hard one. But seriously. I think you could use a little vacation. It might do you some good to take it easy and get away from this Templeton bullshit for a bit."

"Maybe so. But I feel bad leaving Market to you and Sam."

"It's just a trade show. Don't worry about it. The ship-out deadline is today anyway. After that, it's only babysitting reps."

"Thanks Greg." Jack trips over an uncomfortable pause. "Listen—" He's not sure how to word what he is suddenly so desperate to say. "I know I've been a pain lately—"

"Oh shit, don't, man." Greg's words stretch with exasperation. "Don't bother your cracked head over crap like that. Market has been running hard on all of us. Don't make a big deal about it."

Greg's never been a sentimental type. Always leaves the chain latched on the emotional door, one eye squinting through the crack, so Jack doesn't push. At least he got his intentions forced through. "All right. But hey, tell Sam that it falls to her to be a pain in the ass to Rick until I get back."

"I don't think she'll have a problem with that. But you owe me one thing, Jacko."

"What's that?"

"When you get back, crack *me* on the head, would ya? It'll be my turn for a vacation."

Jack laughs. "My pleasure."

"I'm sure. Rest up, buddy boy, and we'll see ya when we see ya."

He hangs up the downstairs phone and walks back to his room, and resting is easier with those previous coarse weeks at work filed down to a softer memory.

It could just be optimism, but by Tuesday, Jack feels markedly improved. The aching of his head often goes unnoticed unless he is up and about for too long, and he avoids bed and sits at the table with his mom in the kitchen or in the downstairs recliner watching TV.

His checkup with Dr. Haizuki is at two o'clock, and his mom drives him over. When they meet with the doctor, he asks Jack if he has reconsidered having the CT scan. Jack tells him that he hasn't. Dr. Haizuki runs through the dangers of that decision again, then proceeds with a complete physical examination.

The large, bulky bandage is removed, and Jack feels naked and vulnerable. He needs to see the wound, the lurking stranger behind his back. When a mirror is held up, he looks through it to the wall mirror behind him and sees a shaved patch on the back of his head. At the center of this stubbled skin, a long, angry gash marks him, like a lower-case 'r', dark with surgical stitches. Bizarre, this suture holding back whatever it is that makes him Jack—as if to break this superficial bond would release some part of him into the very air. He reaches back and, with gentle caution, touches it. It's still sharply tender and swollen. Dr. Haizuki tells him that it is healing well, Jack's motor responses are good, and he can detect no adverse signs that would warn of danger. His wound is redressed with a small bandage.

The following day, Jack tells his mother that he feels ready to return home.

She glances up from her Terry Redlin jigsaw puzzle she is working on at the table. A piece of a tree, or maybe fence post, is pinched between her fingers. "Why in the world don't you stay a few more days?"

There it is—unavoidable, really, and why he dreaded coming here in the first place. She is using that voice, like a buzzing wire ready to snap. This same flustered inflection had been used to say things like, "Why can't you just try to do good in school?" and "Do you have to argue with me about everything?" and "You can't stay in your room forever like this, it's not healthy." This house is a museum to all those strangled emotions of childhood. He needs to get out of here.

She slips the piece in place—it was a section of telephone pole. "You shouldn't push yourself, you know. I can make your meals and you can rest. The doctor said you need to take it easy."

Jack works his foot into his shoe, all the blood in his body eager to help out as it runs into his head and shoves against his skull. "I'll be fine."

"I don't like the idea of you alone in that apartment." Her breath thickens and she coughs, inhales, coughs again. He's been noticing that, too. She coughs a lot, and she takes several naps throughout the day.

"I'm just not going to feel right until I can get myself back into some kind of normal routine. Besides, you've got enough to worry about with Ben and the others coming this weekend. Don't worry about me."

She concedes, but not without several sharp jabs of concern that he stiff-arms with silence. Let her get it out of her system, be Mom one last time. Time will reflect and invert their roles soon enough.

She drives him to his apartment. When he gets out of the car, she keeps her eyes to the empty passenger seat that slowly forgets his weight and she says good-bye. He trudges down the sidewalk and into his door.

Back after five days. The apartment should somehow look different, because the emanations of this place feel different, yet everything is precisely, frustratingly where he left it on Friday night. If he weren't restrained by his own rationality, he would suspect a conspiracy of individuals invading his home and replacing all his possessions with different objects looking exactly the same.

He wanders his rooms, not sure how he is supposed to fall back into normal life. He absently fingers objects along the way— the books on his shelf in the hallway, from Oscar Wilde to Stephen King, from Hawking to Calvin and Hobbes; his high school tennis trophies on his dresser that he keeps planning to throw away but never does; the pocket watch his father had given him six months before he died, now stilled in torpid time on his nightstand. He touches them all, and his other hand moves inexorably to the back of his head, measuring the physical pain of the wound against the emotional sensations of each tactile encounter.

And then, it happens. Much like it has always happened. A meandering thought that strays upon the fringe of the Shrug.

He is diving down, plummeting into a distant darkness, an empty recess in his mind, and his thoughts become dissipating vapors as he senses it, this vacuum of void, and his awareness approaches a fringe, a border, an event horizon, and he can feel its pull against him, and he is losing himself, losing this awareness of who he is, as if his conscious self is catching the current of this massive abyss of absence, churning and turning him inward, a compressive, nullifying force. And he engulfs this force as it in turn enfolds him, and he knows he can just let go, and it would be so easy to, and feel so right, to just lose himself, lose everything, to find balance. The remnants of

Jack ache with the compulsive, irresistible urge to succumb to this force, to collide into it, and break through, like some cosmic drain wrenched open. It would take just a nudge, just a push, just a shrug…

He is looking at the ceiling. He doesn't know for how long. And what about him? *What, where, who?* These humid questions slowly condense against his cold mind into single drops of thought that trickle down into his awareness. As they pool and seep, he is finally conscious of himself asking these questions, and a dry panic evaporates the moisture from his mouth as he realizes those answers are not readily available.

What?

The *what* is that something has happened, something *bad*. This is a certainty even if nothing else is.

Where?

The *where* is here. And here is familiar, familiar as home. And home is the apartment. Yes. He is fairly certain that the apartment is where he is, and that the apartment should mean something to him, though it is not enough.

Who?

The *who* is him, the one asking this question, the one in the apartment where something bad has happened. Something bad that has happened to him. And he is…

He sits upright, the pulse of pain returning to his head. He's on the edge of his bed, one leg on, one leg dangling, his father's watch in his hand. He knows who he is, where he is, and what has happened. He also knows that *that* has never happened like this before. He has never experienced it with such magnitude. Ever. This was a numbing emptiness of incredible force that tried to swallow him, and it was terrible and horrible because, for a moment, he wanted it. He knows absolutely that he has, just moments ago, sank deeper and closer to the actual act of the Shrug than he has ever gone before.

And it happened involuntarily...beyond his control.

He stands, head swimming, and the final important question sounds in his head.

When?

He turns to the clock, and he stares. He gawks, because the clock appears to be terribly misinformed. What it says can't be possible. But, whether he stares at those red digital numbers on his nightstand in surprise, anger, frustration or desperation, the clock remains stolid.

The *when* is 4:23pm. The *when* is almost an hour from the time he stepped into his bedroom.

He has been unconscious for an hour.

Jack's stomach surges, he feels a swelling pressure in his throat, and he dashes to the toilet, reaching it just in time to throw up.

Part Four

THE DESCENT

-16

Fear like a blindfold in the silent, darkening apartment. Light and sound are only agitators. Anything he sees would offend, any noise shrill, any smell rank.

He paces through the shadows, and the words in his head, spoken with severity in that eastern accent, are impossible to shut off or quiet.

Is your vision blurred? Are you dizzy? Are you involuntarily losing consciousness?

Liz. He'll call Liz. It's time to tell her. She'll tell him what to do.

Brisk strides take him to the phone and his arm makes a spastic lunge for the receiver.

Christ, no. He can't. He can't face her disbelief, her disappointment, her revulsion that she wouldn't hesitate to release on him. She would tell their mother, and his mom would tell the doctor. Besides, twenty years ago, maybe he could have torn that sapling secret up by the roots. Now he can't even get his arms around its trunk.

Get to the hospital, then. Get some help.

They'll ask questions. They'll scan him. What else would they do? He can't allow that. Especially after this last episode, it's obvious the nature of the Shrug has become far more precarious, and another scan is too great a risk. But not getting medical help could mean he will only get worse, and the consequences will be fatal.

The issue of the Shrug itself aggravates his panic. It had come upon him unbidden, out of his control, and that means it could occur again. Only next time, perhaps it will happen. He has never wanted that. That's why he devised the rules in the first place, so no accidental or personal situation could cause it.

What the hell does he do now?

He lies down on the couch and tells himself to calm down. Just calm the hell down. He's been overdoing it, that's all. He had probably just lain down, fallen asleep, and had another vivid dream like he had after the accident. When he woke up, he had been disorientated and so he panicked. Not surprising considering the head injury.

He cycles this through his head for a while, enough maybe not to believe it, but at least accept it, and that allows him to turn on the TV and stare at the screen with a glazed distraction until, after a time, he does a pretty good job of thinking nothing at all.

He nods off eventually on the couch, more as a forfeiture of wakefulness than a commitment to sleep. And he has fitful fragments of dreams about his father, about surging forces, about an infinity of nothing.

The next morning, he tries to keep his mind shut off. He makes coffee, brushes his teeth, showers, gets dressed, and fixes breakfast. Each menial task a reassurance, like hearing the rattle of keys in the coat pocket after tearing a room apart to look for them.

He quails to the clock striking seven. He should be leaving for work, ready for a day of checking emails and adjusting layouts and studying new product specs. He takes quick, darting glances around the room.

The apartment is a mess. He can take care of that.

Swift strides to the cabinet under the kitchen sink for a dust rag and furniture polish. He goes to work on the living room, swirling the rag over the dust-covered occasional tables and his desk. Good. That's better. Neurotic as hell, maybe, but whatever works. He scrubs with a circular fury, watching the gloss finish return to cloudy surfaces.

He plugs in the vacuum, pushes it over the carpeting as it howls and grunts, and he has an implacable wish to put a face to Pauline, draw upon her image. It would be a foothold, a way to ground himself. To focus on a feature—an eye, a mouth, a cheek, an ear. He could be anchored by such a detail.

The apartment smells like burnt hair and hot motor by the time he shuts the vacuum off. He burns some incense Liz had bought him on some long ago birthday, her way of telling him to mellow the hell out. Opium trickles into the air. Vacuum put away, he sits in front of his computer to rest. His head hurts again. He should take a pain pill. Later, maybe. He wants to know if she's written. When he checks his email, he is not disappointed.

FROM: *Iamsurfacing@illinoiscable.com*
TO: *jack@shouldlendtheworld.com*
SUBJECT: Re: Solving the Riddle

Mr. Jack,

It sounds like you received an impacting lesson on the fragile nature of life! I'm glad to hear it sounds like you passed. Rest yourself well, and use the time to reflect upon the temporal glories of the world—such as yourself!

And, though your head wound sounds quite severe, it didn't seem to affect your cognitive abilities, as you have cracked the first code of Pauline! I knew you could do it. Now, buckle yourself in; the ride takes some adventurous turns from this point on. The next clues to revealing the wonders of Pauline follow:

0671214500

0817216731

0840713843

Hint: *Integers Silently Become Names.*

Follow these clues to their destination, and you reveal the deeper mysteries of myself. Have fun, and don't let me down, Jack!

Moving on. You wanted to know what I thought about your website. Hmm. You couldn't ask me an easy question, could you? Well, it is an interesting premise, with a seemingly simple and absolute proposition: All or nothing. I myself could not imagine ever being in such a state as to wish for nothing. I am saddened and troubled by those who would, even in jest, vote for it. Just how does that affect someone in their everyday life, having this seed of desire in them that longs for nothing? Where is there even a place for love, respect, joy, fulfillment, or even desire when one harbors such emptiness in them?

That is why I fret over you, Jack. To even propose the question is to look into the abyss, and you must be careful not to lose your balance on such a precarious edge.

Of course, the question that really begs being asked is: what is *your* vote, Mr. Jack? Is there a reason within you to keep all this something from becoming nothing?

I await your answers most eagerly, Mr. Jack.

-P

Jack rests on Pauline's parting question. He strains to remember when he last attempted to answer it for himself. He struggles to recall any of his old answers. For so long, he has evaded this question—his rules removed himself from the equation. Now, someone else has posed the question to him.

Is there a reason within you to keep all this something from becoming nothing?

The sun has moved to clouds, the day withers to gray, and Jack dwells over everything he can no longer control, tries to think of a time when he could, and his thoughts of work and life and people collide against the Shrug.

The autumn air helps to clear his head as he strolls down his block to the convenience store for some lunch. He had planned to shop on Saturday to fill his empty refrigerator, but a certain bout of unconsciousness in a hospital bed had intruded on that task.

The street he lives on isn't a major road, but is an access to downtown and intersects a block ahead with one of the major Terrapin highways, so traffic at this hour is steady, the cars passing by at their usual ten to fifteen miles over the speed limit as people claw and bite at whatever extra moments they can get between their teeth to gnaw on.

In the store, he is as impatient as his appetite, and quickly selects the long-warmed meat and bean burritos that he told himself last time he would never, ever buy again. The teenaged attendant with the lip stud does not disappoint by making any attempt at courtesy or cordiality as he rings up Jack's purchases with a bitter, mute malaise. Jack heads home.

Burrito in hand, he sits back down at his computer to tackle Pauline's latest puzzle.

He takes a bite of salty sawdust wrapped in a tortilla shell and studies her clues. It's got to be some sort of alphanumerical code. But the numbers all start with zero and the repetitions seem contrary to words and language. He rereads the hint: Integers Silently Become Names.

The reference to integers must reflect back to the numbers. But, *silently become names?* This makes him reconsider his discounted theory that it's an alphanumeric code. As he looks longer at the hint, he notices something odd. Why did she capitalize every word in the sentence? This is, after all, a librarian. No spelling errors or grammatical clumsiness in any of her emails. Likely the capitalization is intended.

Suddenly the whole thing makes sense. So, this is some kind of scavenger hunt, then?

He does an Internet search, finds the Terrapin Library site, and loads the catalog search page. He clicks on Search by ISBN #.

Integers Silently Become Names.

International Standard Book Number.

He keys in the first group of numbers and waits. The search brings up a book and an author. *Surfacing*, by Margaret Atwood. He vaguely remembers the novel. It had been assigned reading in his college lit class, and hadn't left much of an impression. A trudging, mostly introspective story where nothing much happens and then it ends abruptly. The Professor had given him a 'C+' on his paper. But something else tugs at him about the title. Surfacing. Surfacing.

Her email address. *Iamsurfacing*. It must be a favorite novel of hers. Or perhaps there is some sort of relevance in the story to her life.

He keys in the next ISBN number. This time it's a far more familiar title—*Pride and Prejudice*, by Jane Austen. Another book forced on him, not once but twice; first in high school, then again in college. And another book woefully lacking in any dramatic action. *I'm going to have to toss some David Eddings or Chad Williams her way*. He types in the final number.

When the title appears, it surprises him. Certainly he knows the work. Who wouldn't? But, to include this particular piece into the mix says volumes about who Pauline Swanson is. Although many people might include it on a "must-read" or a "most influential" book list, it's no small statement that she had him find it.

The search has responded with *The Holy Bible*.

So, Pauline Swanson has a solid religious grounding and enjoys books with strong female heroines in conflict with themselves and/or their environment.

Jack is ready for his reply.

FROM: jack@shouldlendtheworld.com
TO: Iamsurfacing@illinoiscable.com
SUBJECT: Re: Re: Solving the riddle

Pauline,

Your puzzles are getting more challenging! You had me stumped for a bit there. But I finally cracked your clever little hint, and it was plug-and-play after that. Of course, it is only a semi-victory I suppose, as I would need time and some handholding to learn just what profound insights could be garnished from the titles you provided me.

Surfacing, for instance. I did actually read that book back in college, but I have to confess, I never really understood it. It takes place in Canada, right? But I don't think your intention is to inform me that you are Canadian.

Now *Pride and Prejudice* I know, but I will tell you right now, I am no Darcy! I'm probably more like Mr. Bennett I suppose; down-to-earth, a bit detached and out-of-place to his surroundings. I am going to guess that you have something in common with Elizabeth, then?

And your final clue: *The Bible*. Will you think less of me if I tell you that I haven't read it front to back? I was always more of a New Testament kind of guy. I'd let Sunday mass fill me in on the meatier bits of the Old Testament when I went to church.

This has been an interesting way to get to know some-one. I suppose I should expect as much from a librarian. Now me? I'd be more likely to list King's *The Stand*. Have you read that? I'm thinking maybe not.

You ended your message by making reference to me looking into the abyss. And now, I suppose, you wonder if the abyss is looking back at me? Just how do I answer this? I do feel sometimes that I have unwittingly been cast upon the edge of some great chasm, and that paths that appear to take me away from it actually draw me right back. I do not want to sound odd, but lately I have felt that there is some great conflict taking place, of oppos-ing forces, which we are all apart of, and yet completely detached from. Does that make any sense to you? If I can sound even more insane for a moment, I can't help but feel that there is something I am supposed to do, some action or decision to make, that will provoke an outcome from these polarized forces.

Wow, that does sound totally crazy, doesn't it? You're probably wondering what kind of wacko you've gotten yourself involved with. But, nonsense or not, it just feels good to have someone to discuss this with.

Well, I'm looking forward to your next message, though I shudder to think of what puzzle you'll throw at me next!

Take care,

Jack.

-15

On Friday evening, Jack gets a call from Liz. Is he is up for another round of gaming and finishing off Asterrak? He responds with an absolute yes, desperate to get out of the apartment. And fantasy seems far more desirable then reality. He tells her he'll be over within the hour, and packs up his computer.

He's a little nervous driving to Liz's place. He should be taking it easy. But it's only a five-mile trip, and he can avoid the main highways to get there. He takes the trip slow and cautious. No troubles. Just making a big deal out of nothing. Curbside to Liz's place, he steps out of his car, hoists his CPU up from the back seat, and heads in.

Len is here, long and lean across his usual spot on the couch; Liz must have calmed down. He looks better, only slight discoloration clouding his jaw line. The swelling is pretty much gone, and he is far more like his old self, other than the perpetually clenched jaw that makes him seem pissed off about everything.

"Jacky," he says with a wave, and it sounds like a threat through his wired-shut mouth.

"Hey, boyo." Liz is up on a chair against the wall over her computer, arms hyper extended, little black cut tee shirt rising halfway up her blanched back, steering a framed portrait left and right into place. She lets go, hops off the chair, and flames a cigarette as she gives the painting a quick study. "How're you feeling?"

Jack sets the computer down at his designated spot at the kitchen table, eyes darting to the picture. "I'm good." Sounds almost convincing.

He walks up to the painting. Here's something he hasn't seen for a long time. One of the last things she ever painted. He's never been able to look at it for long; that portrait always stares back a little too hard. "What are you hanging that up for?"

She gives him the same grin she'd worn that long ago night when she had called out his name from the doorway of his bedroom and clicked her camera. "Oh would you give it a damn rest already? If you don't like it, don't look at it."

The painting is a swirl of blues, browns, and blacks, heavy strokes of somber color wisping around a tenebrous face and draining into a resentful storm of two dim eyes. His eyes. Eyes that had still been hating his father after a standup, clenched-throat blaze of words between them that had sent him barreling down the stairs to stew on his bed. That's when Liz had appeared.

"Jack."

He glared at her.

Click.

"Fuck off!" he had yelled and prayed his father hadn't heard and thought it a final retort.

Her reptile smile only needed the flick of a forked tongue to complete it. "It's not the end of the fucking world, brat. Just another goddamn day."

She had brought the painting home a week later from college, a blowfish chest of pride. "Well? How do you like it? I call it, 'The Day The World Ended.'"

He didn't, not at all. Not because it wasn't any good, but he couldn't stomach himself looking back at him with such hate. He told her it was all right as he kept his eyes away from it. She had shown it to their father next.

Two days after that, she moved out.

"That is so fucking awesome," Len says through that vise mouth and sips his beer from a straw. "You gotta get back to painting, Liz."

Liz sits down with a smoky huff. "I don't 'gotta' do anything." She looks at Jack. "And Mom's flipping out about you refusing some scan. What's that all about?"

One of the very subjects Jack was trying to escape by coming here. "Oh, please. Not you, too."

"Well, it is kinda weird that you'd refuse it like that. Besides, you're making me have to put up with Mom's whining. And *that* I don't appreciate. So what is it? Are you freaked out about radiation or something?"

"Something like that."

Liz puts up her hands. "All right, all right. It's your brainpan, chum. Just overcome with sisterly concern is all."

"Well, don't blow a fuse or anything."

"I'll keep my ampage low, bro."

Jack walks to the kitchen into a cluttering mess of greasy pans, chicken bones, and an empty frozen chicken box. He takes a beer from the fridge as he shouts back to Liz, "Thanks for driving my car back from the bar, by the way."

"Yeah. Maybe you can bring some beer next time to show your appreciation."

Jack takes a swig from the can, wonders if he should really be drinking at all and takes another drink as he walks back to the living room. "Hey, I'm not the one who goes through it like water."

"That's bullshit," Len mumbles. "I could never drink water that fast."

"Len, how long is that mouth of yours going to be wired shut?" Jack asks.

"Two more weeks. Liquid diet until then."

"Ouch. Sorry, man." Jack sets his beer down in a clear spot on the table. "I have to grab my monitor and keyboard. Only one trip if I can get a hand."

Liz stands up. "You're an invalid, so I suppose I'll give you one."

They walk out together across the dark front yard and to the curbside, where so many private talks have taken place under the cold confessional of night.

"So, everything settled between you and Len?"

Liz falls heavily against Jack's car, tying her arms across her chest. "Yes. No. I don't know."

"Okay. And that means?"

"It means that everything is back to status quo, and I don't know if that's good or bad. I just don't get why he can't figure out that he and I will never be."

"You're kind of throwing some mixed signals his way."

She frowns. "Like what?"

"Sleeping with him might have given him and idea or two."

Her eyes narrow. "Hey, I told him it didn't mean anything. He said he was cool with that. It's not my problem if he decided to throw a bunch of meaning into it."

He's never been able to figure out if she believes these emotionless outbursts or if she's selling it. And if it is a pitch, is it to him, or to her? Jack can't handle any hostility right now—he needs a night that isn't laden with conflict and antagonism. If he doesn't say something, though, he'll be betraying Len. "Go ahead and tell him a million times that it doesn't mean anything. It won't matter. It still means something to him. And I'm not totally convinced that Len doesn't mean something to you. Problem is, you go through life keeping only the best pieces. You love the rose and curse the thorns, so you chop it off the stem and wonder why the flower dies."

Jack watches her face tighten and he wonders why he said anything, but her trademark cock-sure grin breaks the wave of anger. "Listen, Len is a big boy. He can think for himself. I've been honest with him. It's his prerogative if he wants to fuck me, or tell me to fuck off." She hacks a dry laugh. "And just who the hell are you to be talking to me about relationships anyway?"

Jack drops a hand against the hood of the car and leans. "Now what's *that* supposed to mean?"

Liz shrugs. "Nothing. Just that you don't exactly get involved with anyone. When was the last time you were with someone, Jack? Huh?"

The question catches him off-guard, and he rewinds his memory. How long? Four years? Five? It was the last year of college. Sara Flemming, a Psych Major he shared a Trig class with. Tall, slender, and attractive in a cute athletic way, always wearing shorts and tube socks and running from one place to the other. She was out of his league, really, but college never really had leagues, not in that way. She kept staring at him in class, and he started staring back, and the ground came up on him fast. They spent a few months together. Then, like a blindside blow, she said they were over. He asked her why. She said that whatever it was she had found so intriguing about him had just become tedious. She said she was tired of meeting him for the first time, whatever that meant. It hit him hard, but it didn't take long to recognize that the loneliness after she was gone had an ironic similarity to the three months he was with her.

"What should it matter to you?" There's an edge to his words that he didn't necessarily intend.

"Settle down. I'm not calling you queer or anything." She pushes herself off the car and her body sighs. "You just don't let anyone get close."

Jack squints at her, befuddled. "I don't know what the hell you're talking about." He kicks at the concrete. "I'm just me." When he looks up at her, he can see something uncomfortable fidgeting behind her eyes. "Liz, what is this, anyway? Are you trying to get me to open up to you?"

She's quiet, scratching at her arm like she's bothered by a rash, looking just below his eye line. It's a Liz he has never known—passive and somewhat insecure. Jack feels over-reactive, wanting both to hug her with aggressive affection, and cringe from an expected static shock of wintry contact. Submitting to neither impulse, he maintains a stagnant stare.

Her voice turns quiet. "That night, at the bar. When you fell. That really fucking shook me up. All that blood…running out of you. I was positive you were dead. You looked all pale like a corpse. I completely lost it, Jack. I got on my goddamn knees, used my hands to try and stop the blood from running away." She glances at her hands, then hugs her shoulders with crossed arms. "I think Ox finally pulled me away so they could get to you. It was Len, you know, who had your head in his lap with his jacket, trying to stop the bleeding. Len, moaning through his broken, bloody mouth, holding you together." Liz's eyes are red and straining as she looks back at him. "And there I was, blood on my hands, just looking at you." Her voice tightens and hitches. "What the fuck was I doing, Jack?"

It's too much. He can't see her raw and exposed like this. "Liz, don't-"

"I wanted to fucking throttle Len. He was with you and I was held back. It should've been my lap you were bleeding into. You were going to be gone, and I wasn't going to get that last chance, to be your sister."

The bond between them, always slack and dragging along the ground, is suddenly a taut vibration, and the secure comfort is also a snaring constraint. Her naked, unguarded gaze yanks on that cord. He drops his eyes to Liz's black, bulky boots that suddenly seem too big for her feet. "Liz, it was a crazy night. Just forget about it. I mean, being brother and sister is just a flat fact. Nothing changes that. But we're also friends, and I like that. Kind of seems more important, really. We aren't forced to be. We weren't born into it."

Len saunters out to the end of the walk. "What the hell, I thought you were grabbin' the monitor, not buildin' one. What's up?"

Liz averts her puffy eyes and Jack looks over to him. "We're coming."

Len's eyes hold on Liz, her back to him, and he wipes a scrutinizing hand across his mouth. "Yeah, sure." He turns and heads back toward the house, then stops. "You're not talkin' 'bout me, are you?"

Liz's arms flop to her side. "Christ, Len. You don't hear us laughing, do you?"

Walking again, Len sends up a spindly length of middle finger over his back.

Jack offers Liz a pursed smile. "I suppose we should get inside."

An absent wipe of her eyes, and they are dark and opaque again. "Yeah. I need a beer. These Hallmark moments really dry a girl out." She cracks a grin as she sniffles and runs her forearm across her nose. "Hey, I don't know what the hell I'm trying to say. I just know that I really mean it. You know?"

"I know that, sis." His smile feels better, sincere. He moves back to the car door. "Alright. Grab the stuff on the back seat, would you? I'll get my monitor."

She moves to the other side of the car. He gets his arms around the monitor and hoists it up.

"Hey. Liz."

Her head pops up from the other side of the car.

"You know, that painting really is incredible." He stands there, the monitor an intimate weight, lugged between here and home so many times. Not so heavy tonight.

She swings the door shut, keyboard and mouse in hand. "I know." She winks.

Five adventurers—Lady Ca'drannia the elven warrior, Lillith the halfling rogue, Orson the Sorcerer, and their two friends Xaneth and Dunidun. A long journey across the hostile lands of Teladrial to find Ghuul's Gate, where Asterrak used the power of Vyst'tel's Staff—that which he stole from the Dwarves—to enter and destroy the Lord of the Dead.

Their enemy is a god now. He knows they are coming. He is

ready for them.

A host of undead guardians await. A terrible battle ensues outside the Dwarven ruins on the edge of the world. Ca'drannia falls. The paladin Xaneth calls upon his god. Heavenly light turns the dead and brings life to the elven warrior.

They enter the old dwarven ruins where Ghuul's gate resides and rest in the dank, damp temple ruins.

It's a good night. No hard feelings from last time, and no one dies. Jack let himself be submerged into this alternate reality, and it's a sudden, icy sensation to so easily step away from the people and the history of this other world by simply clicking "quit."

Jack and Len are disassembling their systems and packing up while Liz roams the game world forums on the server's website. "So you're sure that scroll is in the temple ruins?" Len asks her for the second time. " We don't have a chance against Asterrak without it."

Liz huffs. "I told you. The stories are in the History forums. Cyggthul Ragdall wrote down the words Vyst'tel gave him to activate the staff so he wouldn't forget them. He hid those words somewhere in the temple. I've been messaging the DM's, letting them know exactly what we're looking for and why. But I can't guarantee we'll find anything."

Jack finishes unhooking his system and takes the last swig of his beer. "Knowing the DM's, we probably *won't* find it. When have they ever made it easy for us?"

Liz is obstinate. "Well, the precedent is set right in the history forums. They have to honor it."

Len laughs sarcastically. "Yeah, right."

Jack slips into his jacket. "So when are you heading over to Mom's tomorrow?"

Liz turns from her screen, her face slack. "What are you talking about?"

No surprise that she's forgotten. He sighs. "Tony, Chris and Ben are in town, remember?"

Her face remains blank for a suspended moment, then her eyes clamp shut with a wince. "Oh, *shit*."

"Mom'll kill you if you don't show up."

She slumps in her seat. "I'll be there. Christ. When are you heading over?"

"Oh, sometime around one o'clock I suppose."

She grumbles. "Fine. One o'clock."

Len stands and stretches. "The bonds of family. How do you find room in your chest for that big heart of yours, Liz?"

"Eat me," Liz snips.

"Only if you ask nicely."

Jack hoists up his CPU. "Well, I'm out of here, guys."

"Take 'er easy, Cap'n." Len gives his salute.

Liz sulks. "See you tomorrow."

It's close to Midnight when Jack returns home to his apartment, and he doesn't realize just how tired he is until he reconnects his system and sits down at his computer desk. This is the latest he has stayed up since the accident, and his eyes are puffy and burning with a mixture of fatigue and the thick atmosphere of smoke from Liz's place. He is eager to crawl into bed, but first he keys www.shouldiendtheworld.com into his Internet browser.

The site is an embarrassment, a shameful exercise in self-indulgence that he has since avoided. He has read none of the hundreds of emails from visitors, and he hasn't checked the website postings, but his morbid interest works away at him.

His home page loads and he views the tallies on the voting.

207 for saving the world. 15 for erasing it.

Browsing over the existence-loving voter's submissions, his concentration blanks out quickly. There's nothing new, nothing profound. It should probably worry him that no one seems able to come up with a perfectly sound, effective argument for sustaining existence, only sentimental babbling, religious ravings, and jokes.

The PUSH THE BUTTON column manages to maintain its disturbing, enthusiastic call for world annihilation. It may only be seven percent of the vote, but they're still out-cheering the pro-existence faction like underdog fans at a high school basketball game.

The seven new entries are just as disquieting and less coherent than the previous posts, and Jack is just about to shut down the computer for the night, when he's drawn into the final entry.

Submitted by: *themessenger@VOID.com*

The human race is predetermined for its ultimate demise. At a genetic level, we are hard-wired for our assured destruction. Freud established this in his definitive work, Beyond the Pleasure Principle. He maintains the theory that "the aim of all life is death." This is because all life resists change. As we began from nothing, so we struggle against the turmoil of change as we come into being. Why else does a baby cry when born? In existing, we follow our primary drive, "the instinct to return to the inanimate state." Everything in existence is driven by entropy. Elements decay, cells die. Intelligence interprets these desires subconsciously with destructive and disastrous decisions. Thus, even though we consciously desire peace, we make war. Though we wish a healthy world, we actively pollute and destroy it. We are ensuring our own destruction.

Jack leaves the website, but that post holds strong to his thoughts.

Is humankind really on an unavoidable path of destruction? The argument is oddly comfortable to wrap around. He doesn't wish for some cataclysmic end to everything, but to believe the proposition is to remove all the exhaustive burdens of hope, offering instead the easy dependability of resignation. More importantly, it would begin to suggest a purpose and meaning to the

Shrug that he otherwise has been unable to discover around or within him.

Some small part of him has always believed that humankind, on its present course, could never hope to last. Humans have an innate counter-intuitive reaction to survival. How else could the lump sum of history be argued? Otherwise, the news would be spilling out reports from across the globe announcing, "World leaders unite under results from surprising new studies revealing that war, violence, intolerance, and aggression are not solving world problems."

He rubs his eyes and focuses back on the computer screen. He's too tired to mediate a full-blown philosophical and sociological debate in his head, and he isn't ready to dig footings for the foundation of a belief. Better to continue trudging along the complicated landscape, pitching tents of temporary ideology in convenient clearings.

He checks his messages and fixates on the familiar sender in his bulging In Box. He compulsively opens the letter.

FROM: *Iamsurfacing@illinoiscable.com*
TO: *jack@shouldlendtheworld.com*
SUBJECT: The third and final riddle!

Mr. Jack,

Well done solving the last riddle! I am quite impressed. One day, we will have to discuss these works, as the layers of meaning they contain run far and deep, and have special significance to me, each in their own way.

But my goodness, Jack, I found myself in a far deeper, darker place reading your last email! Here I am, revealing myself to you through mysteries and riddles, and meanwhile you become more encrypted the more you reveal. You have become quite a challenge to me!

So, you sense some terrific battle between polarized forces. Oh, my good, dear Jack, but for the darkness of night, we would celebrate the day!

Of course a battle rages. It is all around us. It has been waged from the beginning, and the struggle will last until the final days. The fact that you recognize this fills me with hope. Now you just need to understand what the struggle is all about. Realize this, and perhaps your role shall become clear.

I would like to meet you sometime, Jack. The time for written words is drawing to a close. There is, I think, so much yet to be said between us, but these words cannot be shared from a distance for they will diminish as sound dissolves to echo over a chasm.

But now, the third and final riddle I provide to you. And, since you shared with me a glimpse of this abyss of which you step upon the edge, I am obliged to reciprocate in similar fashion. But I have to give you fair warning...this one you will not solve on your own. I'm not ready for you to know this answer. There will be a time and place to reveal it, but not now. However, for me at least, this is the necessary first step. Here it is:

> *This seed to sow*
> *Never to grow.*
> *Yet heart will reap*
> *regrets to weep.*

> *A piece from me,*
> *a lot for thee,*
> *A hundred twice,*
> *Two score and thrice.*

The mysteries of Pauline are revealed for you to puzzle out. Perhaps, if one day we meet, you will be able to fit these pieces snugly into their proper place within the bigger picture.

In the meantime, Mr. Jack, I will look for your footprints on the edge of the abyss, and follow them to you.

-Pauline

-14

It's a reluctant drive to his mother's the next day. He doesn't like feeling this way, but he can't help it. He's never been close to his older siblings, and is only diminished when he is with them—shadowed and transparent.

When he arrives, his brothers and sister and their families fill the rooms with their lives, and he becomes a pocket of emptiness, a bubble swelling against their fluidity, rising past them to break at the surface.

Tony hoots from the living room couch. "Nice bald spot, Friar Jack."

Christine drops her dishrag and dashes from the sink right for him, a full recruit of their mother's. "Oh my God, Jack, what in the world are you thinking? Mom told us about you not wanting to get a CAT Scan? I'm shocked they'd even release you without one." The worry lines under her big drooping eyes wriggle with every exaggerated inflection.

Ben strides past from the door, tall and broad and flat-headed, fisting grocery bags in his hand with his wife Tina beside him. "Ease up on him, Chris. Half of the medical profession is just quackery and incompetence, anyway. They just want to pump up the bill." Ben is dusting off words their father had so often brandished from the hip.

Tina is prim and pretty, but her dainty figure carries no meat on her body to hide her age. "Oh, Lord. Here we go." She blows blonde wisps of hair from her face and starts unpacking snacks and drinks from the bags Ben set on the island.

"We dropped Jack on his head as a baby plenty of times. Once more isn't going to make a difference." Tony's rough, pocked face breaks into a grin.

Their mother, sitting next to him, swings a backhand across his shoulder. "That's terrible!" She covers her mouth as she titters, then coughs out the rest of her humor. She looks tired.

Tony pats her on the back. "Okay. No more being funny. We're killing Mom."

That brings out another gurgling fit of giggles from her. "Garsh, yes. That's it! No more."

Christine wanders back into the kitchen to scrub dishes again. "Well, it's certainly better to be safe than sorry. That's what insurance is for, isn't it?"

"Darling, Jack can take care of himself," Tom says as he cleans his glasses on his cardigan, slips them back onto his hourglass head, and turns another page of the paper.

The television plays a low volume screaming and yelling as almost naked teens wiggle their butts to hip hop on some Florida beach. His niece Kim sits on the floor, her dead stare gripping the screen, boasting her sixteen years like an engorged pimple. Every so often Tony tosses a throw pillow at her or nudges her with a foot and her face storms with angst. "Dad, stop it!"

His other nieces and nephews are nowhere to be seen. Ben and Tina's kids are at college; they rarely make it here other than for holidays. Tony and Sue's younger one, Anthony, has to be around somewhere, probably rummaging through basement rooms. And

Christine and Tom's three little imps of mischief are probably hunting down trouble outside. Maybe Sue is with them; Tony's wife is a pied piper of children, loves being in their attention.

Liz is late, as usual.

Christine finishes with the dishes, Ben and Tina put out chips and soda, and they all sit and talk. Jack listens to them fill each other in on the latest developments in their lives, talking about their work, their homes, their vacations, their kids. They laugh and share, and it doesn't take long for them to reflect back on their father and the stories that have become almost mythological since his death.

And Jack hides under their words, ducking behind the tales from their childhood, an eavesdropper to his own past.

"Jack, remember that time you got yourself stuck up the tree in the front yard and Dad had to pull out the extension ladder to get you down?" Ben laughs.

"Oh, yeah! I remember that," Christine exclaims. "How'd you end up in that tree anyway?"

Tony's narrow face alights. "Dad's watch. He broke Dad's watch."

Jack only recalls the event as his brothers and sister speak of it, smiles and laughs lightly with them. But listening to this story of himself is surreal, because the moment seems fractured from the existence of others. He does remember it, though.

He had been eight, and taken the watch from his father's dresser in the bedroom. The old wind-up pocket watch with the long silver chain riveted him. His father had been very protective of the watch, telling Jack that it was special, given to him by his father. When Jack asked why it was special, his father said, "It keeps time, Jacky. Keeps it right in here. See? We have to borrow time. This watch owns it." As his father wound the watch Jack came to believe that if he didn't keep it wound, time would stop and everyone would be stuck in place.

Jack took the watch that one summer afternoon while his parents were shopping so he could see how it worked. He wanted to see this time the watch kept. He began to disassemble the time-piece, removing the face plate and back plate, marveling over the small, delicate cogs and wheels that moved with perfect, dissecting fluidity, those tiny gears that somehow had the strength to churn and chop time forward, one piece at a time. Jack could feel his heart pump at each tock of the clock, and he knew the watch that kept time was also lending each beat to his heart.

Jack found a small screwdriver from an eyeglass repair kit in the junk drawer, put it to the watch, and turned it against each screw he found. Case screws and set level screws and wheel bridge screws lay beside the watch casing, and as he lifted out the wheel bridge to see deeper inside, the wheels of time fell all about him, rolling across the table.

And time did stop. He was frozen in a moment of perpetual regret and confusion, stupefied by what he had caused to happen, and more and more confused over why he had done it in the first place. Wedged between one moment that would not pass and another that would not come, he fled.

Outside, he could only think to get off the ground, as if the world would somehow revolve past him and he could be free of it. Before him was the towering maple in their front yard, looking like some ancient, wizened beast wresting against the grip of ground as it strained for the sky. Thoughts of the watch were already slipping past as he struggled for the first branch, scrambling and clutching for a hold. He hung from a low limb, his feet dangling above the ground, and he swung his legs up to the branch, entwining them around it. He hoisted himself onto the sturdy limb and stood. The remaining branches were within easy reach.

He only looked up, climbing toward the blue of the sky, beyond the grasp of the ground, and his head swam from the height. He stopped when the limbs began to sway and buckle from his weight. He sat there, one hand clinging to an upper branch with his legs locked around a lower. The motion of thin, rubbery branches moving up and down made him feel weightless and floating, the pendulum-like rocking providing a new time, transcending the earth. He was keeping time now. He was holding it within him. He looked out over his yard and the neighbor's, to the woods in the distance and the horizon that terminated the distance, and everything below and beyond him was elsewhere, frozen in the broken time he had left it in. The world did not move past him. He was moving beyond it, possessing and possessed by the current of time he now held. Infinity folded around him. And within those folds was nothingness. He wanted to slip between those folds, a fetus in the womb, floating in the fluid of emptiness surrounded by eternity.

"Jack! Jack! What the hell...?" His father's voice, a thin echo from the world rising up from far, far below. "We've been looking all over for you!"

"Oh my God, Walt, get him down, get him down!" His mother's cries were distant. He was moving out of reach.

"Jack, goddamn it! Get your ass down here!"

These voices didn't exist anymore. He was above it all now. Beyond everything.

"Jack!"

"Jack?" Christine's hazel eyes are amused with a tinge of concern. "You fading again?"

Jack smiles with embarrassment. "Just remembering. I hadn't thought about that for a long time."

Tony laughs wryly and shakes his head. "Some things never change."

"Jack's always been a drifter," his mom says. "Walt used to call it wanderminding. Do you remember that, Jack?"

Jack does, and the memory finds the hole his father's death has made.

Liz arrives by 2:30, Sue returns with the kids, and they play silly board games and laugh loud and obnoxious the way his family always does. At four, his mother begins supper, fending off all her children's insistence that she not bother, fatigue in her eyes and slowness in her steps. Christine and Tina immediately step up to help her. Sue plays Uno with the kids, Tom reads a Noam Chomsky book. Ben and Tony head downstairs and Liz looks at Jack, then follows. He trails after them.

Tony plops himself down on the couch. "Man, she's looking old."

Ben says, "That's what happens when you only see someone a couple times a year."

"No, it's more than that. I was talking to Christine on the phone last week. Mom's been telling her about her problems."

Ben meanders through the room, looking at pictures and picking up family trinkets that sit atop the old family furniture. "What problems?" He turns over a heavy, spherical marble owl in his hand.

"She's been seeing the doctors regularly. On top of the emphysema, she's got high blood pressure, weak heart, arthritic joints—serious stuff."

Liz has found her place in the recliner. "What do you expect? She's seventy-five. Old people have problems. Nothing new there."

Ben makes a face. "She's not seventy-five. She's only seventy for Christ's sake."

Liz rolls her eyes. "Oh, sorry. My mistake." She grabs a magazine from the stand next to her and starts flipping through it too quickly to read anything.

Tony leans forward, elbows falling to his knees. "Just seems like maybe we need to do something."

Ben looks at Tony. "What do you mean, 'do something?'"

"I don't know." Tony says. "Maybe its time she sells the house. Check in to an assisted living place."

"Oh, I don't know." Ben considers. "That seems…rash, doesn't it?"

"It's not like sticking her in a home. These are like apartments, only with special amenities and facilities on-site."

Liz tosses the magazine aside. "Aren't those places expensive? Where's she going to get that kind of money?"

"From selling the house," Tony says.

Ben is shaking his head. "Tone, I don't know. Seems pretty severe. What about a retirement community?"

Tony rubs at the stubble on his head. "Retirement communities aren't going to take care of her. I'm serious, I'm worried about her. I don't think she can live on her own anymore."

Jack is withdrawn to a corner, and when he speaks, his voice sounds detached from the room. "Maybe you should talk to her about it."

Ben considers this for about a second. "Mom's not too sensible when it comes to things like this, Jack."

Tony nods. "She probably won't want to leave all the memories behind."

Liz wears a sour face. "It's her life. She can do what she likes. If she wants to stay here, let her stay."

"It's not that simple," Ben says. "There's her well-being to consider."

"So that gives you the right to swoop in and take control of her life?"

"It's called responsibility, Liz. Not something I'd expect you to understand."

A bitter laugh clears her throat. "Yeah. Whatever."

Tony shifts in his seat. "Maybe Christine can talk to her and feel it out. Mom tends to open up to her more anyway."

Ben rolls his shoulders and looks at everyone else with square-shouldered indecision. "I suppose. Guess I can look into some of these places and see what the costs are."

Jack looks around the room at his brothers and sisters, unable to say what he wants to say. He is pinned under a cold stone of thought. He knows what he sees when he looks in his mother's distant and slippery eyes, and no rest home will draw her back from it. His mother is finished with this world. She is like a weary vacationer at the end of a trip, and all the sights and stops, the scenery and the souvenirs, have become a bitter goading to the transience of the journey. Now there is only the end, the final destination.

The return home.

-13

Monday morning arrives like a haunt. The alarm startles him; he hasn't heard it in over a week. The frenetic beeping is a demand to resume the routine. Within the foggy haze of sleep, he responds to it without question.

He walks to the kitchen, pours water for coffee and flicks the pot on, then drags his feet to the bathroom to brush his teeth and shower.

Hot water and steam thaw his frosty sleep, but his misty perception remains. He dresses and walks back to the kitchen. Reaching for the coffee pot, he discovers he forgot to scoop in the coffee grounds and has instead prepared eight cups of hot, cloudy water. There's probably a metaphor here somewhere, but he's too muddled and groggy to waste time on it. Instead, he grunts, pours out the water, and starts over.

On the stoop, having his morning cigarette, he keeps jerking a hand to his pocket to make sure his keys are there so he doesn't get stranded on the stoop. Slap the keys, puff a few times, panic, slap the keys. His brain won't register the confirmation of touch. Or just doesn't believe it. It's a morning for disbelief.

So many days ago he was knocked into oblivion and forced to choose between his safety and the perpetuation of the universe. Now, it's Monday morning and time to go to work. "How's it going, Jack?" Greg will greet when Jack enters the office. "Oh, just peachy, Greg," Jack will answer. "What's new, Jack?" Sam will ask. "Oh, you know. Same old, same old," Jack will say.

He's having a terrible time with this scenario.

His throat tightens as he drives down Carrington's small downtown Main Street, crossing the railroad tracks and approaching the Templeton offices. He's been down this road too many times to count, but today he strains his eyes on every street sign, worries over his next turn, doubts his bearing.

He knows how to lie. He knows how a lie feels—the chafe of humid heat. He's flush with it now, and he has no idea why.

He takes a left into the lot and parks in his normal space at the normal time. The same cars fill the lot, and the short walk to the office is unbearably familiar. The damned door to his office area is still in its normal place, and Greg and Sam are in front of it, outside, having their normal before-work cigarettes.

And Jack feels like his skin doesn't fit.

Greg flags him with a wide boisterous wave and shouts, "Look who's here! It's Head Wound Harry!"

Sam sputters on her exhale of smoke.

"Hey, guys." Jack steps up onto the concrete platform to join them.

"How are you feeling?" Sam's dark round sunglasses probably hide the red of a weekend hangover.

"I'm all right. Feels weird being back. Seems like I've been gone for a long time."

Greg cranes his neck to look at the back of Jack's head. "Well, your brains look like they're staying in, so that's a good sign."

"Not like you'd need them for this job." Sam says.

"So what's new around here? What are we working on?"

Greg sluffs the question from his narrow shoulders. "Who knows? Been doing Market maintenance, mostly. Rick just got back from High Point on Friday. He was a moody bastard for most of the day—no surprise there. Seemed to loosen up a bit in the afternoon. We had a nice, long talk."

Greg says it like Jack should know what he's talking about. He doesn't, and it makes him anxious. "What about?"

"Oh, nothing special. Just trying to get our department running smoother. Get him off our backs a bit." Greg tosses his cigarette away and heaves a sigh. "Well, time to do the dirty, I guess." He bends down, picks up his briefcase, and leads the way inside.

Nothing unexpected, nothing different. Printouts of ads and point-of-purchase signs lay about on tabletops. Furniture catalogs spread-eagled at computer stations. The long straight path of cubicles is a quiet bustle of business; keys click, the occasional phone rings, conversations softly drone.

Jack drops into his chair, turns on his computer, and stares at the unfinished projects still on his desk from two Fridays ago, now sprinkled with post-it notes calling out changes and additions. The revisions mean printing out seven more copies for Rick, who will take them to five department heads, to the CEO, and to Chuck. Each will see something different, want something else, and Rick will pander to them all, wag his tail, thump his leg.

He opens up his task list and watches the projects run down his screen. Old projects long-neglected, still flagged by the impotent little red exclamation point of priority. Current projects caught in the vicious circle of corporate bureaucracy, swatted back and forth between the egos of management. Below these, all the half thought out whims of Rick, the thunderheads of brainstorms spattering from his mouth. All of them duly noted, then hoped to be forgotten.

The screen blurs, tirades of tasks press against his eyes, and he looks away. He reaches back behind his head, touches the bandage, feels the blunt pain under the gauze, and knows he's not ready for any of this.

His phone rings. He grabs the receiver.

"Get in here." It's Rick. He sounds cocked and loaded. Before Jack can reply, Rick hangs up.

Note pad and pen in hand, he walks down the hall to Rick's corner office.

"Well, look who decided to grace us with his presence. What did you do, beat your head against the wall one too many times?" Rick smiles, but he doesn't have the knack. It's always just varying degrees of smugness.

"I'm fine, thanks for asking."

"Sit down."

Jack takes a seat, pen and paper at the ready. "How was Market?"

"Oh, Christ. What a fucking rat race. Chuck was riding me like a Chihuahua in heat. Lot of orders, though. We kicked La-Z-Boy's ass. Oh, and your recliner sell sheets where a hit."

"Good."

Rick hunches down into his office chair huddle. "Now listen. The whole plane ride back from Carolina, I was thinking. Let's throw these recliner promotions into high gear. We got all this technical crap running all over the page, and who gives a shit about that, right?" He jerks off the air with a fist. "Customers don't give a rat's ass. They just want it to look good and feel good."

"We've been saying that for a long time, Rick."

"I know, I know. So, I'm flipping through this airline magazine, and I'm looking at all these travel ads for Morocco and the Bahamas, and I start thinking, 'Vacation. Relaxation. Getting away from it all.' You know what I mean? So, what about an ad that shows one of our recliners, and the header says, 'Get away from it all…without ever leaving your chair.'" His eyebrows stand for applause. "Huh? Put the chair on a beach or something."

The idea makes Jack tired. "We've tried stuff like that before. It never flies."

Rick's enthusiasm stiffens. "I don't give a shit about before.

Look behind you and you walk yourself into a wall. I want you to go to work on this. Play around with it. See what you come up with in the next couple days."

Days? "Rick, I've got seventeen projects all labeled 'Hot' by you. Things that Bob and Chuck are asking for. Where am I going to get the time?"

"Let me worry about that."

"But you wanted that PowerPoint presentation done by tomorrow."

Rick's left eye narrows. "I'm not asking."

"All right. Fine." Jack stands up. He just wants to get out, get back to his desk, before he says what he wants to say.

"Jack." Rick spits his name like profanity, like it should be dripping down his back. He can hear Rick breathing behind him. "Close the door and get back here."

Jack reaches out and swings the door shut. No escape. He wants so much to be on the other side of it. He turns to face Rick.

"This shit ends right now. You got me? Now."

Jack opens his mouth, and it's pointless because there are no words waiting for him. Nothing but a suspended breath too big for his lungs.

"I don't know what's been going on with you, and I really don't give a shit. There's just the procedure and where you fit into it. And the procedure is, you do what the fuck I tell you to do. If you don't, then procedure is my boot up your ass all the way out the fucking door. I'm sick of the attitude, sick of you telling me how you can't do whatever I tell you to do. I'm just sick of *hearing* you."

He's free falling, his bowels squeezing into his throat, and his head throbs.

Rick bolts up, sending his chair rolling back, and he leans in. "I gave you this fucking recliner ad to give you a break, settle you down. Greg tells me you're stressed out. I don't fucking know why. I'm the one taking the heat. I'm the one with the target on my head. But fine. Jack's stressed out. Okay. We'll throw Jack a nice, fun little project. And then you piss on it. You gotta buck everything I throw at you." Rick jabs a stiff finger at him. "Not any more."

Everything is wrong. Everything is too big. He can't swallow. There's a pressure between his ears, and when he speaks, his voice is canned and muffled. "Get your finger out of my face."

Rick's jaw clenches, muscles blistering. He gives Jack a long, scalding stare and the finger moves past Jack to the door behind him. "Get the hell out of my office." He grabs his chair and sits down, clutches the armrests as if he's on a bucking Brahman.

It's pushing against the heels of his feet—the mass of the world. Too much. Too big. He's overcome by proportions. How can he inhale against this inordinate mass all around him? His hand fumbles for the door and opens it. "You're so small." He walks out, closing the door behind him.

He walks back to his station, and he can't be here anymore. He stands before his desk, his chair, the papers, tape holder, stapler, phone, and it doesn't make any sense. Just debris, pieces that don't fit together any more. Maybe they never did. He moves past it all, moves it all into the past, behind him. He moves on.

"Smoking already?" Sam, from her desk, looking up at him. "Jack?"

"This isn't working. Sorry." He keeps walking.

"What?"

Greg's phone rings. "Yeah…yeah, all right…." The clack of the receiver replaced, and Greg steps around his partition. "Jesus. What's up Rick's ass? Hey, where are you going? You okay?"

"Have to go. Sorry. I'm sorry."

"What are you talking about? Did Rick do something? What's happening?"

Sam steps up, looks at Greg and then at Jack. "Are you feeling all right?"

He reaches the door, pushes it open. "No. I don't feel right." He looks at Sam and Greg, Greg who had once been so tall, hadn't he? Doesn't matter now. "I'll see you around."

"Jack! Hold it. What the hell's going on?" Greg's phone rings again. He hisses out a "Fucking Rick…" and storms down the hall to Rick's office. Jack is just outside as he hears Greg pound on Rick's door.

A short walk to his car, but it goes on and on. He tries to think about what he's just done, but his mind is stuck in an angry feedback loop, replaying everything as it happens. Every step. Every sound. Amplified and distorted and echoed. He drifts to the driver's side door.

Sam's voice is far away as she shouts from the doorway. "Call me, Jack! Call!" He looks at her, and Sam, the building, the Templeton sign, have all lost dimension. He thinks he nods to her, but he really isn't certain because the world just isn't standing still anymore.

Part Five
THE ABYSS

-12

Floating is simply falling with nowhere to fall to—plummeting in a vacuum with no awareness of the descent.

He should be thinking about many things as he drives home from Templeton. Did he just quit his job? That's a good question. Why? Another choice topic for consideration. What will he do now? There's a valid subject. But these thoughts have no buoyancy on the surface of his consciousness. Instead, one question keeps plaguing him—annoying and obscure and persistent.

Who am I?

It's pathetic, and he wants the question out of his head. He tries to hold it under, to drown it, but it persists.

If Templeton Furniture Industries is out of his life, what is left?

He remembers high school, floundering aimlessly to the constant frustration of his father. "Get your head out of the goddamn clouds, Jack," his father would say from Jack's bedroom door, and Jack would brood happily on his bed. "You're messed up in the wrong crowd, Jack. They're dragging you down," his dad would lecture from the dinner table, and Jack would resent him with sublime satisfaction. "You've got no direction, Jack, and that'll get you nowhere fast," his father would admonish from the garage, and Jack would drive away with silent smugness. And the bad grades, detentions, and meetings with teachers continued, until finally his father turned to apathy. "I give up, Jack. Go ahead, ruin your life." And Jack smiled to himself as if a long, hard battle had finally been won.

After high school and on his own, college and work were a distractive challenge to the nagging constriction of emptiness. He started to excel in school, as if all that incoherent anger could find expression through discipline and study. And, after a life of feeding off the disappointment of his father, there was the newfound exhilaration of receiving his father's pride.

Landing the job at Templeton after college made him a man to his father. Walter Cross' son, his little Jacky, working for a Fortune 500 company, making decisions that could mean millions of dollars. He knew without a doubt that, to his father, this was tantamount to the first tribal hunt—drinking the black cardiac blood of the slain deer. Of course, being the modern, Midwestern Caucasian tribe of the Cross family, rather than the blood of the kill, his father had tossed him a can of Pabst and slapped him on the shoulder.

"I'm proud of you, son."

Not those words exactly, but that's what he had meant.

When the cancer began to consume his father, Jack requested extra projects from Rick, worked later and on weekends, and headed up independent projects on his own. He was Rick's golden boy then. Innovative cross-marketing concepts, advertising campaigns that busted through new markets, all handed over to Rick on a silver platter. Jack hadn't cared. He didn't want credit.

He never mentioned to anyone that his father was dying. Several times he had outright lied to Greg and Sam. Shame was nursed by the comfort of the lie. At least, for as long as it could last.

He had watched his father die. Stared into the gape of his vacating eyes.

They were with him in the end—Jack, his mother, Liz, and Christine who had been there the past month helping with those final days. All of them in the living room while his father sat in his favorite recliner, dignity lost to baby blue pajamas draped over an emancipated body, flimsy tan slippers that did not hide the humility of frail, bruising ankle and purpled heel. The hospice nurse and her annoying serene smile at his father's side.

It happened fast and cruel. His eyes rolled and his hand twitched as he gurgled broken breath. Not his father. Absolutely not. It was repulsive, like God had wriggled into that fleshy costume for a grotesque pantomime. No peace, only pain and fear. His mother could no longer cry, just moan and whimper, eyes peeled white and mouth wrenched open.

And, reflected in the horror of those dimming eyes, what his father was seeing before him during that last, rattling breath.

Nothing. Emptiness. That nullifying force swallowed his father from the inside, and Jack stared into it.

They stayed in that room for an hour with his father's wasted, expired body still in that chair, Jack battered numb by the void emanating off the husk of Walter Cross. His father seemed impossibly far away, as if he had never existed.

After the funeral, Jack went to mass with his mother, and the recitations were a hollow drone, the sermons just so many echoes rebounding from the church ceilings. He was sitting in that room again with his dead father.

Jack stopped going to church after that.

Now, his job is gone. What's left? What does he have to hold on to? He is fading to transparency, lingering like vapor. And it really doesn't seem so hard, to just surrender to it, skim the surface of this vacuity and its promise of comfort.

"Sir! Can you hear me?"

For a second, he panics. He's overslept, late for work. Get up.

Hurry. But it all feels wrong, and when he opens his eyes, he's looking at the dashboard of his car.

"Can you hear me?" A muffled shout from behind the window of his car door. A sheriff peers in, all brown with rural authority.

Nothing makes any sense. Where is he? When is it? What the hell is going on?

The sheriff raps hard on the window and gestures for him to roll it down. For a moment, Jack can't remember how, and looks foolishly for a crank handle. Then he sees the power window button. The car is stalled, but the key is still turned. He presses the button and the window whirrs down.

"Are you hurt?"

"What?" The question confounds him.

"Sir, are you injured?"

He looks around for the first time and wonders why there's barbed-wire fencing covering the hood of his car. Might be related somehow to the field where his car appears to be parked.

Flickers of memory. Templeton. Rick. Walking out. Driving home.

Now, there's the interesting thing. Jack doesn't remember actually *arriving* home. He recalls leaving Templeton, and then...

The hungering maw overcoming him. That familiar, irresistible void. A brief image of his father, far below him, at the trunk of a vast, towering tree, telling him to hold on, hold on Jacky, don't let go.

"Are you all right, sir?" Irritated annunciation.

Jack turns to the man. "That's kind of relative, isn't it?"

The sheriff looks annoyed and his voice narrows. "Are you hurt?"

Jack gives himself a quick appraisal. Everything seems to be working—well, other than his head, obviously, which lately becomes absent at the most inconvenient times. "I'm all right."

The sheriff steps back from the car, arms at his side, hands hovering over his hips—cowboy at the showdown on highway 39.

"Please step out of the vehicle, sir."

Jack opens the door and stands. His head swims for a moment, but he remains upright and faces the officer. Before him are the deep ruts of tire tracks running through the torn open barbed-wire fence in a gradual arc all the way up the embankment and to the road some three hundred feet away. It must have been the muddy ground that finally stalled out the wagon. That, and the fence.

The sheriff is short and wiry, face thinly cut at severe angles. His broad-brimmed hat half-conceals his eyes in shadow as they study Jack. "Let's see your driver's license, sir."

He digs for his wallet, pulls out his license with clumsy fingers, and hands it over.

The sheriff examines it, then looks back up at Jack. "Mind explaining what happened, Mr. Cross?"

Jack isn't prepared for split-second thinking—he only remembered his own name a few seconds ago—but the last thing he wants this official to know is that he blacked out behind the wheel of his car. "Well, I don't know. I was just driving, and something darted out onto the road—"

"Something?"

"A cat, I think. I swerved to miss it and I guess I lost control."

"A cat."

"Maybe a raccoon."

"Uh-huh." The sheriff looks behind him to the road and his eyes follow the tracks back to the car. "That's a long, even run for being out-of-control."

Jack forces his expression to remain flat. "I guess I was a bit panicked."

A gesture to the neat little ruts by the car. "These tracks don't even look like you tried to stop."

"I kind of froze up when I left the road."

"That barbed wire didn't even make you think about the brakes, eh?"

"Like I said, I was out of sorts at the moment."

"Yeah." The sheriff's scrutiny intensifies with a squinted eye.

"Why didn't you answer me right away?"

The question is thick on the air, and Jack catches himself scratching his arm for no reason. "I guess I was just shocked."

"Sir, you didn't look shocked. You *looked* catatonic."

He has to turn this around fast. "Listen, I just lost my job, okay? I was already freaked out about that. Then I'm suddenly heading off the road into a farmer's field. I guess you can say I've had a real shitty day and my brain just kind of punched out for a bit."

Suspicious wheels turn under that broad-brimmed stiff sheriff's hat. "Have you been drinking, sir?"

Jack shakes his head adamantly. "Absolutely not."

"Drugs?"

"Never."

No blink of eye, shift of feet, twitch of hand—the sheriff is a dubious block of law-enforcing rock. Finally, he takes a step back. "Alright, Mr. Cross. I'm going to give you a Breathalyzer. If that confirms what you say, I'll only ticket you for inattentive driving. And there'll be damages to pay. Stay here with your vehicle. I need to run your license, and I'll call in a tow truck to get your vehicle clear."

Exhale of relief makes Jack feel like he hasn't inhaled since leaving his car. "That's fine, officer."

The sheriff turns and walks to his car on the side of the highway. Jack steps back into the wagon and grabs the steering wheel to keep his hands from shaking.

A lungful of air shoved into the plastic tube of the Breathalyzer makes Jack lightheaded and makes the Sheriff satisfied. The tow truck arrives and undoes the absurdity of a Subaru flossing barbed wire in a farmer's field. Ticket in hand, station wagon no longer pretty but operational, Jack is allowed to drive home. He does so, stunned and wide-eyed.

10am on a Monday and back in his pathetic rental brochure

snapshot of an apartment. Not where he expected to be at the start of the day. Has he ever liked this place? Department store art hanging on bland white walls boxing in ready-to-assemble furniture and a Templeton SKU675-35 Moch-A-Rama sofa. Manufactured, leased living.

No. He's never liked it at all.

Keys are dropped onto the stand by the door, windbreaker is peeled off and thrown onto the kitchen chair. He stands there and takes up space as the battery-operated pendulum swings to the tock of the clock. Otherwise, the buzz of silence.

In his bedroom, to stare down his bed, where he can sneak and slip under the covers, close his eyes and find comfort in unconsciousness. Let Templeton and the blackout and all this mess dissolve in a solution of sleep. The mound of pillow propped up against the headboard, fitted sheet on the mattress rippled like windblown sand, a copse of quilted blanket piled along the edges—sweet oasis of avoidance.

To turn around right now, he could almost expect to see his father standing at the doorway, ball-bearing eyes of accusation. He would wither from that glare now, a face so different from the one in his dreams, though Jack feels no less small in those visions—helpless and lost.

He yanks away from the bed.

Back in the kitchen, he grabs the phone book from the stand and tosses pages about.

"Saint Mary's Hospital." The woman's voice is pleasantly sanitized.

Throat crimps, silence suspends, then Jack says, "Dr. Haizuki, please."

-11

The bus makes slow progress to the hospital. It carries four passengers. The hard, rigid face of the elderly man at the front faces the doors. The deflated gaze of the middle-aged man in a crumpled corduroy jacket across from Jack looks past him to the window. A brooding girl with matted hair two rows ahead fingers the spangles on her wrist. Their faces show the same dejection he feels. Nothing so desolate as that accelerated groan of engine without the chatter of voices. The speechless dread of destination.

He could have driven to the hospital, but the deep scratches on the hood of his station wagon were an effective reminder of the consequences.

Big city buses have never bothered him, but public transit in a small city is block-by-block affirmation of a lost privilege. Every turn of the bus made independent of his will only reinforces the awareness that he is losing control of his life.

He knows what he wants from Dr. Haizuki. The question is, can he get it, and will it be any help? He has to do something, but there's little hope the visit will solve anything. He certainly can't tell Dr. Haizuki about the Shrug, and he won't allow any scans. This entire trip is probably pointless, but were he to fall from a great height, he would flap his arms if only to distract him from the imminent approach of ground.

The ride is a grind of time, twice as long as by car. When the bus finally pulls up to the main entrance of the hospital, he exits behind the shuffling, hunched-over old man who Jack is positive will not survive scaling the steps to the pavement. He tries to ask the man if he'd like help, and he's cut off by a petulant grunt as the old man dangles one foot over the edge, lowering himself slowly to the curb as he clutches the bus railing. He finally meets the ground, stabilizes and scuffles off to the hospital doors.

Jack trots ahead to open the door for him, and the old fellow huffs as he passes. He thinks, The second set of doors is all yours, buddy, and passes the man on the right.

Jack checks in at the nursing station and takes a seat. As he waits, he convinces himself to leave three times, is determined to tell Dr. Haizuki everything twice, and is just coming to the definitive decision that he is absolutely incapable of making a decision when Dr. Haizuki appears.

"Mr. Cross, hello." The doctor extends a hand.

Jack accepts it as he stands. "Thank you for seeing me, doctor."

"Oh, please. No 'thank you's. It is what I do, of course." He gestures down the hallway. "Come. This way."

Behind the nursing station and through a sliding glass door, he follows the doctor into a small examination room. Haizuki closes the door, sits at a desk against the wall, and gestures to the chair beside it. When Jack sits down, Dr. Haizuki folds his hands on his lap over his stark white lab coat. "So, Mr. Cross. How are we feeling?"

"I feel fine at the moment."

Dr. Haizuki raises a dark eyebrow. "At the moment? And what of the other moments?"

"There have been…symptoms, perhaps."

The doctor's congenial countenance tapers to concern.

"Explain, please."

"I've experienced a few blackouts since the accident." He's fidgeting, and his awareness of it only makes it worse.

"Blackouts. You are meaning complete loss of consciousness?" Jack nods.

"Just recently?"

"Once this morning, and once about six days ago."

Never a good thing to see alarm on a doctor's face. "Six days ago? Why would you not contact me then?"

An inarticulate stammer is his only answer.

"Mr. Cross. What you are telling me is no insignificant event. No, no. This is quite severe."

More nodding. More squirming.

"What about pain? Dizziness? Memory loss? Have you experienced any of these conditions?"

"Not really. But there's been disorientation after the blackouts."

"So of course you will now consent to a CT scan immediately."

It means the same thing, but a headshake is so much easier than saying "No."

The doctor sucks in a breath. "Mr. Cross— "

"Dr. Haizuki. My position is still firm. And, it can't be explained either."

"Then you leave me impotent to help you, Mr. Cross, outside of exploratory surgery. And I am strongly opposed to such a procedure without having any idea of what we are looking for or where."

"And I don't think I'd be too eager to go through that myself."

"So we are at an impasse." The physician has become unmoving, intransigent, right down to his index fingers that stay rigid as his hands rest on the tabletop, unable or unwilling to relax and curl back into place.

"I came here because I need to know something."

Doctor Haizuki's accent becomes more prominent. "But there is nothing I can tell you, Mr. Cross. You give me no ability to answer on your condition." This has all become personal to the doctor—every gesture, every word, steeped with resentment. When Jack thinks about what to say next, all he wants to say is "I'm sorry."

"Please. Just tell me. The original scan you ran when I was first brought in. Before the error. Was there any reading? Any data at all?"

Head turns from side to side, as if Jack were offering him a forkful of slop. "No. Nothing that could in any way answer to your condition."

"But there was *something*, right? Some data output up to the point of the error?"

Hesitation. "Of course. I've studied it extensively, but the area scanned was clean. The error occurred near the point of the injury."

"Was there anything that seemed strange? Out of the ordinary?"

"I don't understand. Just what is this all about, Mr. Cross?"

"Is there a way I could see the scan? Is there a…a printout or something?"

A swipe of irritation at the file on the desk and the doctor pulls out a black film printout. "You can look at it all you would like, Mr. Cross, but if you think you can diagnose your condition by this, you are mistaken. There is nothing here for you to understand, and nothing to clarify the cause of your blackouts." He tosses the film toward Jack and it slides to the edge of the desk. Jack takes it.

And of course the doctor is right. The cryptic data reading down the side is a stack of meaningless numbers and codes. The image itself Jack knows to be the top of his head—a slice of brain in a bone frame. But there is no flagged pin pointing to the Shrug, no flashing red button. The scan ends abruptly with a small blob of white at the center of the termination. Incomplete and indecipherable. Might as well try to understand Sanskrit.

The film dangles in his hand as he starts to put it down, catching the fluorescent lighting from different angles, and something appears that he hadn't seen before. A closer look and it's gone again. He moves his face in, tilts the printout back and forth.

There.

He points to that area of the scan as he offers it back to Dr. Haizuki.

"What is that?"

The doctor at first seems to ignore Jack, but with a click of his mouth, he leans forward to focus on the point of the image where Jack's finger is. Studies and draws closer. Finally, he drops it back on the desk. "It is nothing. An artifact of the error. Nothing more."

Jack looks at the film again, at the faint, thin arc of line radiating away from the small fuzzy white area blotting the center of the scan. It makes him think of his old physics books—the first, early pictures of particle collision data. Whether desperation or intuition, this hairline arcing path seems important.

"Could I please take that with me, doctor?"

Haizuki's glare lacquers his agitation. "If you wish a second opinion, we are required to pass on your records. You have no need to take them yourself."

"No, no. It's not that. Honestly. But I would really like that printout, just the same."

"This is highly unusual, Mr. Cross. It is not normally our policy to relinquish files to patients personally. Your records are, of course, available to you. It is standard, however, to keep them within medical channels."

"I'll give it back, I promise. But…I really need to take that."

The doctor's normally soft dark eyes strain as he looks from the film to Jack. "I must tell you that your behavior is very suspicious. Considering the circumstances, I could even say…irrational." Carefully, delicately said with impeccable bedside manner. But still threatening.

Of course it's irrational. Everything about this crazy situation is inconceivable. That's why he needs something—anything—to prove it otherwise. And that CT scan is the first chance he's had in almost thirty years to tell him once and for all if he's insane. And if he's not…

Well, he'll cross that bridge when he comes to it.

"Doctor, I sympathize with your position. Really. But, all the same, I object to the insinuation that curiosity in my own medical records would be called irrational."

"Mr. Cross—"

"And just because I find myself in an uncomfortable situation that forces me to withhold private, personal information does not mean that I am suddenly unable to make rational decisions."

Haizuki's hands assume surrender, palms out and raised to the shoulders. "Now, now. Please don't mistake genuine concern for an…accusation. Oh, no."

Uncomfortable to be this way, to play the aggressor just like his dad to the poor carnation-haired waitress when he had cut into the medium-rare steak he had ordered at some dive diner only to see the faint blush of pink against grilled-gray meat. Or the electronics salesman who tried to sell him a three hundred dollar extended warranty on a TV and his father asked why he'd want to buy a TV from a store that was so certain their product would fail that they encourage their customers to buy insurance. Jack had watched more people bend and break to that sneer of in-your-face common sense drilled into them.

"Doctor, I appreciate everything you've done for me, and now I'm asking you to relinquish my file."

Haizuki sets the CT scan down and pushes it toward Jack. "I cannot begin to think of what possible use it would be to you, but…take it if you must."

Jack reaches for it, but the doctor's fleshy, fawn-skinned hand remains in place. "There is one condition. You must allow me to at least schedule an EEG for you."

Jack draws back. "I can't agree to any intrusive scans."

"But this is not intrusive. Simply electrodes placed on your scalp that receive electrical data from your head. It will not show details of the injury, or any physical complications if they have occurred, but it will at least alert us to abnormal brain activity caused by the injury."

He doesn't like the sound of it. It may be safe, yet what really is safe when it comes to the Shrug? "I don't know."

"Please."

He could just take the scan. He has every right. But it would be better to make some kind of concession to the doctor. Besides, scheduling an appointment doesn't mean showing up to one. "Fine. But can you schedule it for Monday?"

"That is a long time from now. I would prefer to get you in here sooner."

"Monday is the best I can do."

"You seem quite determined, Mr. Cross, to not let me see into any part of your head, be it by scan, or by being open and honest with me. For your sake, I hope you change your mind before it is too late." Haizuki's stare is passive but penetrating— probing like an x-ray. Jack focuses upon the film until the doctor's hand draws back.

"Maybe soon, Doctor. Maybe I'll be able to come back to you and tell you everything. But not now. Not until I find some things out. Thank you for letting me have this, though."

Dr. Haizuki merely nods once and stands, closing the folder and putting it under his arm. "I will schedule your EEG for one week from today. I'll have the nurse call. In the meantime, take care of yourself, Mr. Cross, as you are quite determined to let no one else do it for you."

On the bus ride home, Jack can only sit there and hear Dr. Haizuki's warning.

Before it's too late. What absolute severity those words intone. He may die. A grim realization, tasted and spat out many times since the accident, but as he sits in the window seat in the middle of the Terrapin public bus heading north to his apartment, he swallows it hard.

Back home, he is focused and resolved. Granted, his plan is as transparent and thin as cellophane, but at least it's a next step. And the CT scan he still clutches in his hand as he sits down at his computer just might be the crucial clue to everything that has overturned his life in the past week.

Jack brings up a search engine and types in a name from his past that just might help him.

"Mark Bennings" +physicist

It doesn't take Jack long to locate him. After sifting through the first page of search results he ends up on the Fermilab website. The Fermi National Accelerator Laboratory is home to the most powerful superconductor in the country, located about forty miles west of Chicago just outside of Batavia, Illinois. Fermilab's website lists all current engineers and what projects they're working on. Jack learns that Mark has been at Fermilab for almost three years now, after having worked a postdoctoral position at the Cyclotron Institute for five.

Jack has no idea if he can simply call the Fermi National Accelerator Laboratory and ask for someone, but he tries it on a whim. They take his name and number and say they'll pass the information on to Dr. Bennings.

A half-hour later and Jack is answering his phone.

"Jack! Holy shit, this is a blast from the past!" Mark has the same excitable, bouncing voice, now cured with maturity.

"*Doctor* Bennings. I'm impressed. No more Busch beer for you, huh?"

Mark erupts into laughter. "Oh, man. Those where the days! So, what are you up to now? Where are you? What are you doing? Come on, give me all the juicy details."

"Well, nothing as ground-breaking and significant as you, that's for sure. Still in Terrapin, doing graphic design at Templeton Furniture Industries." He finds the truth uncomfortable and unnecessary, so he lets the lie slip. "Just a desk-jockey for the corporate machine."

"Married? Kids?"

"Nope. How about you?"

"Five years next spring. Natalie and I are expecting our second in December."

Jack stumbles in awkward silence. Mark? Married…. with kids? An obsessive, single-minded science nerd like Mark settles down and raises a family, and Jack is one week away from his thirtieth birthday, alone and jobless.

"You should try it, Jack. I'm telling you, coming up with a grand unification theory wouldn't give me half the meaning in life that a family has. It's a world-changer, my friend."

"I bet." Jack can't find volume to his voice. "What about you, Mark? What are you working on now? It's gotta be incredible working there."

Mark is pure vocal energy. "Oh, Jack. It's unbelievable. Really. Right now, I'm mainly focused on the KTEV Experiment. Basically looking to resolve the antimatter deficit in the universe by searching for direct CP violations in 2 PI decays of the neutral kaon."

"Uh…okay."

Mark chuckles. "Yeah, I know. Sorry. It's the bane of being a quantum mechanic. People ask, 'What are you working on?' and then real quick they regret it. Basically, we're creating proton collisions at one tevatron of energy—that's one trillion electron volts, Jack, the highest energy in the world—to create pions and kaons. Problem is, we have to isolate the kaons, so we need a vacuum window strong enough to support thirty tons of pressure, but thin enough to let the pions escape."

"That's cool." Whatever the hell that means.

"Well, for us physics types, it is. But hey. Enough about that. What's up, Jack? What made you decide to hunt me down after all these years?"

"Mark, I wish I could tell you that this is just a friendly call, because it's great to be talking to you again, but I was hoping you could help me out."

"Don't worry about it. I'm just glad something happened to actually make one of us look the other up. So, how can I help?"

Jack's listing eyes glance at the CT scan. "I've got something here I'd like you to take a look at if you could. It's a long shot, but I'm thinking maybe you might have an opinion about it."

"What is it?"

"I'd rather you just looked at it."

Humored curiosity seeps over the line. "You're sounding kind of mysterious, Jack."

It's getting so easy to lie now, like a reflex. "It's just an odd little thing that's not easy to explain over the phone. So, is there a chance I could drive out and see you sometime?"

"Definitely. I'm a bit swamped right now, but next month would work great."

Not the answer he was hoping for. He needs Mark to see the scan before the EEG on Monday. Besides, who could say if he even had a month? "Actually, I was hoping for sometime this week, Mark, if there's any way."

"This 'odd little thing' of yours seems pretty important."

"It's just something I need to find out about, and I happen to have this week open to me."

Jack can hear a faint flipping of pages over the phone. "All right. How about Friday? You can meet me here. I'll have a visitor's pass ready for you at the front desk. I can give you a tour of you'd like."

"That would be great, Mark. Thanks a million."

"Hey. You can stay with Natalie and me, huh? I'll stock up the fridge with Busch. It'll be great."

"I can't wait. Looking forward to meeting Natalie."

"All right, then. It's a plan. Now, I better get back to it. Do you need directions here?"

"I'm good. The website is pretty clear."

"Great. Take it easy, Jack and we'll see you on Friday."

He hangs up. Direction. He has a course. Too soon to allow the burgeoning hope of a solution take root, but if he can just be nudged further along—if the visit with Mark could give him some idea of what to do next—it would be worth it.

Illinois. It will be a long trip on the dismal escort of Greyhound. Not something to look forward to. But, there is another reason to go to Illinois, isn't there?

He's compelled to his chair at the computer, finds Pauline's last email and clicks "reply."

FROM: *jack@shouldlendtheworld.com*
TO: *Iamsurfacing@illinoiscable.com*
SUBJECT: Guess what?

Pauline,

Sorry it's been a bit since I emailed you last. Life has been, for lack of a better word, interesting lately, and I'm just now trying to get a grip on it all.

So, I'm not sure how interested you will be in this, but it just so happens that I'm going to be in Illinois in a few days. I'm getting together with a friend on Friday—he works at Fermilab, about 40 miles west of Chicago—and so I thought, since you brought it up in your last email anyway, how about getting together? I'm assuming you live in Illinois judging by your email account. I'll be arriving by bus. I could come down any time this week, actually, as I find myself suddenly with an ample amount of free time.

This is a bit uncomfortable for me to ask, as I realize we barely know each other and have only been corresponding for a couple of weeks. I hope I'm not out-of-line to suggest it. You could choose a neutral territory for us to meet. Maybe a coffee house or something?

If this interests you at all, let me know. And please, please don't feel uncomfortable just telling me "no" if the idea doesn't sit right with you. I'd understand completely.

I think it would be really nice to meet you in person, though.

Anyway, I hope to hear from you soon.

-Jack

He has nothing else to do but wait for Pauline to respond. He looks at the TV instead of watching it, jumping from the couch too often only to find zero messages in his inbox. Near three o'clock, a rumbling stomach reminds that he never had lunch so he fixes a sandwich.

He eats, and he can't stop looking at the clock. The clock's hands tell him he shouldn't be here, that sitting in his apartment at this time on this day is simply not allowed. Liz, his mom—they have no idea he's not at work. His little secret, his mystery life.

And they won't find out. Not for a while. It would only pile more worry onto his mother, and by what Tony was suggesting on Saturday, she has enough troubles without Jack's help. Because of this, he can't tell Liz about it. Even though he trusts Liz not to say anything to their mom, it doesn't mean she wouldn't inadvertently slip something out in casual conversation.

All the lies that have already been said, and all the truths that have not—to Dr. Haizuki, to his family, and now to Mark Bennings—are merely the foundations for bigger lies yet to come.

And then there's Pauline. The one opportunity to be completely honest with someone, to say all the things he's never been able to discuss with anyone else. Besides, there's something about her, as if she could make the world change direction with a word.

At five-thirty, Jack's phone rings.

"You never called me."

"Sam." He's thrown off, turned around. Is it actually possible that he just saw her this morning? "I'm sorry. I've been…busy. Time slipped away from me."

"What do you mean, 'busy'? You made plans today?" Her laugh is jagged and her voice cadenced with sarcasm. "Eight O'clock, go to work. Eight-fifteen, quit job. Nine O'clock, get hair cut—"

"No. That's not what…I just, I went to see my doctor."

That brings her down a notch. "Jack, are you okay? I mean, we were really worried about you. What happened?"

As if he could even answer that for himself. " I don't know. I had enough of Rick. I couldn't take it anymore."

"What did the doctor say? Is your head still giving you trouble? Are you still not feeling right?"

"No. I'm fine." Reflexive; a verbal flinch. "I may have rushed coming back, but there's no problems."

"You're not really quitting, are you?" Her voice squeezes with a pleading lilt. She's probably pouting.

"I walked out, Sam. Not much chance that I can just show up tomorrow and say, 'Whoops, how did that happen?'"

"But you really *can*, Jack."

"What?"

"You still have your job. Greg talked to Rick." A low chuckle. "Greg screamed at Rick. Holy shit, Jack, you should have heard him. Not too often Greg blows a gasket, but when he does—" She whistles over the phone.

Jack is flabbergasted. It never even occurred to him that he could go back. That part of him had been amputated and cauterized. But his chest swells at the thought of Greg screaming at Rick. For him. "But, what could Greg have possibly said to Rick to make him want to take me back?"

"Well, first he beat him up over coming down hard on someone who just suffered a head injury, asked him if he wanted to kick his grandmother in her artificial hip next. Then he reminded him that you could feasibly sue for damages because of blatant disregard for your condition. *Then* he refreshed Rick's memory about all the things you've done over the years to see to it that Rick didn't have his ass dropped on the curb years ago."

A gust of air escapes. "He said all *that?* Holy shit."

"Rick stewed in his office for half the day, then called Greg back in late this afternoon. He says you can take a few more days off, make sure you really are better, and then come back. All this will be forgotten." A bloated pause. "*So?*"

He could have it all back—the job, the security, the normal life. It's right there for him; he just has to reach out and grab it.

Now he's lying to himself. The ultimate deception. Nothing has changed. The offer is made over a chasm, and he's just being drawn to its edge. "I can't."

The line is hissing silence.

"Sam, it's amazing what Greg said, what he did, but I...can't. It's over."

"You're just going to quit." Her words are finely chopped.

"It's what I have to do."

"Jesus, Jack. That's pathetic. You're throwing away four years."

Relentless Sam. The woman who can perch on a tree stand in November cold with squint-eyed, vapor-breathed patience for five hours waiting for that twelve-point rack to stroll into her gun sights. A single mother who beat the odds and grappled for a good job, benefits, a future.

"Sam, listen. Maybe… maybe this is all for the best, you know? " That sends a leaden groan from the other side of the line. "I wasn't happy at Templeton anymore. You know that. This way, I can move on and maybe find something right for me."

"God, you're being so stupid, Jack. You think you're going to find something better? Wake up. This is the world. Time you started dealing with it." She's cold again, like that distant night at the bar, the long-ago Wednesday after the meeting on the stoop. She's in the past now.

Jack is tired of talking. "Well, we'll see."

"You'll see, all right," Frosted with stubborn contempt. "But by then it'll be too late."

Jack flinches to those words, words he has heard already today, that are skipping across the liquid surface of his time, rippling out toward an unavoidable and final event. He is speechless to them.

"Well, I gotta fix dinner for the brat. Take care of yourself, Jack." The line goes dead.

Later that evening, a reply from Pauline is waiting for him.

FROM: *Iamsurfacing@illinoiscable.com*
TO: *jack@shouldlendtheworld.com*
SUBJECT: Re: Guess what?

Mr. Jack,

How exciting this is! A chance for us to meet face-to-face. Of course I am interested! It's the opportunity to flesh out the mysterious Mr. Jack.

And I just may be able to pull some favors and take some time off of work as well. That way, I can be sure to devote myself to your care and be the best host I can be.

I live in Skokie, which is just north of Chicago. I think the perfect plan would be for you to come here and I can meet you at the station. You should come up on Wednesday. That way, I could give you a vigorous tour of Chicago on Thursday, and get you to your friend on Friday. It'll be good times, Jack!

If for any reason you need to reach me, my number is 847-355-0906, but don't call me unless you positively must! I don't want anything to dilute the magic of our first meeting! It'll be so wonderfully awkward!

Let me know when your bus is arriving, and I'll be there.

See you soon, Mr. Jack. (How exhilarating it was to write that!)

-P

Jack purchases his tickets that evening. The bus will leave Wednesday morning at 6:43am and is scheduled to arrive at 2:23pm. He makes reservations for a hotel room in Skokie for Wednesday and Thursday night and emails Pauline to let her know when he's arriving and where he'll be staying. Everything is neatly set in place. And he can't shake the oddly exciting, nervous notion that he is planning an escape.

His mother calls after that, and when she tells him she'd like to have him and Liz over for dinner tomorrow night, she sounds different, out of place, and he asks her if everything is all right.

"Can't a mother ask her children over for dinner without causing a stir?"

"I'll be there, Mom."

-10

Tuesday morning and desperate for a diversion from this suspended day, he walks to the library a mile away and hunts down Margaret Atwood's *Surfacing*. When he tries to check it out, the puckered and spectacled woman with the topiary hairdo draws attention to the fact that his card is three years out of date. He'll have to get a new one. He stares back at her, a sloshing dread in his gut that *this* could be waiting for him tomorrow at the Skokie bus station—a hedge-haired, crumple-faced book monger.

He passes the day reading. Researching. Looking for Pauline between the lines of fiction. But he finds something else. He can relate to the main character, this unnamed woman. Her journey to her past is mystical and haunting, the search for her missing father a dark, inward quest, and all those around her, friends and companions, are oblivious. He falls into a passage:

> "I'm not sure when I began to suspect the truth, about myself
> and about them, what I was and what they were turning into.
> Part of it arrived swift as flags, as mushrooms, unfurling and

sudden growth, but it was there in me, the evidence, only needing to be deciphered. From where I am now it seems as if I've
always known, everything, time is compressed like the fist I
close on my knee in the darkening bedroom, I hold inside it
the clues and solutions and the power for what I must do now."

A lifetime of stumbling over a stammer of truth, now to
discover this verity of verse pressed between the pages of some
book—words that have waited for the relevance of moment—the
sting only now felt from the slap at birth.

He sets the books aside to find his suitcase and travel bag. To
pack for his trip.

He knows he shouldn't chance the drive, but asking Liz for
a ride would only draw questions. Just a short trip, anyway. His
focus is intense upon the road as he makes his way across town.

This dinner invitation is suspicious. Holidays, birthdays, the
occasional weekend—these are normal. Not a weekday out-of-
the-blue invite. Something is going on. Something has happened.

He makes the turn onto his mother's street, and when the
front of the house is revealed around the long grass hillside, he
doesn't have to wonder anymore. The answer stands in obscene
clarity of royal blue against white, stuck into the ground of the
second tier of terracing, swinging against the breeze.

For sale. Keening Real Estate.

In the driveway, he kills the engine and steps out. The
dimming day is unusually warm this close to November—the
autumnal colors dull and droop, but still add a vibrant throe of
life to the approaching pall of winter. He leans against the car,
stares at the sign, and surrenders to the moment. He turns his
face into the changing breeze, exhales the green and breathes
deep the golden brown.

"So you're really sure about selling the house?" Jack only intends to sound concerned, but to his ears it comes off almost spiteful. In the air, the scent of sweet meat in the kitchen charges his memory. His mother's meat loaf, her trademark dish, glazed in caramelized brown sugar barbecue sauce. His father's favorite. He can't imagine this smell in some Berber-lined elderly apartment.

"Well, it's not the sign in the yard that's for sale, Jack," Liz says and gives him a poor-poor Jack pat on the back as she slips past and snuggles up to Frig at the kitchen table.

His mother shuffles over to the oven and turns it off. "This house is too big. Too much for me." She opens the oven door and bends down for the steaming glass pan. "Keep mashing those potatoes, Jack. They'll be lumpy." A soft grunt as she uprights herself and takes the meat loaf to the table. Small, single-serving loaves of breaded beef simmer in the pan.

Jack absently prods at the bowl of potatoes with the masher. "Just seems pretty fast to up and move to Oregon."

"Well, we'll see how fast it is when this house actually sells. The agent says the market's not that good right now. Could be months." She expels a breath as she sits. "When the time does come, though, Christine and Tom will find me a nice place, and they'll be there to help out if I need it."

"I think it's a great idea," Liz says, "if it's what you really want. Go for it."

"Well, I certainly don't feel good about giving up this place. There are a lot of memories here. But I have to say goodbye to it sometime, I suppose. Nothing lasts forever." Her eyes wander the room. "It's a pity one of you kids couldn't have taken it, raised a family here, but Ben, Tony and Chris are gone, and you two certainly seem to be in no rush to start a family."

Liz snorts. "Way to get your digs in, Mom."

Jack carries the mashed potatoes to the table and sits down. "What about money? I mean, this house has been paid off for years. Can you handle taking on the expense of a retirement community?"

His mom wears her worry comfortably, like a Sunday blouse. "Well, it'll be a challenge, but with the sale of the house and social security, I should be fine for a long time, barring medical bills."

Jack looks across the kitchen table to Liz who has moved her attention from the conversation to Frig. She leans into him and whispers something that screws his lips into a snide grin. His mother's attention flitters between them, her smile tight and posture wilted.

She folds her hands. "Shall we say Grace?"

Jack shares a darting glance with Liz and they drop their heads to their plates.

"Bless us, oh Lord, for these thy gifts, which we are about to receive…"

Jack mumbles along to his mother's nursery-rhyme chant, Liz a guttural accompaniment. A tenor tongue intones clearly above them, and Jack brings his eyes up to Frig.

"…from thy bounty, through Christ our Lord. Amen." His mom looks at Frig. "Thank you. It's so wonderful to have some-one other than the muttering twosome join me."

Frig grabs the serving spoon and digs into a loaf of meat. "We've always said Grace before a meal. Used to it."

"Well, isn't that nice? I didn't know that about you. Really, Elizabeth tells me almost nothing. Are you Catholic?"

"Protestant."

"Still go to church?"

He plops a heap of potatoes on his plate. "Yeah. Usually."

Her smile is razor sharp as she looks at Jack and Liz. "Well that's wonderful."

Liz returns a terse grin. "Touching. Pass me that spoon, Frig."

Jack watches his mother shift and straighten, rearing like an old bull with memories of the charge. "Now, just what kind of name is Frig, anyway?"

Liz drops the spoon to her plate, the clank and clatter cracking the conversation in two. "It's just a name, Mom. We've been over this. God, you can't let it go, can you?"

The hurt and innocent expression is almost compromised by the calculating eyes. "I'm only asking." A congenial cock of her head back to Frig. "I mean, you *do* have a real name, don't you?"

From deep in Liz's throat, a low rumble. "Mother…"

Jack watches Frig, and the metal head youth, in his finest eveningwear tonight with a striped button-up shirt slung loose and open over his Metallica t-shirt, hair held away from his face and in a rubber band wrap of ponytail, is unfazed by the scrutiny. He chews casually on a bit of meatloaf, then runs his napkin across his face.

"It's Chester."

Quiet. The only sound is Frig's fork clinking against his plate as he hacks off another lump of loaf.

Liz's eyes bulge and her head turns slowly to Frig. "*Chester?*"

Frig nods to her and swallows.

A long look, at him, at the table, at him again, then she belches abrupt laughter and slaps the table, writhing in her seat. Jack feels the threat of a chuckle himself, but somehow Liz not knowing Frig's name keeps him mute and staring.

His mother's brow rises to Liz's hysterics, then she lifts a serving bowl with perfect, oblivious composure. "Corn, Chester?"

Jack walks the brick path of the yard under the cold, distant stars, and the blackness above engulfs.

Selling the house. Moving away. Should it really bother him? His visits here have been sporadic and short, and his mother only manages to annoy him lately. Yet, whenever he says goodbye and heads home, he ends up being annoyed with himself instead.

She'll be happier near Christine. They're close, share everything together. It makes perfect sense to get out of this big house full of moldering memories.

He turns around when he reaches the shed and starts to walk back. As he looks down, he studies the individual bricks of the walkway he passes over, how some are shoved upward, unable to resist the churn and shift of ground that surges to every winter freeze. Back at the porch, he runs his hand along the railing. Flashes of his father swabbing his bald head as he digs the footings, sweat beading and dripping from his red nose. He can still see the old muscles pulse on those broad shoulders. Had his father considered how temporary it would be while he was building it? Did he think about strangers one day passing idly across its boards, calling it theirs?

Once his mother leaves here, it'll no longer be Walter Cross's porch; there'll be no more story to it. It'll just be dry, dead wood, a means to get from out here to in there.

The door opens. Liz steps out and lights up.

"Where's Frig?" he asks.

She wags her polished black thumb at the door. "In there. Helping Mom with the dishes."

Jack stares.

"Yeah, what the hell, huh? I came here with a brooding rock star and I'm gonna leave with a church-going momma's boy named *Chester*. Shit."

"Well, he's still got the tattoo. Just flash that at Mom if things get too cozy for you." Jack rests his forearms on the railing, leaning into the dark distance.

"You wanna tell me what's bothering you, boyo?" She joins his lean beside him.

"What do you mean?"

"You've been pretty quiet all night, and you got that look."

"What look?"

"That look you get when you're about to make me regret asking you what's wrong."

Jack retreats from the rail, stuffs his hands into his jeans pockets, and treads a tight circle of pacing. "I don't know. Just strange, I guess. We're going to be the last of the family here. Everyone else will have moved on."

Liz picks at a fingernail. "So?"

"What do you mean, 'so?' I'm just saying. Dad's gone, Mom's leaving. Ben, Tony and Chris are long gone. And here we are."

"Right where I wanna be—at a safe distance."

Her emotions are running on autopilot tonight. He hates that. "Just forget it."

She pushes herself forward, passing a hand through the scrub brush of her black locks. "Sorry, I just don't get it. You're acting like we had some kind of tight family unit. All close and loving and shit. Just what family did you grow up with? Oh, yeah. You missed the best years, didn't you? You were just the baby of the family then." She reaches out and squeezes his cheek before he can pull away. "Cute wittle Jacky." She shakes her head. "You missed Ben being the walking asshole, power-tripping all over the place. Little miss prissy Chris turning her nose up to everyone. Tony was never around—whatever he could do to stay away from Dad. And Dad would just come home from work every night, push us out of the way, and head for the liquor."

It's a rant he's heard before, standard Liz exaggeration, that necessary pinch of tragedy to the drama of her life. With his toe, he prods at a loose nail coming up from the deck board beneath him. "I think you make too much out of it."

"We get along now because we're not together. We respect Dad now because he's dead." She glares through the snaking smoke that rolls from her lips. "And maybe that's even too little, too late."

He doesn't want to look at her anymore, but he's mired in the bitterness that glints her eyes. "I don't know why you need to hate him so much. I don't get it."

She blows an exhaustive breath. "I don't hate him. I just resent him. Big difference."

"Ah. Right."

"Hey. There was never any way me and Dad could ever get along. He never got me, and I never got him. But, at least I didn't expect him to change. He never returned the favor." She jerks her head, like shaking off a sour stench. "Whatever. You remember it however you want to. Knock yourself out. I better check on Chester." Her cigarette is a red streak arcing into the night as she goes back inside.

He moves toward the door to follow, but on impulse reaches out and gives the railing a shake, tests its integrity. It gives a bit to his force, old wood squeaking against rusting nails. He could come back, tighten that up with a few screws.

No reason, though. No point. It will be someone else's porch soon enough.

Part Six
THE CUSP

-9

Jack wakes up at the normal time Wednesday morning, and as he stands in the shower under the wash of hot water, he realizes that he hasn't brushed his teeth yet, which he always does before showering. He can still taste the sourness of sleep coating his mouth, and he bothers over this oral neglect as he lathers his hair. How could he forget?

He scrubs out shampoo with scouring fingers. Now he's wasting time obsessing over meaningless thoughts. Better instead to focus on how best to rearrange his post-showering routine.

And what the hell does it matter, anyway? He's not going to work, never going to Templeton Furniture again. The routine, clothed and sheltered by him for so long, quivers from naked exposure to the raw elements of the unknown. Out of the shower and in front of the mirror, he smirks a perverse little grin at the reflection in the mirror. He sees that regimented part of him—that list-maker, that linear planner—and turns away from it to hang up his towel.

No shelter for you, my friend. No refuge. Die.

Overcome by this whim of bravado, he recklessly shuffles his entire morning program, putting on his deodorant before he shaves and combing his hair before finally brushing his teeth. On the counter is gauze and tape for a fresh bandage. He ignores them and steps out of the bathroom with tapestries of St. George slaying the dragon fluttering in his mind.

Clothes are slipped on, breakfast is eaten. He packs up his bathroom items for the trip and bides his time at the kitchen table with coffee and cigarette, not caring if he stinks up the place. He doesn't want to be on that stoop, not today. He stares down the clock until it finally tells him to gather his suitcases and leave.

The drive to the downtown bus station is quiet and short. The pre-rush hour traffic is sparse, the morning cold and calm, and Jack is crisp as the morning air and sharp as the sunrise shadows upon the dewy grass. He sizzles in his seat and drives too fast on the downtown streets with the window open and arm out to the nipping air. He pokes once at this odd euphoria with thoughts of his condition, his unemployment, but quickly decides to let the fragile mood be.

The Greyhound bus station sits in a decaying corner of the meager Terrapin downtown. The small metal-framed box of a building rests in the middle of a fractured blacktop parking lot that flakes off the ground like an old scab on skin. He pulls his car into a back parking space, joining only two other vehicles. He grabs his overnight bag and his suitcase from the back and bustles into the building.

The station is simply one room of old scuffed linoleum, plastic chairs, and fifteen-year-old vending machines and video games. It smells like sweat with an undertone of bleach. The suggestive exterior did not disappoint.

At the ticket window, the attendant is slumped over the counter. She's thin-haired and wire-framed, wearing five decades of life with weathered resent. She watches a morning news show on the small television mounted to the wall and sniffs every so often to the reporter's story, or the reporter herself—there's no way to be sure. He steps up to the window, places his bags on the ground, and smiles at her.

"Hi. I have a seat on the 6:43 bus to Skokie. I booked ahead."

The attendant keeps her attention on the television. "Name?"

"Jack Cross."

She rummages through a metal file bin and withdraws some paperwork stuffed into a Greyhound ticket folder. As she opens it and pulls out the tickets and information, she doesn't seem to actually look at any of it. "Charge it to the card number on the reservation?"

"Yes, please."

She heaves a sigh and turns away from the broadcast to handle the transaction. A bony finger stabs at the keys of the credit card machine. "Damn thing's slow," she mutters. "We got a slow line."

Three seconds later, a receipt prints out.

She tears off the printout and drops it in front of Jack. "Sign." Her attention drifts back to the television.

Jack scribbles on the receipt and pushes it back to her. "Is the bus on schedule?"

"Mm-hmm." She slides his tickets and receipt copy to him and lowers herself back to the counter, Jack apparently no longer an object existing within her perception.

He grabs his bags and walks to a row of chairs where he sits down and waits. A middle-aged man with thick stubble and shoulder-length greasy-black hair, looking as worn as his jeans and army tee shirt, sits in the far back corner, one hand holding the handle of his canvas knap-sack as if to keep it at bay. He watches Jack, and Jack feels completely uninteresting.

Other stragglers begin to arrive ten minutes before departure, but it's a sparse load for the trip. That's fine with him; he wasn't looking forward to almost eight hours on a crowded bus.

At six-forty, the driver steps in and announces they are now boarding. Jack and the other passengers move to the exit, bags in hand, and stop beside the bus where luggage is being collected. Jack removes his book from the suitcase before his luggage is yanked away from him and tossed into the storage compartment.

He's already a hundred pages into the story, and he figures eight hours on the bus will get him close to the end.

He has no idea if he understands Pauline any better by reading it, but trying has forced him to read deeper into the narrative and brush against some underlying meaning of the story. However, what he touches he doesn't understand so much as discern its substance. He recalls the professor in his literature class lecturing about her trip being some kind of archetypal quest, and it is fairly obvious that she's driven by more than the desire to find her father on this island she travels to with her friends.

On the bus, he takes a seat mid-way back. As it rolls away from the station, he thinks about his own journey. Does he really know what he's searching for? Does he have any idea what he's going to find? He recalls Pauline's reply to his first email.

I find you can waste far too much time looking for things when you don't know what you are searching for and don't know where to look; meanwhile, you become distracted to all the things that life is throwing your way to discover.

Jack nestles into his seat and opens his book, but he is slow to focus on the words as he imagines just exactly who he will discover when he first meets Pauline Swanson.

It is a long ride, yet passes faster than he imagined. He reads his book against the distraction of rolling farmlands and woodland patches blurring past his window. As time and scenery flows by, he becomes extremely aware of the motion and momentum of himself flowing past the locations—a slippery exhilaration that leaves him unfettered to the moment.

As Skokie draws near, he begins to second guess what seems more and more to be a rash act—meeting a woman he knows virtually nothing about and has only corresponded with for a couple of weeks. Just who is Pauline Swanson? How old is she? What does she look like? What will he talk about with her? Why in the hell did he set himself up for such an uncomfortable and potentially disastrous situation?

But she doesn't know him, either. It is a means for escape. Likely, he'll be able to make an educated guess as to which of the waiting people at the Skokie bus station will be Pauline. Just look for a lone woman intensely scrutinizing each individual who steps off the bus. Should this woman, for example, be a forty-seven year old with shaved head, stamped with tattoos and stapled by piercings, wearing army boots and a shirt proudly declaring, "I walk with Satan," he will calmly, briskly walk past her and dive into the nearest cab, telling the cabbie to "Just drive!" and never look back as he speeds way.

But these extreme visions exclude both the suggestive nature of her emails and his unshakable, instinctive draw to Pauline. Of course, how someone presents themselves in text can be very different than how they are in person. And, based on recent experience, he suspects his instincts may be operating on an agenda disparate from his own.

It's just shy of eight hours into the trip when the bus leaves the main highway and takes the exit to Skokie. It lumbers down the road amid the dense and crawling afternoon traffic for three or four miles, then turns off onto a side road. The station comes into view. Jack doubts, rethinks, and regrets. Maybe he *is* brain damaged to have talked himself into this.

The bus pulls into the gate below the large parking ramp next to the station that, by Terrapin standards, is a stellar edifice of commercial transit. Everything darkens under the heavy concrete ceiling of the parking structure. Jack looks to the wall of darkened windows running along the entrance of the station, trying to bore through the tinting to catch a glimpse inside. Only faint silhouettes of people look out, and he wonders which of them might be the shape of Pauline Swanson.

The bus whines to a halt beside the passenger entrance where it hisses and idles. The passengers in the bus are already standing and making their way down the isle. He follows them as the driver's voice over the speakers squelches "Thank you for riding

Greyhound, and have a pleasant day." He exits and waits in the small line to retrieve his bags, then turns and walks to the doors of the station.

He's not in Terrapin anymore. Bright walls zip with sharp, sporty stripes of color and tough gray carpeting withstands the station's foot traffic. Eighties pop music wafts about the station's spaces and posters tantalize with the landmarks and hallmarks of U.S. destinations. The smell of the place is spring exhaust and Jack just keeps moving.

He steps through the roped walkway, swinging left, turning right, following his fellow passengers through the cattle-driving corral of the disembarkment area. They gradually dissolve into the crowd of family and friends there to greet them, or stride purposefully to the exit. Others meander and wait to load the next bus. Jack reaches the end of the roped-off lane and his eyes pan the room, his grip tightening around the handles of his bags.

There is no trouble spotting her. Jack locks on to the eyes of Pauline Swanson.

He'd be giving himself too much credit to think he would have spotted her by her clothing, though the long, floral-patterned skirt blossoming burgundy and blue, navy blue sweater draping over round hips, and anchoring black clogs certainly complete the ensemble of frumpy librarian. He would be bold to say the long, thick mane of tumbled dark hair immediately identifies Pauline Swanson, though the feral locks almost hum her name. Perhaps he would have been caught in the desperate searching of those mahogany eyes that, dark and deep, crouch in a pounce behind the cover of articulate brows. Her lips, thinly splayed to breathe a soft secret or curl around irony, are certainly the kind Jack could imagine forming the words of Pauline's emails. Cream skin on fleshy cheeks touched with rosacea soften the sharp, sloping nose that holds round wire-framed glasses in place, and are the final pieces to the collage of Pauline Swanson.

But in the end, it is none of these things that draw his attention directly to her as he stops mid-step ten paces from her. It is, instead, the sign she holds, written in bold black letters against white, which says simply, MR. JACK.

She takes hold of his gaze and her eyes flex. And he has yet to rediscover forward momentum.

"Breach the gap, Jack," she beckons huskily, and Jack obeys.

The static din of chatter around him muffles to an obscure background rumble the closer he moves to her. When he stops before her, he feels bound to say something significant, but is struck dumb.

"Pauline," he says simply, looking up to her six-foot meaty frame two inches over his. She looks to be in her early thirties, though a silvery wisp runs down the side of her cascading dark chocolate hair. She's not beautiful, not ugly, but she definitely is something.

"Jack." A broad grin and flaring eyes. She holds up her sign. "Your limo awaits."

"Nice touch. I couldn't miss you."

She gives a quick burst of low laughter. "I have a gift for making myself known. Your trip was good? No hazards, no pitfalls?"

"Smooth bussing."

"Good." Hands are thrust onto her sides as she arches her back, all the posture and scrutiny of a sergeant sizing up a new recruit. "So. Mr. Jack. Let's have a look at you. Hmm. Yes. I do believe…mmm-hmmm…without a doubt you are completely *not* what I had expected. Most definitely."

"I'm not sure how I should take that."

"Oh, I wish you wouldn't take it. I haven't actually given it to you yet. But, you should feel very, very good about it. I would have been disappointed if you ended up being exactly what I expected. I mean, how mundane to be so easily assumed. Please tell me I'm not what you expected."

Jack shakes his head. "I don't think so."

"Well, that's good." She tosses her sign into a nearby trashcan and turns her head, surveys the surroundings. "Well, isn't this exciting? New and wondrous experiences are afoot in the throng of a busy bus station. My heart is racing with excitement. How about you?"

His tongue has forgotten its function—words stumble over it. "It...certainly feels like the cusp of something eventful."

She leans into him, those dark eyes surging. "Every breath is drawn upon the cusp of an event, Jack." She searches his face for something and nods once with an affirming purse of her lips, then snaps to attention. "Hungry?"

Jack gives a tentative bob of his head.

"Great! A culinary adventure awaits. I know just the place." She pivots tightly on her heels and her broad steps and pumping arms propel her to the exit. Jack, slow to react, must trot to catch up to her.

But not before he turns a fleeting glance out the window for signs of a taxi.

-8

Jack follows Pauline down the streets of Skokie in the mid-afternoon hustle. It's a meandering stroll with Pauline taking a commanding lead. He expected to leave the depot for Pauline's car, but as they stroll further from the station, Jack assumes this perfect place to eat must be a convenient walking distance away. Shell shock from their initial meeting still dazes him. He follows her, trying to orient himself to the new surroundings and work out the stiffness in his legs and the travel lag that muddles his perception.

Pauline points to areas of interest as they walk past, presenting them like shiny baubles pulled from her pocket and held between her fingers. Each location, every landmark, accounted for with respect and enthusiasm.

"That's the tattoo parlor where I got my first tattoo." She gestures to a building ahead of them. "I got it after a life-defying tragedy I wanted to embrace forever."

That baffles him, but he won't probe the subject—too soon. He nods attentively and looks through the window into the dingy, whitewashed parlor squeezed between two large brick buildings.

The sign displays a fiery bird and says *Phoenix Tattoos*.

"Carlos. That's him right there, with the black beret. I was a canvas to Carlos' art. It seems there is nothing better you could hope to be in this life."

Pauline points across the street to an ice cream parlor on the corner called *Eastern Delights*. "Have you ever had Asian ice cream?"

He had no idea there *was* such a thing. "Can't say I have. Not much of a market for it in Terrapin, I guess."

"Oh, you must try the saffron-pistachio. It'll be like I'm tasting it for the first time through you."

Jack swallows. "Mmmm. I can't wait."

She keeps moving, a zealous tour guide, and his legs pump to keep up, knees knocking into his suitcase and bag. He's spoken little, and that makes him self-conscious. He needs to speak up, to claim his place. "How long have you lived in Skokie, Pauline?"

"Oh, about ten years now. Ever since I finished college at Evanston."

"Do you have family in Skokie?"

"No."

That was uncomfortably concise. Jack retreats to quiet safety again.

He can't stop staring as she struts her heavy, bouncing steps and looks up, down, and around her, stopping to peek inside storefront windows wide-eyed and grinning as if seeing everything for the first time. Somewhere under the drapery of clothes and her big-boned girth is the suggestion of curve, the tease of voluptuous feminine lines, but the burdened determination of her stride manhandles the sexuality of shape.

She leads him away from the road, through a small park of grass and trees and pathways webbing out from a central gazebo. She plods up the steps and leans over the gazebo railing, smiling like she has found some secret place and is inviting him to share. The rumbling motors and rubber-thumping tires of traffic are distant, leaving the chitter of squirrels and squawk of crows to call out the bustle of nature's rush hour.

They must have walked two miles by now—the luggage gaining weight with each step. He sits on a bench against the gazebo's half wall and drops his bags. "So, where is this place to eat, anyway?"

"Oh, about two more miles, I should think."

Two more miles? He can't remember the last time he walked four miles anywhere, with luggage, no less. Then still to walk all the way back?

His expression must be telling. She laughs her deep, eruptive chuckle. "Are you in a hurry?"

He feels heat in his cheeks. "Me? Oh, no. This is fine."

"It's better than fine, Jack. It's a beautiful fall day and we're able to actually experience it, not just watch it pass by through a window. We can touch it. We can hear it. We can *smell* it." She grabs at the air, snatching a handful in her fist, and brings it to her nose. She sniffs deeply, eyes closed. "Oh, that's the stuff."

"I can't argue that, I guess." He opens and closes his hands, working blood back into them, tendons tight and hot. "I was just wondering about your car at the station."

She looks confused. "Car?"

"I just didn't know where you had parked and if you might get a ticket."

"Well, it's possible I suppose, if I *had* a car, which I don't, so I guess we don't have to worry about any tickets."

"Oh." The exclamation falls from his lips. When she wrote that she'd meet him at the bus station, a vehicle had seemed implicit.

Pauline brushes aside a thick coil of hair from the front of her face. "Jack. What's the matter?"

He shakes his head, embarrassed again. "Nothing. Really."

"Do you think I'm strange for not owning a car? Am I some kind of aberration of social predilection because I choose to avoid the machinations of modern gluttony and ego?" It's all said with a smile, but he detects offense behind the whimsy of her words.

He shifts uncomfortably. "Listen, I didn't mean anything by it, I was just wondering, that's all."

"Jack, we may not always say what we mean, but we always mean what we say. Are you that afraid to talk to me?"

"I wasn't trying to say anything, okay?" That was a snap. Too harsh. He looks away quickly, and he can't stop thinking, *Mistake. This is all a big mistake.*

She laughs, a boil of molasses. "I make you nervous, don't I, Jack?" She waggles clawed fingers at him. "Who is this peculiar woman leading the hapless young man?"

Home seems insurmountably distant from him now, this park and the street and the city utterly foreign. He grabs the edge of his bench and will not reply to her.

He feels Pauline's eyes target him, like she's going to say more, but instead she hitches a breath and looks off to the distance, passive and thoughtful. "Can you sense it?" she asks.

She's like a book with missing pages, sentences that end abruptly to new paragraphs and ideas. He stares, helpless.

She draws a reflective breath. "It's all around us. The season is dying. It's a sweet surrender. The breeze anticipates it. The trees that dressed in celebration of it now shed their colors in a humble homage. The birds sing a prayer of love for the death of life. Listen. It's like the answer to every question you've never asked."

Jack stands up. Her back is to him, hands on the railing, head back and hair rustled by the breeze. In the forty or so minutes he has been with her, he's felt unbalanced and small, wading in a conversational undertow. But he sees now, he recognizes what he had missed before—her insecurity, her absolute discomfort and nervousness. A spooked deer bolting full speed into a fence with goggled eyes, escaping where there is no exit. He watches her, wishes she would speak those last words again, those first words she has spoken that aren't costumed in plastic jewelry. They are cold and disrobed. They are kindred.

He suspects he thought wrong before. Maybe she is the missing pages.

Of all the things that come to mind to say in reply, he instead offers a wavering smile when she faces him again, and he gives in to dry, brittle words. "I'm really lost, Pauline. And I'm scared." He feels the familiar flush in his cheeks. The words were unintended, unbidden. He's rolled over and exposed his belly to a purring lioness.

Pauline draws close, sympathy rounding her features and relief in her consoling voice. "I know, Jack." She offers him her hand, and he accepts it, realizing he could go no further without it.

-7

It's a corner café that Pauline leads him to at the edge of the downtown Skokie business district. Outside the doors is a pungent smell like burnt bread. The large, green awning overhanging the entrance has "Capos and Cantos" screened in a flourishing white script. When Pauline's hand slips out and away from his to open the door, it seems strange that it would have ever been there in the first place. He tries to remember what it had been like, having some small part of her wrapped within his grip as a tiny bit of him was wrapped in hers, tries to imagine what it would be like to have it again. He can't, the moment is gone, but the warmth of skin that lingers on his palm is like a pleasant notion he closes his fingers around, well kept.

Inside, the aroma is sharp and roasted in the spacious establishment moderately filled with a college-aged crowd. They cuddle their lattes and chug their microbrews as they chat. Many stroll past the collections of local art, photography and sculptures that color and texture the room. Moody acoustic guitar accompanying the bitter verses of a female voice feathers the air.

Pauline leads Jack to the counter at the back of the café. A pale waif of a girl with an erratic burst of flame red hair looks over to Pauline from the shushing cappuccino machine

"Swan Song! How you doin', girl?"

"I couldn't be bad if I tried, Jazz."

Jazz squirts a dollop of whipped cream into the oversized cup, adds a dash of cocoa, and sets it on the other side of the counter, shouting "Thirty-seven!" and then skips over to Pauline. She lunges her upper body over the counter and gives Pauline a shoulder-wrap of hug. "Oh, where have you been?" She falls back to her side of the counter, and her eyes flit briefly to Jack before settling back on Pauline.

"Jazz, I require your rapt attention." Pauline peers down at her, curled brow an accent to her intensity, and gestures with a flourish. "*This*…is Mr. Jack."

Embarrassment seems to be a perpetual emotion around Pauline. He flushes and smiles.

Jazz looks him up and down, dubious flare of nostrils, and thrusts out her hand. "Greetings, Mr. Jack. I'm Jasmine."

Jack shakes her hand, gently at first, but more firmly as he reacts to the small girl's girded grip. "Hi there." His voice sounds meek and it annoys him.

Jazz seems unprepared how to proceed, maybe skeptical. She's broadcasting to Pauline some question or comment that Jack is caught in the middle of that bears his unspoken name. He'll be forced to speak soon if they don't.

Jazz whips out her pad and pen and stands at attention. "So, what can I get you?"

Pauline looks up at the chalkboard menu. "I believe I would like my usual unusual, please."

Jazz nods. "Ah, yes. Excellent choice. We have some particularly unusual items today for you."

"Surprise me, my dear."

"Byron's been playing around with a new dish. You can be our guinea pig. What about you, Mr. Jack? Are you feeling adventurous?"

Jack rolls his shoulders, glancing at the menu. "Actually, I'm feeling like a turkey sandwich."

The '*tsk*' Jazz cracks with her tongue as she writes up the order slaps Jack like a C-minus. Pop quiz at the menu, and Jack's already disappointed the staff. She looks up from her pad, licking the tip of her pen with all the flare of challenge. "And to drink?"

Pauline orders a chai tea, and Jack asks for a nut-brown ale. Never had it before, but maybe it will make up for his turkey sandwich.

They pay for their order, receive a number, and move off to a large wooden booth against the window.

Jack hangs his coat on the hook at the end of the booth and stuffs his suitcase against the wall on the seat. "I take it you come here a lot."

"This is my home, Jack."

"Seems like a nice place."

"Oh, right now it's just a mild-mannered café. But in the evenings, it magically transforms. Music, poetry readings, and the blood-rushing, caffeine-induced energies of creativity flood the room."

"Sounds like your kind of place." The last time he put himself into a throng of exuberant people, he had been knocked into oblivion and his life turned inside out. Of course, it's doubtful Ox and Len will be strolling in anytime soon to attend a poetry reading.

Pauline glows and her voice softens. "Perhaps you'll even see me perform here tonight."

"You're a musician?"

"Of a sort. Poetry. The music of words."

Jack smiles to the thought. "I should have known."

She rests her cheek in her hand, elbow on the table. "Don't expect that to be your last surprise about me." Her finger twirls a lock of hair, wraps it tight.

"I wouldn't presume. So, do you have a regular...um...gig here? With poetry?"

"Oh, you won't be seeing my name in lights. I just sign up for the open poetry readings. Anyone can." Her stare is heavy on him, anticipatory, and there's a queer sense that Pauline already knows this conversation and is coaxing him through it with bemused sympathy. "And what about you, Jack? Graphic design at an undisclosed furniture company. What exactly is it that you do? Other than creating bizarre little websites."

"Nothing so interesting as poetry. Really, I just pitched the concept behind the product with pretty pictures. Worked and slept. The job took up most of my time."

"You're speaking in past tense. Have things changed?"

Was that intentional? Guarding the truth has been as natural and thoughtless as blinking in the past week. "Well, you'll notice I'm not at work right now, and this isn't exactly vacation time for me." Instincts provoke a pause, but Pauline's warm attention is soothing encouragement. "I quit. Well, not in so many words, I guess. I walked out. But one way or the other, I am now unemployed."

"Why did you do it?"

Precarious footing on that question. He doesn't completely know the answer to it himself, any more than he understands why he's here with her. "Seemed like the right thing to do at the time, I guess."

She's staring, mulling over his words or challenging his answer. A broad smile alights on her face. "Well, congratulations, Jack."

"I'm not sure if it's really something to congratulate me for. I mean, I walked out of a secure job with good pay without any prospects to fall back on."

Her smile holds strong and she claps her hands together on the table. "Oh, yes. Congratulations are definitely in order. You're in the middle of a momentous life change. Your mettle will be tested. You will learn and grow. Perhaps, if you're dedicated to the task, you may just improve yourself."

Pauline, the human horoscope. His sardonic chuckle is little more than a grumble. "You certainly have a rosy outlook."

"Jack, are you telling me that you were happy with your life up until now? Things were working out for you? I may have missed something, but that's not the impression I've gotten. So, how could you possibly be anything but happy by this change in your life?"

Good question. She makes sense, yet the dread that hangs about him is caused by so much more than just the loss of his job. But he's not ready to tell her everything. Not yet.

Jazz walks up to their booth balancing a wide, round plate shoulder-height. She places their drinks in front of them, then sets a plate before Jack. Golden-crusted bread, thick folds of turkey on a ruffled blanket of romaine lettuce, slabs of red tomato, all dripping with cheese and sauce under lush curls of sprouts. This sandwich deserves a standing ovation.

"Full service," Pauline says. "I'm honored."

Jazz winks at her. "The benefits of being a preferred customer." Before Pauline, she places a bowl of what looks like raw shrimp in a diarrhetic brown sauce seasoned with weeds. "This, darling, is the latest foray in delectable delights courtesy of Capos and Cantos. Prawn Ceviche—butterflied raw king prawns marinated in fish sauce and served with fresh chili, garlic and bitter melon."

Pauline glows approval. "My taste buds will be gawking tourists in an exotic land of taste." She marvels over the dish that, to Jack, looks slightly more appealing than the dead fish he once saw a seagull gutting on the Lake Superior shore during a weekend road trip to Duluth with his parents.

He gives his turkey sandwich a clumsy smirk. "My taste buds will stick to familiar comforts, thank you very much."

Jasmine angles a frown at him. "Now, just think of everything you'll miss out on with an attitude like that."

He glances back at the spongy pink prawn flesh in the gastric brown liquid. "Indigestion and nausea, I'm guessing."

Jazz shakes her head. "Pauline, you have your work cut out for you. Make sure he gets back to the retirement home before curfew."

Pauline laughs. "Oh, don't underestimate this one, Jazz. I have tremendous hopes for him."

Jack thinks he is smiling as Jazz walks away, but the smile burns as Jazz's comment lingers. He tries to mollify the simmering humility with a swig of beer and peers out the window at the increasing congestion of traffic.

"So, just what are you looking for, Jack?"

She's inclined toward him, scrutinizing, when he returns his attention. "What do you mean?"

"You are a man on a quest. And your face doesn't hide much."

Jack is deflected by her words and he pans over the artwork on the walls—just blurs of undistinguishable shapes in random color from where he sits. "Well, I don't know if it's that, or if I'm running away."

"Mr. Jack now seems to want to argue semantics. Whether you're running *to* something or *from* something, the action is still the same."

"And what makes you such an expert?"

"Oh, Jack. Don't you think I've ever looked in a mirror? I've seen those eyes looking back at me."

"And what is Pauline Swanson looking for?"

She takes her fork and lazily nudges a prawn. "I'm reformed. I'm not on the long quest anymore. I've watched the flames of my future on the horizon too many times to step willingly into that conflagration. No. I quest for the day now. It's all I can afford."

His throat swells and he can't get his voice above a whisper. "I think I'm stuck there."

Pauline raises her chai tea. She opens her mouth to speak, but looks troubled. "I would like to propose a toast, but I've just realized I still don't know your last name. I can't give a proper toast without your full name."

"Oh. It's Cross. Jack Cross."

A smile wriggles on her lips. "That's quite a burden to bear, Jack." She lifts the glass higher toward him. "Well, then, a toast to Jack Cross, and to the changes before him. May his quest be fulfilling rather than fulfilled, and may he never limit himself to his expectations."

Jack brings his beer bottle up to her glass. "I'll drink to that." A swig from the bottle of nut-brown ale, then the turkey sandwich is in his hands. He takes a big bite, the crisp, flaking crust breaking away with a soft tang of full-flavored wheat and oat. The moist turkey against the crisp greens, tomato and sauce is so full of flavor that the insides of his cheeks tingle. He can't help but hum with satisfaction. He wipes the corner of his mouth and looks up from his plate. Pauline's attention is fixed upon him.

"So, you can enjoy things." She beams, and Jack never wants to forget that someone has looked at him this way.

They eat and their talk is casual. Is this comfort he's feeling with her? Or is he just becoming accustomed to being uncomfortable around her? She's so different, so completely unlike anyone he's ever known. He enjoys watching the forkfuls of food finding their way carefully to her mouth. She's not a dainty eater, but each heaping scoop is attentively chewed and savored. Between bites, she probes details of his life—about Terrapin, his family, his interests.

"So, you're interacting with all these different people, and the game really allows you to do all these things?" The topic has turned to his on-line gaming with Liz and Len as he finishes the last bite of his sandwich.

"Well, the game itself is fairly limited, so you make up for it by emoting your actions in text."

"Emoting?"

"Sure. You type something like, 'reaches into pouch' or 'brushes hair from face.' You just bracket the emote, and that's how you do things that otherwise couldn't be seen or done."

Pauline runs a finger along the bottom of the bowl through the brown fish sauce, brings it to her mouth and folds her lips around it. "Emoting. I like that. But I still don't understand the object of the game."

"Well, there's really no object. You're inventing and playing out stories. Sometimes a DM will step in and throw a twist in the storyline."

"'DM?'"

"The dungeon master. They kind of lurk in the background of the game, stepping into a non-player character or dropping a new character into the game. They'll usually play an antagonist to your storyline and try to make things interesting."

"Very strange, Jack. It sounds like some kind of bizarre little alternate reality."

"Well, it's a nice escape sometimes."

"Oh, I see. Escape. Very interesting." She moves in, lamp of interrogation pulled closer to his face. "And just what role are you playing now, Jack, on this latest escape of yours?"

He laughs nervously, leaves it for her on the table as his answer. Hero or villain? Is that the question? Oh, no. He couldn't possibly move himself toward either extreme. He's just not that important.

Pauline pushes her empty bowl away from her and stretches with a contented moan. "Well, are you ready to begin the long, arduous trek to my place?"

He sags to the weight of a full stomach and resents his luggage. "How far is it?"

"Oh, Jack. Don't disappoint me now. Embrace the adventures before you."

He groans and pushes himself off the bench. Slipping into his jacket, he says, "You're very odd sometimes, Pauline."

"Mmm. I swoon to your charms." She grabs his overnight bag and he his suitcase, and he follows her through the café and out the door.

Pauline takes a mere three steps to the left and opens the door immediately beside Capos and Cantos. She holds it wide and, with a sweeping motion of her arm, gestures inside. "After you, Mr. Jack."

He actually questions what she is doing, where she could be leading him, for one surprised second, not because he is dense, but because he could just as easily have expected Pauline to muscle up a manhole cover and take him down to a subterranean world.

"You're having way too much fun at my expense."

"You practically beg for it, Jack."

The stairs are steep and long in the darkened stairwell; each creaks a different note of age. Reaching the top, he waits in the dimly lit foyer. Pauline is right behind him, keys jingling as she steps up to her door.

She unlocks the deadbolt on the old, paint-peeling door, but opens it only a crack. "You are about to enter my inner sanctum, Jack. Are you quite certain you are prepared for this?"

"I, um, thought so, until you asked me." A teetering imbalance has been pushing up under his ribs since meeting her, and he still can't figure out if he wants the feeling to stop, or never go away.

Pauline nudges him further off-kilter by seeming to reply directly to his thoughts. "You're trying to figure me out, aren't you?" She laughs. "My poor Quixote wants to battle windmills."

That simple, innocent word—'my.' Possessive. She is taking ownership of him, either as guardian or as master. He struggles with his own docility that wills, that wants to cling to her leg, submissive and protected.

She swings the door open. "Enter, Jack. Welcome to my domain."

Her place is overwhelmed by books. They claim all available space against the walls of the large living room. Several bookshelves bulge and sag with volume upon volume. There might once have been some attempt at a system, but that system has succumbed long ago to the literary infestation.

The apartment itself, despite the disarray of books, still manages a well-worn comfort. Thick sunlight fills the apartment, distilled by the dusty atmosphere, and glimmers as the sluggish air churns. This fuzzy radiance seeps from large windows that overlook the street, and the light mellows on plastered butterscotch walls. The hardwood floor, though dull and hazed with ground-in dirt and worn finish, looks soft and warm. No pictures hang, the bare walls span like desert sand, but a cross takes prominence on the main wall opposite the windows.

To the far end of the living room, tucked into a small alcove, is Pauline's computer, the monitor and keyboard crowding the top of an old sewing machine desk. Jack holds on this, the incongruity of technology upon the antique utility, and he shares an intimacy with this computer and the wooden chair stationed before it.

Pauline steps in and around him, directly to the red, red couch in the center of the room. She drops onto it with arms wide across the rest and the back, and she dominates the apartment. "So now I have you," she intones. "Alone, and at my mercy."

"It appears so." He stands narrowly in the entryway, a flood victim on a sinking stone.

Pauline says nothing for a time, and Jack responds likewise. Her eyes crawl over him, and he is desperately casual in his formal discomfort.

"So," Pauline says. "Do you plan to stand there all day, or are you up to the challenge of risking the living room?"

"Yeah. Sorry."

He sets his luggage down and moves toward the chair at the computer, but the disapproving cock of Pauline's head makes him quickly divert to the couch, where he clings to the far corner.

"It's a nice place," he says. "I like it."

"Oh, I more than like it. I worked downstairs for several years, and when this apartment opened up, I didn't even think about it, I just grabbed it."

"How long have you been here, then?"

"Eight years."

The pauses between their words are palpable, seconds that stack between them like blocks.

"How did you like working in the café?"

"It was a good college job."

"Is that how you met Jazz?"

"Yes."

What did they call it in English classes? Caesura pauses? In context, they are much more resilient, unwieldy, like a grindstone.

"You two are close?"

She gives an odd look that confuses his question, pulls in her lower lip with her teeth. "Occasionally."

Something about that answer in the wrappings of her expression compels him to discard that subject. His eyes wander, and he reaches for a book from the stack beside the sofa—Norton's Anthology of Woman's literature. "I don't think I've ever met someone with so many books." He opens the heavy text and flips through its onionskin pages.

Pauline sits. Stares. "Hmm. Yes. I have a lot of books."

"You're not going to tell me you've read them all, are you?" Jack looks back up and Pauline's fingers thrum against the cushioned couch back. She is expectant. Waiting.

He closes the book, squinting as the sun lowers in the sky and comes into view through the window, bright and hot. "What?"

"You're horrible at small talk."

"I'm…what?"

Pauline brings one leg up, folds it and tucks her foot under her as she shifts closer. "You're talking, Jack, but you're not really saying anything."

He stammers to her ardent glare. "I'm not following you."

"Talk to me, Jack. Don't distract me."

"What do you want me to say?"

"What do you want to tell me?"

"I-" Sitting doesn't work anymore. He stands and paces, silent, not for lack of words to say but from a congestion of words that lodge in his throat. He came here to talk, didn't he? To open up to someone? Why now does it feel like psyching himself up to jump off a cliff? Pauline's insistence that he actually does have something to say only goads him to prove her wrong. "I'm not getting you, Pauline. We've known each other now for, what? Two hours? Two hours and a few emails. Small talk seems a pretty normal thing."

"Ah, normal." Pauline puckers. "Yes. And you're all about normal, aren't you? You wear normal like camouflage. Why *are* you so obsessed with normal, Jack?"

He tries to laugh, but the nervous titter that crumbles from his lips is damning. "Obsessed with normal? Where do you get that from? You barely even know me."

She sits up straighter. "Oh, I don't know. Let's see. You're first email to me was an emphatic browbeating of how normal you are. You cringe at anything that doesn't strictly conform to Midwestern cuisine, and even the idea of not owning a car is subversive."

His fingers pick at the buttons of his shirt. "Wow. That's a bit of an exaggeration, isn't it?"

"Oh, perhaps. But so is your cover of banality."

He takes a hasty step toward her, rushing to speak. "I'm not hiding behind anything." His pacing stalls, that automatic response clogging his mouth like cotton, twist of a wince a mute confession. This woman is some kind of antigen to untruth. Even those things that he, up to this moment, has fooled himself into believing, suffocate within the squeeze of her appraisal.

Pauline's chestnut eyes under the shadow of her tumbling dark hair dare him to stand by his statement.

He lets himself fall back to the couch, finds an empty section of wall and hides his eyes there. "I guess maybe I've never felt normal my entire life." His words don't seem to hold in the silent room. They drain like hourglass sand.

"You said you were scared, Jack. Isn't it time you told me why?"

That memory, of her hand in and around his, is a gentle brush of phantom contact. Something inside of him, something clenched and cramped, lets go. His hand wanders to the stubbly fuzz of the shaved patch at the back of his head and touches the raise of skin that makes a jagged inch-long run across his scalp. "There's this… thing…in my head. It's almost impossible to describe, but it's like…a hole. Like an…empty thought. But it's heavy. It's heavy, and it's deep."

He can't look at Pauline, because he knows to do so will pinch off this flow of openness, and he wouldn't be able to handle the surging pressure. He has to get this out, so he continues with his gaze downcast, and confesses to her foot. "If I focus on it, I can feel it pulling on me. Pulling on everything. It's been there for as long as I can remember, but when I was young, it was just this odd little bubble of emptiness to think around. By the time I was twelve, thirteen maybe, I started to, sort of, play with it. Explore it. I'd crawl under my thoughts to find it, and the more I concentrated on it, the more I began to…recognize it. That's when I started to realize what it is…what it could do if I…let it take me."

Pauline is so still that the room around her almost jitters. "What are you trying to say?" The answer already rests within her widening eyes.

"Pauline. The website. It isn't a joke." The words stick to his tacky mouth, and he really needs a glass of water.

"Jack, that's…crazy." Her voice snaps with a dry chuckle like pinewood popping in a fire.

"Maybe."

"But…how could you possibly equate this…this *thing* in your head with ending the world?"

How many hours of his life has he spent on this same question? "I don't know. I suppose it's kind of like…hunger, or thirst. How does any living thing actually know what hunger and thirst are when it feels them? How does it know what to do to solve them? I mean, no instruction manual comes with life, yet eating, drinking, sex, birth…all these things are built into us—instinctive—and we know what to do when the time comes. All I can tell you is that there is no question in my mind about what the Shrug is. The only question is whether or not I'm crazy."

It's Pauline's turn to look away, and he's thankful not to be under the scrutiny and shock of those eyes. "Boy, you certainly didn't hold back with this one, did you, Jack? Wow."

"I don't expect you to believe me, Pauline. There's absolutely no reason to. I've never told anyone for this very reason."

"So why tell me?"

"Because…something's happening. Something has changed, and I honestly don't know what to do."

Jack watches Pauline, her apparent struggle to face him, and the air wrings out of his lungs. But then her posture straightens and her head raises, and when she returns her attention, it is Pauline at the station again, Pauline at the café. The Pauline that makes him think everything could be okay. She places her hand on his knee. "Tell me everything."

Over twenty years. He held a secret for over twenty years, not sharing it with anyone—not even Liz, who he gave all the explicit details to of that uncomfortable night with Sara Flemming back in college when they had sex for the first time in her dorm while her roommate slept above them.

And here he is, in a city he's never been, in the apartment of a woman he hardly knows, sitting on her lumpy red sofa, telling her everything. About the CT scan. About the blackouts. About the visions. And she is quiet, but she is intensely quiet, moving only once to get water for him and herself. He doesn't even realize that he is finished until the long silence that follows. She appears pale, though she could merely be losing her color to the fading glow of twilight.

"You have to tell your doctor, Jack. This is serious."

"Come on. Dr. Haizuki will never believe me. My story will only give him grounds to judge me incompetent and he'll perform another scan."

"Then don't tell him about your...Shrug. Just continue to insist on no scans, but ask for treatment."

"I did. That means opening up my head, and I'm not going through that. Not yet, at least. Besides, what if by them poking around in there, they cause me to trigger it? Maybe I'll let him run his EEG, but that's as far as I'll go."

Pauline's brow crowds her eyes, and Jack wonders what she really wants to say that she isn't. "So, you'll go see your friend on Friday. And maybe he'll tell you that there's something to this. What then? It won't change anything. You're already convinced this thing is real."

All he's been doing since the accident is reacting. Nothing is planned out or thought through. He takes a drink of water and swallows slow. "I don't know. I really don't. But I have to play this out. These…dreams, visions, whatever…of my father? I don't know what they mean, but they're important. There's an urgency to them I just can't shake."

Pauline pulls back from him. "What are you saying?" There's a tense quaver in her voice. "That all this is part of some grander scheme? That you're being given a mandate from God?"

"Listen. I'm no messiah, okay? There's no delusion of grandeur operating in me. I don't know if I can even *believe* in God. How can I, if the Shrug is real? You see the contradiction, don't you? Why would God ever allow this ability…unless God is suicidal."

"Jack. You can't destroy God. The very concept negates the nature of God."

"Leading back to the point of whether there can be a God if a power like this exists."

Pauline's face tightens to his words. He's lost her now, pushed her too far. But then she hops up and walks to one of the bookshelves with stiff-stepping determination to rummage through the piles. She comes back with a small soft cover book and holds it out to him.

"What's this?" He looks at the thin paperback, relieved to see it isn't the hefty bindings of the Bible in her hands.

"*Systematic Theology.* Written by Paul Tillich, a Christian philosopher. Take it."

Jack does with reluctant curiosity. "Are you going to try to save my soul, Pauline?"

She sits down again and grabs her water. "You're the one who believes all this is happening for a reason. Maybe this is *my* purpose, Mr. Jack." She taps the book he has set in his lap. "One of the concepts Tillich tackles is the nonexistence of God."

This takes him by surprise. "I don't think Sister Rosanna would approve."

"Who?"

"From grade school. Forget it."

"Listen. Tillich is attempting to explain the nature of God. He writes that it's futile to try and argue the existence of God, because God can't exist. For God to exist would be to strip away the very aspects that make Him God. God is beyond existence."

"Okay." It's always seemed perfectly straightforward. Existence, nonexistence. Something, nothing. What she's suggesting applies levels and layers to concepts that by their nature completely disallow them.

"Don't you see? You think you can undo existence, right? Turn everything to nothing. By doing this, you believe you would undo God in the process, therefore God can't exist, because the possibility to destroy God precludes the existence of God."

"Right."

"But, if Tillich is correct, how can you destroy something that doesn't exist in the first place? God is beyond the concept of existence, and, in so being, eternal and indestructible."

There's an apparent logic to this, though the obscurity of the concept makes it difficult to feel out its edges. He pages through the book and tries to contain the idea within his reasoning.

One finger makes slow, even orbits around the lip of her glass. "And, Mr. Jack, if you accept Tillich's tenet and how it relates to your situation, then you would have no choice but to accept that God factors into this Shrug."

Jack curdles to that line of reasoning. This is exactly where he doesn't want this conversation to go. "Look. I don't think I can accept that all this is happening because of some greater plan of God. No offense, but I just don't have the faith for it."

"Why not? You yourself told me you sensed something moving you toward a decision or action. Are you telling me you can believe this, and yet so stubbornly refute God? It seems to me you should have a far greater problem with that contradiction than with the concept of God."

His mother should be here. She'd eat this up. "And what if there's no great plan, Pauline? No guiding force in the universe?

What if everything is random and coincidental? Look around at the world. Natural disasters, wars, strife. I read a response on the website the other day. It says that the human race, maybe existence itself, has a predilection for its own destruction. How could God fit into this kind of emptiness?"

Pauline shakes her head. "Jack, who in the world sold you the concept of life promising anything? You think you're owed an Eden, so you declare the world a hell. The world is what you make of it. Nothing is offered here. You have to offer yourself to it."

"They're nice words, Pauline. But I'm sorry, it just sounds like another didactic sales pitch to me." He sets Tillich's book down on the coffee table. "And you should be careful bringing God into this. If the Shrug is part of some grand scheme by God, doesn't that inevitably lead to me using it? Otherwise, why give it to me?"

"It's the height of presumption to question God, Jack."

His eyes have a terrible urge to roll. "Oh, Pauline. I'd expect a response like that from my mother, but not from you. It's a copout."

"No. It's faith."

"Same difference." As he says it, he knows it's a mistake, that he's made it personal, and seeing Pauline recoil to his words drops a load of regret into his stomach.

She stands up in the gathering darkness of the room, facing away from him, and turns on the floor lamp in the corner, a stark light that bleeds shadows. "And *that*, I believe, will conclude this discussion." She walks back to the shelf and begins to shuffle paperbacks about in what looks to him a meaningless reorganization.

He stands, but keeps his distance from her. "I didn't mean that. Not how it sounded."

Her laugh is acidic. "*Don't,* Jack. Really. You don't have the verbal coordination to keep your balance on this tightrope."

Jack slumps back to the couch, boiling in his acceptance of her words. So, now what? He can't just sit on the couch and wait for the tension to pass. These strangled moments never seem to relax in time, not until all the air is choked out. Forget apologizing. He'll only mess it up. Just try to get onto a new subject and get past this.

And so he is resolved. But two attempts of opening his mouth to a voice trapped by his clenched throat bring him no closer to relieving the taut silence. He goes for a third try just as Pauline steps in front of him. "It's imperative that we get ice cream."

His mouth is still open, still silent, still frozen stupid. "All right."

She walks ahead of him to the door, swings it open, then turns and glares at him. "And if you order Vanilla, I'll scream."

-6

Whether it is the walk to Asian Delights or the Saffron-Pistachio ice cream, by the time they finish eating Pauline returns to her "usual, unusual" self, and Jack is thankful enough of that to suffer the musty, spicy-sweet taste lingering in his mouth.

As they make their way back, he risks a question. "You never said if you believe all of this."

"Does it matter if I do?"

"Sure it does. To me it does. I mean, I'm not expecting you to believe, but I'd still like to know, just the same."

Pauline slows her lunging stride. "So. I say I believe you. What changes? It will always be this thing that either is or isn't. If it is, still nothing changes unless you decide to change it. It all comes down to you, Jack. The real question has to be, do I believe in you? And to that I say, I do. Even if you don't believe in yourself. How about you, Jack? What do you believe in?"

"I don't know. I believe in this, here, right now. This moment, being with you."

"Oh, Jack. That's the one thing you have no business believing in. It's no wonder you haven't any faith. You won't find it in the present. The present is just a figment of your imagination. A fiction between what has already happened, and what hasn't happened yet. Get out of the now, Jack. You reek of it. You're sick with it."

"I wouldn't even know how."

"Take my hand, Jack. I'll lead the way. We'll mourn the past and hope for the future together." His arm is tugged as her motor gears up.

"Where are we going?"

"To our time machine, Jack! Poetry Night at the café. You're going to hear me read."

Back at her apartment, Pauline excuses herself to her bedroom, saying she needs to "dress the part of poetry." It's ironic, since he always imagined women poets to dress like librarians. While he waits, he realizes that he should call the hotel to make sure they hold his room. After he tells the clerk that he'll be checking in late he hangs up just in time to be taken completely by surprise when Pauline returns from her bedroom.

"And just what are you staring at, Jack?"

He thinks, *if I had seen this when I came off the bus, I just might have found that taxi,* but he says, "You look nice," and tries hard to find some way to believe it. But the tall, big-boned woman before him, made uncomfortably taller by the black high-heeled shoes that pinch her feet, the black stockings over thick legs that run up and up to the short, split black skirt, and the emerald green mock-wrap that folds flesh between arms and breasts and glitters with studs that sparkle her chest, only make him feel embarrassed for her.

A heavy, red-glossed smile and a leer lined in jade steps closer. Sultry waves of musk waft against him. "Shall we make our descent, Jack?"

It's an entirely different café to the one at lunch when he follows Pauline into Capos and Cantos. The counter is the same, and the menu, the art and sculpture. The tables are as they were, though pushed back from the front to make room for a microphone stand and portable PA equipment that crowd the small platform of the makeshift stage. But the atmosphere is kinetic. The audience fills most of the tables and booths, and others mill about at the front, or move from table to table talking. Though mostly college-aged and haphazardly dressed, the occasional thirty- or forty-something patron peppers the pulsing crowd. No one seems to simply speak; they make their points with wild gesticulations and their faces bulge and flare with emphatic expression. It's a cacophony of melodrama with a mocha aroma.

Pauline plunges into this crowd, those heels putting her a full head above most. He struggles as the tag-along, smiling when introduced, then withdrawing to the silent head bob and smile. She keeps to the vehemently dressed group that hovers around the sign-up sheet on a table just off-center from the stage area. She scribbles her name on the list and shares inside jokes with the others.

Jack has no idea how much time passes before a stout, butch female with short spikes of hair and a lip stud muscles the mike into her hands and welcomes everyone to Wednesday Night Poetry. Cheers and applause follow as the lights dim to a moody gloom. Pauline leads him to an empty table a few rows back from the front.

One by one the poets step up. It's easy to figure out who the regulars are. They rarely introduce themselves; emotion slathers their words as they incant their verses. He doesn't know what kind of poetry he expected—his only familiarity is the love sonnets, odes and ballads forced upon him in Lit courses—but after two or three poets, it's clear there will be no sonnets or odes tonight. The two male poets who recite are just thickly sardonic, but the women rage with hostile metaphors. He's unable to lock on to their full meanings, their words like water through the grip of his mind, but he understands enough to squirm in his seat and keep dropping his eyes to the table. When he looks over to Pauline, however, she basks in the often violent sexual themes, responding to a dramatic line with inarticulate outbursts of approval, hooting like a beered up football fan at the end of each reading.

After the seventh poet leaves the stage, the MC resumes her place at the microphone. "Alright, kiddies. Next up, our own Swan Song...Pauline Swanson!"

The applause and cheering is the loudest of the evening; Jack can't discern his own applause other than for the numbing pain of clapping too hard as he competes against the others. Pauline's slump-shouldered ambulation to the microphone contrasts the confident skyward angle of her chin. She waits for the crowd to settle.

"Just one for you tonight. It's titled, 'Role Model.'" She begins to read, her voice running like hot wax from flame:

> "I looked up to you,
> reveling in your height.
> The world turned without me
> and I lost balance.
>
> I looked up to you,
> feeling hands on my shoulders—
> your strong guiding grip—
> and I surrendered.
>
> I looked up to you,
> taking your warm offer
> in my cold isolation,
> and I trembled.
>
> I looked up to you,

swallowing your words like cream.
You churned out a smile
as I began to choke.

And I look up to you,
gagging on your sticky sweet lies
that drip down my chin,
and I spit them in your face.

I looked up to you."

Her hands drop to her sides as a welling silence suspends in the murky light of the room. In this absence, Jack draws a thin breath. Then, a concussive burst of barking cheers and applause crashes over him, a wave of sound and energy. He stares at Pauline, her words still adrift like flotsam. Pauline looks directly at him, much in the way Jack must have looked at her when he told her about the Shrug. How many seconds go by before he remembers to clap?

Jesus, why would she read that tonight? To him? Maybe he misunderstands. Maybe it's not what he thinks. He's never had a knack for interpreting poetry. It must be symbolic, not meant to imply the literal act.

He tries to relax. It's not Liz reading this, after all. It's Pauline. Of course it's metaphorical. That's what poetry is all about.

Pauline is halted several times by the kaffeeklatsch beatniks who dowse her with praise. She accepts each compliment with a broad smile and a stiff posture.

When she returns to the table, Jack stands up until she takes her seat, feels foolish for doing so, and sits back down. Pauline delivers a final impaling stare—he can't force any words to come—and then she faces front.

The remainder of the evening blurs.

Up the stairwell with the slushy sonance of voices from the café through the wall, to Pauline's apartment. Jack prods their prickly silence.

"I suppose I'll need to call a cab to get to the hotel."

"Sorry, Jack. I didn't think about that."

"Oh, that's fine. I should call for one now, though. It'll probably take awhile."

Inside, she walks over to the refrigerator and snaps a pink piece of paper from under a Skokie Public Library magnet. "I have a number here. United Taxi Service. I use them every now and again."

"Thanks." He dials the number, requests a cab, and repeats Pauline's address as she feeds it to him. "Forty-five minutes," he tells her after he hangs up.

Pauline slips out of her shoes, rolls down and removes her pantyhose and slinks onto the couch. "Time enough for us to resolve the day. Sit down, Jack." She pats the couch, velvety upholstery dusky red in evening light—curvaceous, rapacious.

Jack sits beside her.

"You are bothered by my poem." Her painted lips imply amusement, but her darkly stroked eyes interrogate.

"It was very good. It seemed to be the favorite of the night."

"Yes, it went over very well. But you're troubled by it."

He just wants to forget about the poem, move beyond it. She enjoys making him squirm, no doubt about it. "Well, I'm not sure if I completely understood it, but it had some disturbing images. Wasn't that your intention? To shock the audience?"

"That's certainly the reason some read tonight. But the essence of poetry is concentrated honesty. I try to be true to the art form. I'd like to know how you feel about mine."

He can't avoid answering her; she has him cornered. "It was uncomfortable, I guess. It made me sad. A little angry. The person in the poem, she subjected herself to such humiliation. She was so vulnerable. Wounded. That's how it seemed to me, at least."

"You see her as the victim, then."

"I don't think I could see it any other way."

"Maybe she is the aggressor, the manipulator. Sex can be a weapon, much more so for a woman than a man. A man becomes exposed and overtaken by sex. The woman wields it, holds it out like a sword. Men are willing to walk into that blade believing themselves invulnerable."

"I don't know. When so much has to be lost in the process, I can't help but see a victim on both sides."

Pauline slants toward him. "So you believe she has lost something in doing what she did. She's been marred by her actions."

Jack tugs at the welting around the pillow he's propped up against. "I don't know."

The reddened imprint of her shoe runs across the arch of her bare foot folded under her leg, deep enough to look painful. Could this be a poem? The truth below her thick ankle, in the creased and inflamed skin inflicted on her as she stood and confessed before an audience? "Why are you doing this, Pauline? Are you forcing me to judge you? Because I don't like it. I don't even see a point to it."

Her fingers glide up and down her thigh as she nuzzles into the corner of the couch, crash of chocolate hair breaking against crimson cushions. "Jack. What's happening here?" She waves a hand about her. "This here. You and me, in this place, at this time. What are we doing?"

His insides are warming like an oven, his outside cool and prickled with flesh bumps; he could sweat ice. Outside, blue neon glows from a bar sign across the street. Goosefeather Downs Pub. He throws his gaze there, Pauline's face in the foreground beside it. He swallows. "I have no idea what you're asking me."

"Why did you come here? Why did you come to see me? You said it yourself—we hardly know each other. Yet you, you of all people, throw yourself willingly into the unknown."

"I just wanted to meet you. Is there something wrong with

that?"

"You can be very frustrating, Jack. Every time I think I gain some ground with you, you put up your defenses. You didn't come here to gain anything, to build anything. You came here to tear down. To destroy."

"Jesus, Pauline, will you stop talking in riddles?"

Her visage cracks. "Please don't use that name in that way, Jack. And I'm not speaking in riddles. Relationships are a destructive process between people like us. There's so much ruin to bulldoze away before anything can be built in its place." She becomes soft and seductive. " I'm your wrecking ball, Jack. You recognized that right away. That's why you replied to my first email. And you can be mine." She sidles closer to him, and his heart thumps against his ears. "Smash me down, Jack. Tear me apart." Her face is close, her voice a husky exhale, her hand sudden and warm on his thigh. "We'll sift through our rubble together."

Jack doesn't withdraw, he can't, and he stumbles into the kiss, his lips fumbling like a misspoken question. Pauline's lips insist and force, the weight of her body heaving onto him, and he is overtaken by her abrupt passion. He struggles against her frenetic motions as his mind flames white. This isn't what he wants. Her tongue slides over his upper lip and he clutches her tightly to him, responds to her surging rhythms, driven to desperate compulsion. This is all he wants.

Pauline moans as she straddles him, her hands frantic, clawing for his waist, between his legs. His thoughts simmer and bubble to vapor; a lusty hiss of steam. The button of his pants wrenched free, zipper undone, her hand slides in and finds him. He slips his hand under her skirt, to the silken seam of her underwear, probing deeper, feeling the soft, fleshy warmth between her thighs, his breathing heavy—

Her legs lock, her body jerks back, breathless, and pulls her hand away. "No," she pants, and her face is drawn and porcelain.

The blood is pumping between Jack's legs. "What? What's wrong?" His words sound distorted and detached—not him at all.

She pulls away from him. "That can't happen." She pushes her skirt down, won't look at him. "Shit." She laughs like braking pottery, eyes wide and glistening. "This isn't going to happen, Jack. Not like this. Not now."

He lies there, gaping, his pants peeled open and his face still flushed. "Why? Did I do something—?"

"You didn't do anything. Damn it."

It's the second time he's heard her curse, and in the span of seconds.

"It's me. But—" She takes a moment for breath and composure. "This isn't right. It's not what we need right now. Not this way. It'll be a mistake." Her head upturns, hands covering her face. "Stupid."

He thinks, *This is exactly what I need*. But the anger, the fear—whatever it is that widens her eyes and drains her face to a pallor—breaks his voice and smothers his craving. "Okay. That's…that's fine. Sure." He struggles to zip and button himself with clumsy fingers and so much less available space.

Her eyes blotch red and glisten. She speaks, not to him, and he can barely hear her. "I can't believe it." Laughing again. A sobbing sputter. "I dropped my sword."

He hears, but he's not sure he understands. Afraid to understand. "What?"

"Oh, touché, Jack." Something about how she says it ripples his flesh and he wants out from under her. But when she faces him again, her tears run from a vulnerability he's yet seen from her.

She draws him up and wraps her arms around him, loose but firm. Her mouth brushes his ear. "I want you, Jack Cross," she whispers, "but you're not ready for me yet."

-5

This is more than he bargained for.

Jack isn't an insomniac, but has suffered sleeplessness infrequently throughout his life. Most often, a strange location or worry over a following day means counting ceiling tiles all night.

In the hotel room, while foot traffic thumps back and forth and back and forth down the upstairs hallway for absolutely no logical reason he can think of at 2:53—

He looks at the digital clock on the nightstand for the seventeenth time.

—2:54 in the morning, he faces the dread combination of being anxious about the upcoming day in a strange bed.

This is more than he bargained for.

For the first two hours in bed, he thought about his day with Pauline. Not a day, actually—nine hours. But it seems like a week had been packed into that day—a month. More. He has asked himself a thousand times just what exactly happened to lead up to that sudden, bizarre encounter on her couch, and he'll likely ask himself a thousand more before his consciousness finally exhausts itself to sleep. There'll still be no answer.

For the last two hours, it's been the far more troubling question of whether or not he wanted it to happen. Just how does he feel about the strange, quirky, frumpy, interesting, perplexing, mysterious, captivating Pauline Swanson?

Did he just answer his own question?

He reaches for his cigarettes on the nightstand for the twelfth time and doesn't take one. He hasn't had a smoke since the quick stop at a Burger King in Madison during the bus trip. He's barely thought about a cigarette since first laying his eyes on Pauline. Does that mean something?

Right now, it means his nerves are twitching and squirming for a cigarette, but somehow, investing almost twenty hours on an unwitting withdrawal makes it seem a waste not to keep it going.

This is more than he bargained for.

What the hell does that even mean? Bargained? Such a stupid expression, and it keeps needling his thoughts. He has negotiated no price, no outcome, no results in this trip.

Has he?

Sure he has. He's haggling a cheaper price on a costly decision— using Mark to confirm or deny something he already believes, using Pauline to confide in—to come away with some notion of a decision he's been unwilling and unable to make on his own.

Maybe this is exactly what he bargained for.

When he left Pauline, they agreed to get together tomorrow morning and take the El into Chicago. "I'm going to take Mr. Jack on a day of adventure," she said through the window of the taxi. Jack waved goodbye, and Pauline's whispered words to him on her couch repeated in his head the entire cab ride to the hotel.

You're not ready for me yet.

In their brief relationship, she has yet to be wrong about anything she's said about him.

He watches the two on the digital clock change to a three.

3am.

Christ, he needs to get some sleep.

Tingling muscles and a fuzzy buzz in his head. He's not exhausted, though. Likely the fatigue will hit later, like a hundred pound quilt dropping on him.

For all his worry over this day with Pauline, outside of his initial awkwardness when he arrives, the distractions of the train ride keep last night's uncomfortable situation in the periphery.

Pauline, of course, is just as she was when they first met; she is agog to all that is around her.

She takes him to Navy Pier first. It's a gray, cold day, even more so on the Pier. Wind sheers off the agitated blue-black Lake Michigan are a steady, breath-sucking force. Jack flinches from the wind; Pauline smiles into it. They walk the stretch of concrete that extrudes into the waterscape, passing the empty restaurant patios and the dull glitter of storefronts. The great spindly frame of the Ferris wheel stands too big and too still against the murky mire of sky. Far ahead of them, the end of the pier looks to overhang the misty horizon of indefinite sky and water.

Jack wonders what the allure of the pier is for so many people.

"We're here at the wrong time of the year," Pauline explains. "It comes alive in the summer. Bands, jugglers, crafters, and concession stands everywhere. Right now, it's just the coldest, windiest place in Chicago."

"So why are we here?" Jack asks.

"Because. It's the coldest, windiest place in Chicago."

That, apparently, settles that.

They duck out of the wind and into the mall on the pier, browsing the window dressings of stores and menus of restaurants. Pauline purrs to the occasional outfit that looks too little like Pauline and would show too much of Pauline, and he smiles and says he likes her woolen, high-neck sweater much better.

At Felicity's Fedoras, Pauline snatches his hand. "Oh, yes.

Absolutely. Come with me." And she's off, Jack trying to keep his legs from tangling together as he follows, caboose to her engine.

Eager reverence down along the display wall, her fingers brushing and flittering against cap bill and hat brim, eyes searching always to the next one. A despairing hope in him that she's merely here to accessorize her wardrobe.

"Pauline— "

"Shh. This is important."

She stops before a brown fedora with simple brown band, brim a swirl and curl to the front. The way her hands wander and fondle, he expects that brim to stiffen and shoot straight up. "This just might do," she says.

"Do what?"

She takes it in both hands, ceremonial, and positions it over him.

A quick jerk back. "Oh, no. Listen. I'm not a hat guy."

"Jack. Don't be difficult. Now, perhaps you haven't noticed, but you're not exactly a bald spot and head wound kind of person, either. Time we did something about that."

"I've got nothing to hide."

"Oh, don't you, now?" She moves toward him with the hat again. "Stand still…or you will anger me. This is important."

"So you've said."

His vision is halved by that roll of brim, and his head is hot and constricted by the hug of band and cover of stiff cotton. She spins him round to a mirror. "How does it look?"

"Like I'm about to wrangle an alligator."

"Confidence and adventure. Good! It's working, then."

He takes the hat off. "No, Pauline. I don't think so."

"Jack. You need this hat. Trust me. It's a walkabout hat. For the journey. My gift to you so you have something to remember me by."

Jack steals another quick look in the mirror. Not him. It's too big, like the lightest wind could send it somersaulting behind him. Another look at her, though, and he knows he can't say no.

A quick stop at a bagel place for a late breakfast, and she leads him up the Lake Shore coastline to the Museum Campus that is cradled by Lake Michigan. The sprawling court lays low to the urban setting, ducking under the Lake Shore traffic, and its bleached concrete pathways wind through a meticulous maintenance of greenery. The Grecian architecture of Shedd's Aquarium and the Field Museum lord over this downtown diversion of chiseled culture. His hand keeps going to the hat, to hold it down, and his head keeps tilting up, fighting for his vision narrowed and focused by the shielding rim.

They take their time roaming the Field Museum and its taxidermy displays, Egyptian exhibit, and much of the Evolving Planet exhibit. It's like a dislocation of time walking in this mausoleum of the past; when Jack passes a clock on the wall, he's almost surprised to see the second-hand ticking ahead.

"*Head of a Man*. Third to Second century, B.C. Ptolemaic period. Although the identity of the man is unknown, this carving comes from the Ptolemaic Dynasty, which was founded by one of Alexander the Great's generals. Likely, this man was an important leader, perhaps a priest or a general..."

Pauline is reading almost every informational plaque aloud, like poetry, and her voice lends mysticism to the ancient history around them. He listens to her voice chilled and dried by the cavernous rooms, and this history that Pauline recites is a mythology—these Egyptian statues, these fossils, these remnants of a long ago termination.

Jack moves closer to the smooth basalt bust of gentle alien features. It's an aberration of his present, existing without a maker, without a source, because the source has been obliterated by time. He's not sure he can even believe in it.

He pushes closer to the glass, fights against the mass of this temporal abortion held in stasis. All he can see is the hairline cracks and the crevasse of chipped nose, and he sees his father—working on the house, grilling on a sunny weekend afternoon, sitting up late drinking his manhattans—but Jack can't secure a hold. These images erode to a trembling emancipated hand, a vacant stare, an expired gasp; an artifact of a man.

He's pulled on by Pauline into a forest of bone, amid the murmurs of the people and the hum of ventilation, and Jack is lost to the decay of the moment.

Expansion, all around him, the floor, the walls, the tyrannosaur skull in front of him, even the air, magnified to porous extreme, chunks of emptiness nestled within the transient material around him to become caverns of space. Matter just a sieve, an obstruction, for the even flow of nothingness that chews and scrapes like a river against the bank. Himself a leaf upon the current, carried to the source, returning to equilibrium, to balance. Shedding the weight of consciousness, surrendering to the beckoning vortex, the ecstasy of oblivion.

A hand—whose hand—snags him, he drags against the rush of force, pressure swelling against him, surging around him, the soft rush of noise, indiscernible…

"…with me?"

He feels heavy, his upper half over-burdened, like being suspended upside down.

"Jack, are you with me? Where are you?"

Gradually, a sense of self saturates like cold rain on a cotton shirt. A sound passes from him, a muffled sludge to his ears.

"What? Jack? What did you say?"

He can feel a warm pressure at the extremity of his awareness, and it pulls him.

"Come on. Sit down over here."

Rising. He's rising to illumination. Light. The smell of plaster and age. Shapes coalescing from shadow.

"Jack?"

He identifies with the word; he can take ownership of it. He looks at her. He sees her.

Pauline.

She studies him with eyes that dart about with concern. "Are you here, Jack? Are you with me?"

Jack nods, slowly, the weight of his head threatening to topple him.

"Was that…is that what…" She takes his other hand. "You had an episode, didn't you?"

Jack's mind is slowly clearing. He remembers where this is now; things begin to make sense again. He looks around. They're sitting across from the Tyrannosaurus display on a bench against the wall. The eyeless gaze of the empty skull is upon him, commanding a phalanx of teeth. A few people walk by, staring. "A small one."

"Are you going to be okay?"

"Yeah. Give me a minute." Loss and separation. Does a newborn feel this abandoned, despondent, after being expelled from the womb? He feels like crying, dying. He could just stop breathing right now, no fight in him.

"What's 'wanderminding'?"

The question yanks at Jack's attention. "What?"

"You said that word, just before I brought you over here. Wanderminding."

The haze has burned away now, and everything is stark and naked around him. "I said that?"

"Yes. You were still…somewhere else."

So tired, like waking to stiff white sunlight. He withdraws a hand from Pauline's grasp to shield his eyes from a glare that isn't there. "My dad. He used to say that to me, when I was a kid. He said I'd drift away sometimes…call it wanderminding."

"Drift away. You mean like just now?"

"Not really. Not like this. This is…more intense."

"But you said this was a small one. It's usually worse?"

"Deeper. Stronger. I don't know. Since the accident, it's been more compelling, more insistent."

"Insistent. What do you mean? I don't understand."

Jack leans back against the wall. The hard, cold surface comforts. "I don't really know if I do, either. It's so…impossible to put into words. Remember when I wrote to you about sensing some kind of…conflict…between opposite forces? It's like that. Like I'm rushing through chaos, and then being sucked toward this perfect place."

"What about the visions? Of your father? Is he leading you to this place?"

"No. No. It's like he's trying to keep me from it."

"But what is this place, Jack? What is compelling you?"

Jack stares ahead, his eyes fatigued by everything around him. "It's not a place. It's the Shrug." His breath hitches, and his eyes meet with Pauline again. "It's like it's not giving me a choice anymore."

They leave the field museum, the only words they share rudimentary and functional. Jack's hand is kept in Pauline's, and she offers a smile to his occasional glances as they walk back across the Museum Campus, through the tunnel running under the downtown traffic, and up again to street level.

He's dwelling on the episode in the museum, plagued by the troubling feelings he couldn't mention to Pauline. And it persists—a lingering need that seeps into him after every episode with increasing magnitude.

He wants it. When it's drawing him in, he wants it more than anything in the world. Nothing else makes any sense. Is the craving a deception, or does the Shrug really offer this perfection, this absolute balance? When he is taken by it, there is no more fear and anxiety, no gravity of self pushing down on him like the thumb of God. But, to be extracted from this emptiness is to be placed upon its edge, to become aware of it, to struggle for footing on its precipice, where it overwhelms.

Pauline distracts him. "Let's get you a drink." She crosses the street, walking toward a bar, and he is in tow.

It's a quiet Irish-styled pub called Flannigan's, all dark wood and a deep malt smell, and they find a secluded corner to sit down at a sturdy booth. The bartender appears, big and scruffy. He deals out two coasters in front of them and asks what they'd like. Jack orders a light beer. Pauline just asks for water.

"You're not drinking?" He takes the fedora off and sets it beside him on the bench.

Pauline's grin seems forced. "Most of my regrets cling to empty glasses like foam."

Jack digs his thumbnail into the edge of the coaster. "Sometimes I think you don't really talk, Pauline. You recite."

Her loud, guttural laugh rolls through the quiet tavern. "Jack, I'm impressed. I think those are the most profound words you've spoken since we've met. You're showing promise." Her face tightens with concern. "Are you sure you're okay?"

He nods, dismissing the question. He's tired of thinking, sick of trying to decipher what he can't possibly interpret. His beer and her water arrive, and he takes a hefty swig. "Pauline, I think it's time to turn the tables. I've been spilling my guts to you about everything. What about you? What's your story?"

"That's awfully direct. What makes you think I even have a story, Jack?"

"Well. Certain things you said last night. About needing to tear down the past."

"Oh, don't hold me too close to what I said last night. I was… overcome."

"I don't buy that for a second. More than anyone I've ever met, you say exactly what you want to say."

She rests her hands flat on the table, her eyes targeting him. "You're still bothered by the poem, aren't you?"

He is. The poem she read last night is like a mystery cog to a clockwork, and he wants to know what it turns. She seems to know more about him than he does; he is naked before her. "You don't have to tell me anything. I'm just curious about you. You said I hide behind normality. You seem to be just the opposite, hiding behind some air of mystery."

"We are opposites, Jack. That's how we found each other. We're attracted to our contrary poles. You hid inside yourself; I evacuated from myself."

"What does that mean?"

"Oh, I don't think you really want the graphic details."

"Wait a second. You'll read a poem like the one last night to a roomful of people—to me—and now you tell me you'd prefer to be discrete about your past? I don't get it."

"Jack, you don't want to know this."

Quiet and intent, his eyes lock onto hers, resolute.

Her sigh bears a hint of frustration, a contrast to eager eyes. "Alright, fine. Let's do this, then. What do you want to know, Jack? Do you want to know if I've performed fellatio on guys? Yes. I have. To a great many appreciative gentlemen. The poem? That was a professor of mine. Brilliant poet. And a brilliant asshole. But then, I was usually too drunk to realize. Or maybe I did realize, and that was his particular charm to me. When I think of it now, most of the guys I'd blow were of the asshole variety. I guess you could say I acquired a taste for them." Her laugh is unusually thin and clipped.

Jack draws back in his seat, grabbing hold of his beer as he might a railing on a steep stair. "Pauline—"

"I got quite a reputation, actually. Guys would approach me by referral. One time, the college newspaper editor and his roommate came over, and I did both of them—"

"Jesus, enough."

"I asked that you not use that name in vain, Jack." She's quiet a moment, not quite looking at him, finger swirling her water. "Suffice to say, I was promiscuous in every aspect of life in my college days. It's amazing just how escapist you can be with alcohol and sex without ever leaving the bars of your prison." She sips her water, then tosses her hair back. "Now, I'm a Twelve Step graduate, and learned how to fall in love with myself again. How's that, Jack? Good story?"

He can't speak. Every response that comes to mind collapses upon itself. He didn't want this, not this way. He needs to learn to keep his mouth shut.

She folds her arms and peers low at him. "So now I suppose you're waiting for me to apologize for my past?"

Jack attempts a response, but Pauline doesn't wait for one.

"I owed only one person an apology, and that was me. I did that years ago."

Jack holds up a hand. "Can I just stop you for a second? Please?"

Her lips press, eyes still honed and glinting, and her head cocks.

"I don't know what just happened here. But I wasn't looking for a confession, and I'm certainly not expecting an apology."

Pauline's voice is quiet and no less antagonizing. "Then what are you looking for, Jack?"

His hand inches out across the table, closer to Pauline, but still safe on his side. "I'm just looking for you, Pauline. That's all. I mean, I don't know if I missed something, but it seemed like you were laying crumbs for me to follow all last night. If I'm wrong, then I'm sorry."

She flits a bitter smile and looks down, maybe embarrassed, though he has yet to identify that reaction on her. "No. You weren't wrong."

"So, then...I guess I'm confused."

"Maybe I'm just responding to you making my motives appear so obvious." She reaches out, finds his hand. "Things are moving a bit fast. In a perfect world, this would have been handled more...delicately."

He wants to withdraw his hand—this is too intimate, more personal than the raw, carnal desire last night—but he refrains. "I'm sorry."

"No. I'm sorry. Honesty and openness are one of the medications of recovery. I think, perhaps, I tend to overdose a bit. I just hope I haven't made you too uncomfortable."

"A little, I guess. Nothing I won't get over."

Squeeze of hand, a smile, and she releases him. "I'm very worried for you, Jack. You can't keep avoiding these episodes—this wanderminding of yours."

"I'm not avoiding it. Tomorrow I'll talk to Mark and find out if what I believe is happening is really happening."

"You can't think it'll be as easy as that."

His coaster is frayed and torn along its entire edge. "It's not like I have any other choices."

Pauline fidgets, her glance shies to the side. Like that outfit she wore last night, this unease doesn't look right on her. "Jack. I'm here for you, in whatever capacity you need me to be. If you really believe all this is real—that you truly can do what you say you can—then I'll accept the responsibility of not dismissing it. But, what if it's *not* true? What if this is actually a symptom of something else?"

He's been waiting for this comment, had expected it when he first confided in her yesterday, but her cautious insinuation dulls the edge of her words and the cut is more abrasive. "I know how crazy this all sounds. But you haven't experienced it, Pauline. You haven't seen what I've seen. Felt what I've felt. It's too big, too far beyond anything I could imagine for it to be a delusion."

Maybe it's sympathy pushing at her brow, turning her mouth, but it looks no different than disappointment. "I know it seems that way, Jack. But the mind can be deceptive. You're risking your life over something you can't even prove, that you can't demonstrate."

"Listen. I'm just going to save us a lot of back and forth talk that'll lead us nowhere, okay?" Is he too loud? Too severe? He's trying to seem calm, level, rational. "I've already had these arguments with myself too many times to keep count. The fact is, just like you said, I can't prove it. Not yet. Maybe after tomorrow I can. But regardless, the door swings both ways. Just as it can't be proved yet, it also can't be disproved. Until it can be, I have to play this out like it's real."

"But what about the things you said back in the museum? You made it sound like you're losing control of it, that it might happen on its own. Are you just going to let it happen?"

"No! No, I—" His biggest fear, one he has continued to push from his thoughts in the hopes he wouldn't have to confront this problem. And he's no more capable of addressing it now. "Listen. Give me until tomorrow at least, okay? Maybe I'll have something to back up all of this. Until then, I don't think I have anything to add to this subject."

He can see she is leery of letting the conversation go. She has an agenda, Jack is sure of it, and he hasn't allowed her to bring it to the table. And he's going to do whatever it takes to keep her from suggesting it.

He just doesn't need to hear it. He doesn't want to.

He doesn't need to see a shrink.

The conversation at Flannigan's becomes the fulcrum on which the day is balanced. Jack feels that balance shift, and the rest of their Chicago visit limps by within his passive preoccupation. Jack settles into his seat on the train ride back to Skokie and lets the rush of tremulous motion wear down the malaise of the afternoon.

At just past seven, Pauline guides him back to her apartment. He drops his hat on the coffee table and himself on the sofa. Relaxing his limbs is a sharp pang of pleasure. "I don't think I'll walk again," he groans, rubbing his legs. "I'm permanently damaged."

Pauline moves to the kitchen and pours herself a glass of water from a pitcher. "Truly pathetic, Jack. You are a disappointment to all bipedal organisms."

He falls back to sprawl on the couch. "I didn't know I was their spokesman."

Pauline steps back into the living room and peers down at him from over the couch back. "Well, I don't think you'll find your handsome face on any posters soon."

Jack's eyes close. He lies there, floating on a pocket of exhaustion, like he could just fade away.

He senses her proximity, opens his eyes as she leans over the couch, planting her elbows on the frame. "I hope you had a good time today, Jack."

"I did, Pauline. Sorry if I seemed a little—distant. Just a lot on my mind."

"Yes," she chimes, slinky as silk. She slides around to the front of the couch and sets her water down onto the coffee table. "Just what are we going to do with that bothersome mind of yours?" She kneels down to him and his gaze is held by the suggestion in those eyes gripped by pendulous lids.

He draws himself up against the armrest, ignoring every ounce of weight in his body that resists. "I think I may be a lost cause."

She moves closer to him. He can feel her warm breath, smell the vanilla musk of her perfume. He doesn't move, he won't encourage, but he doesn't back away. There is comfort and arousal to seduction. She leans in. "I believe distraction is your only hope." Quiet. Soft. Just a wavering exhale as her lips press against his.

It's so much easier to succumb to her without question than endure the endless debates that have clamored in his head. To not think, not worry over consequence, is its own provocation. The kiss is soft, slow, it washes over and soothes like a gentle submersion into warm water.

There is no rush, no frantic intensity, that claws at this passion, only gentle exploration. Time does not carry him in its current; it deposits him on the sloping bank of this moment, cradled in the soothing eddies of Pauline's caress. In another world, another time, he could love this moment. He could make it his.

It is a mystical rune when he finds it, an ochre painting in some cave of the past, revealed as his hand eases up the front of her sweater. His fingers run over it, and he expects texture, like a scar, but it is smooth, a reflection, a projection. This glyph, this ward, hums under his skin with cryptic knowledge.

There, on the soft milky surface of her stomach, above her dimpled navel, a Celtic cross, draped by a scrolling banderole emblazoned with a single word: Kaiya. Below this, like the combination to a lock, are three numbers. They prod him, as if he should know them.

243.

Pauline asks him to stay. He wants to. He knows that he can't. If he does, he won't be able to afford the cost of what would most certainly follow.

And there is solace in the isolation he draws around him in his hotel room. It's familiar, an anchor dragging the deep floor. Alone, he can acclimate himself to the thickening swell that mires him.

He has to be honest with himself. There's no room to fit Pauline into his life—not in that capacity. When he tries to consider a tomorrow with her, it's lost in the spiraling vacuum of the present.

Yet, he will still see her tomorrow. She insisted that she ride with him to Fermilab, that she had already asked Jazz to drive him there. They'll be picking him up at 10am. After that, he doesn't know if he'll see her again, and he doesn't want to think about it.

He doesn't want her in his head at all anymore, not tonight, but the tattoo won't leave his mind—the brand that, when they first met, she mentioned being her reminder of some tragedy in her life. It must have something to do with the third riddle she emailed him. He can't remember the entire poem, but the last part of it mentioned numbers, didn't it? A hundred twice?

Yes. And a hundred twice equals two hundred. And then…

That's it. He remembers. "A hundred twice, two score and thrice."

243.

But what does it mean? And what is Kaiya? A name? If so, who?

He considered asking her after he discovered it, but didn't want to pollute the moment with more past. And he can't ask her tomorrow, not with Jazz along. Besides, he knows better than to make the same mistake he made at the bar—this isn't something to dig for.

He closes his eyes and hopes for sleep tonight, a dreamless respite from all the questions, all the problems, all the fears pushing against him. Above all, to escape the seductive lure tugging at him that promises an end to all of these things.

-4

It's a tight fit into Jazz's compact lime green box of a car. Pauline offers the passenger seat, but Jack refuses and stuffs himself into the back with his luggage, though it's such small quarters he feels he is almost sitting between Jazz and Pauline. He wears the hat for Pauline's sake and suffers Jazz's simpering.

Jack is an audience to Jazz and Pauline's banter while he remains silent other than to thank Jazz several times for driving him. Jazz drives with one lax hand on the wheel, the other free to run through her licks of flaming hair, to rest on Pauline's leg when impressing a passionate point, to wave the air and fan the heat of a reaction. That hand feigns coyness with bravado. In the passenger seat, Pauline sits like a driver, reserved and with attention to the road, other than for long moments of attention upon Jazz, looks that not only listen, but seem to remember and recall, to relish and savor. She is not without her smile today, chipped from rock.

They drive south down the toll way, then west through the suburbs, and finally south into Batavia. Once in the small city, it's just a matter of following the signs to Fermi National Accelerator Laboratory that are posted beside the road, no different than if it were a Jellystone campground with the thieving but congenial brown bear waving at the entrance.

Jazz's car turns into the entrance and they pull up to the lowered cross arm of a guard shack. A uniformed woman greets them. "Could I see a form of ID please?" Friendly, smiling like a park ranger.

Jack digs out his license and hands it to her and Jazz does likewise. Pauline withdraws a photo ID. The woman studies the cards briefly, then returns them. "What's your purpose for visiting today?"

Jack pushes forward and tries to get his head up to Pauline's window. "My name is Jack Cross. I have an appointment with Mark Bennings."

She refers briefly to a clipboard in front of her. "You'll just want to keep following this road and take a right where the sign points to Wilson Hall."

The cross arm raises and they drive ahead, passing under a sprawling metal archway of three flared arcs joining above them in a curious misalignment. Jack remembers seeing the sculpture on the website. "Broken Symmetry."

The pastoral setting is surprising, green and rolling as far as he can see. This could be farmland or a large reserve if he didn't know better, and other than a few small buildings tucked into the copses of trees, the first half-mile stretch of road reveals nothing to imply that he is now within a massive governmental complex of one of the most powerful super colliders in the world. In the far distance is a red barn, well kept but quaint, and he must look twice to believe what he sees roaming around it like brown haystacks of hair.

Buffalo.

He asks if anyone else sees them. Jazz laughs. "And I always figured the government ran on *bull*shit."

Onward down the winding road along a small lake to an intersection. A sign calls out Wilson Hall and Ramsey Auditorium to the right. Jazz takes the turn and Wilson Hall stands tall before them.

Pauline gives a deep-throated chuckle. "Wow."

Jack concurs. Maybe in downtown Chicago it would just be another tall building, but here, situated in the middle of hundreds of acres of soft-groomed nature, the Wilson Building is a monolith of white stone. Its steep, sloping sides flare at the base and straighten to run parallel halfway up, sandwiching the glass and steel central wedge of the building. It is a looming guardian planted at wide stance in the cradle of a clear blue lake, peering over the vistas of fading green in the fall day. Other buildings huddle around it, more function than form, leading to a circular structure that is probably the booster ring where particles are sent to gain enough energy to enter the main collider rings.

Jazz drives the car into the large parking lot. "This is it. The end of the road."

Pauline climbs out and pulls the lever to recline her seat forward. Jack grabs his luggage and stumbles out of the back seat, the fedora catching on the car frame, pushing it down over his eyes. He juggles the luggage in his hands to straighten out his hat. "Thanks again for the ride, Jazz."

Jazz waves. "You're welcome again, Jack."

Pauline walks a few steps with him. She's smiling wide—has been for some time. Jack recognizes this telltale sign of stress and frustration.

"And so, Sir Gawain continues on his quest. Don't lose your head, Jack."

"It's not in my plans."

"Will you stop by and see me before you head back to Terrapin?"

"I'm not sure how tight my schedule will be."

She nods and her eyes dig and search. "Something tells me I would be pulling up the rose by the thorns to ask for your phone number."

"Pauline, I— "

She sends up a fast, firm hand. "Quiet. I misspoke, and now offer a retraction. All is well." The over-wound smile again.

He looks back at the green metal bubble of Jazz's car, is caught in the clamp of her stare over the steering wheel, and turns quickly away. He shifts in place. "Well, thanks for everything."

Pauline's smile stagnates. "Oh boy, Jack. You're no better with goodbyes than you are with small talk. Here, let me help you before you completely ruin the moment." She reaches out, snatches his bags from his hands, and drops them to the ground beside him. "Now, let us just pretend for the sake of the moment that we are two people who enjoyed our time together and believe in a future where we will see each other again." She embraces him abruptly with a strong grasp, and he's engulfed. He returns the gesture, timidly at first, but gradually strengthens his grip.

She slowly draws away. He expects her to lean in for the bittersweet kiss of goodbye, but she just looks at him with resolve. "Good luck, Mr. Jack."

The well of words is dry, his nod empty. He longs for something, but the nagging ache is indecipherable.

She turns and walks her ambling stride back to Jazz's car, and Jack watches as they pull away. He stands there as the car minimizes into the distance. He is alone in the parking lot, and all too aware now of what that ache inside of him is.

He's dwarfed by the emptiness of the Wilson Center lobby, a huge, open area with nothing but a wide, arching desk sweeping across its center. Jack peers up past fifteen stories of concrete balconies and open stairwells to the skylight at the top that blooms yellow sunglow, blushing the grays and browns of stone and wood. It's a cathedral of science rising to the sky. If not for the anchors of suitcases at his sides, he might leave the ground, one more dusty particle adrift on the air to sparkle in sunlight and then disappear.

He passes by a few informational kiosks as he approaches the woman behind the deep walnut desk.

"I'm here to see Mark Bennings." His voice jars the silence of the quiet cavern.

She eyes his bags suspiciously, but then her face turns on a smile. "Oh, yes. He came by this morning and had me prepare a pass for you." She reaches out for a badge lying on the desk and holds it before her. "Jack Cross, right?"

"Yes."

She hands him the pass. "You'll need to wear that during your stay. I'll let him know you're here." Phone receiver slips under a puff of short blonde hair as she dials an extension. "Dr. Bennings. Jack Cross is here." She replaces the phone and smiles back at him. "He'll be over in just a few minutes."

"Thanks." Jack withdraws to the kiosks and glazes over the information on summer programs and current projects. All he can see is Pauline's parting smile, those lips sagging to a hope as heavy as regret. She knew, she understood that he would never see her again. Maybe before he honestly did. It's doubtful, though, that she realizes how much he wanted to stay with her, how even now desire digs in with desperate nails as some force of fate drags him by his legs.

The rear doors across the lobby open and there's no mistaking Mark as he flies in. From the distance, he looks as he did eight years ago. His black hair is shorter, but still combed back from his prominent forehead and slicked down, still the brisk gait with shoulders thrust forward, his small frame chugging like an overcharged motor. He speeds across the lobby and thrusts his hand out to Jack.

"Jack! You made it!"

Jack shakes his hand. "It's been a long time, Mark." And up close, he sees the tracks of time on Mark; the thin wisps of receding hair and the extra weight that fills out his cheeks and sags at his gut. Eight years.

Mark beams and stuffs his hands into his khaki Dockers. "God, where does the time go? I swear it was just yesterday we were cramming for your physics final with Dr. Tesklowski."

"I seem to remember slamming beers, not cramming texts."

Mark's laugh is high and rapid-fire. "Weeding out the weaker brain cells, my friend."

Jack tosses a general gesture to the surroundings. "Seems to have worked for you."

"Huh? Oh, yeah! Absolutely."

"It's a pretty impressive facility."

Mark's eyes fire. "It's fantastic. Awesome people and great things happening here."

"Worlds apart from running those shoe-box experiments back at college."

"The toys of God, Jacky-boy," and his grin is sharp. "That's what we play with here." He gives a quick motion of his hand. "Well, come on. Let me show you. You got your badge, right?"

Jack clips the I.D. to his shirt. "Right here."

"All right, then. Follow me." He looks down at Jack's luggage for the first time. "Didn't you drive here?"

"No. A friend dropped me off. My car's on the fritz." The lie, after two days of honesty, feels good, like throwing on casual clothes after a day at work.

"Sorry to hear that. Well, go ahead and stash your luggage at Jenny's desk there. Nice hat, by the way. Didn't take you for a hat kind of guy."

"What? Oh, God. This. I forgot. A present." He walks around the desk and sets his luggage down, zipping open his travel bag and pulling out the CT scan, painfully discrete. A quick tight roll and he shoves it in his back pocket, then leaves the hat with his luggage.

"Jesus, Jack! What the hell happened to you?"

Jack turns quick, startled by Mark, then remembers the scar, that fissure of circumstance into which everything before and beyond is falling. It's become so much a part of him that he no longer takes notice of it. "Nothing. Just a little accident. Looks worse than it is."

"I would hope so. It looks nasty."

"And here I thought I was sporting a good look."

"Oh, you wear it well. Come on. I'll show you around."

Mark is off, down the lobby, and Jack quickens his pace out the rear doors into the cobbled courtyard surrounded by what must be the main operations of Fermilab. It's cold under the late morning shadow of Wilson Hall draping the courtyard. When Jack steps across its terminus, into warming sunlight, he shivers away the shadow's chill.

They turn right and Mark stops at a nondescript door. "I'm sure I don't need to tell you this, but I'm obligated. Make sure you don't touch any buttons or switches or dials you come across."

"I wouldn't think of it."

"I know that. It's just that we had a tour of school kids come through here once. While they were listening to the guide, one kid leaned his back up against the main control panel. He must have put his foot up behind him—you know, just casual-like? Caught the primaries and shut off the entire collider."

Jack's eyes go wide. "Serious?"

"Dead serious. Experiments that had been running for years were wiped out—" He snaps his fingers. "—like that. It's the only time I've seen veteran scientists *weep*."

Mark swings the door open and Jack follows him in to the entryway of a small room. It's a sharp contrast to the Wilson Hall tower, more like a furnace or generator room, themed in an institutional beige highlighted by reds and blues that tile the floor and stripe the walls. There's not much equipment, though two tall cream-colored cabinets stand loaded with switches and readouts ahead of him. A steel-railing stair at the center of the room descends to the bowels of the complex.

Mark stops before a large wire-meshed window that looks into another room. "This is where the particles begin their journey—the Cockcroft-Walton voltage source."

Jack peers into a massive area housing equipment right out of an episode of Doctor Who—the ones with Tom Baker and his ludicrous length of scarf that he and Liz used to watch on PBS on Saturday nights. Two outlandish towers rise two stories on long metallic blue legs covered with bulbous silvery nodes. Silver domes top the structures, connected by a metallic blue shaft. A five-foot diameter yellow tube ringed by large metal disks at ever-increasing intervals run from them, across the room, and through the far concrete wall. Jack expects crackling coils of electricity to run up the bizarre towers while some hunch-backed apprentice cackles with diabolical glee.

Mark explains. "It's basically a large capacitor, a room-sized version of what you'll find in your typical television. The Cockcroft-Walton accelerates ions to seven-hundred-fifty-thousand electron volts and sends them through that tube, which begins the LINAC linear accelerator. The rings you see around it generate electromagnetic energy that keep pushing the ions forward—we call it 'kick and drift'—until they reach four-hundred million electron volts. That's when the ions enter the booster, stripping away the electrons and leaving the protons we want. At eight billion electron volts, the protons enter the main injector and we reach one-hundred-fifty GeV, then finally to the four mile circumference Tevatron ring, where we hit 1 trillion electron volts."

Thousands of tons of metal and concrete, acres of land, and scores of PhD's, all to harness and control something so completely small and elementary as a proton. "How many protons do you send through at a time?"

"I'll show you." And Mark is off, walking past the two main consoles of switches and into a hallway whose one wall is nothing but components of detection equipment.

Mark points to a small screen that looks like a spectrometer. A light blue line steeps up, plateaus, and cascades down across the screen, twitching slightly. About every four seconds, the middle of the line peeks, like a slow steady heartbeat.

"Every time you see that blip, a proton enters the main injector. They're sent at varying rates depending on what experiment is being run."

"How do you focus the path of the protons so perfectly that you get a collision? Magnetic?"

"Well, yeah, but not the way you're thinking. We're not just sending two protons straight at each other from opposite directions. Remember, they're sailing through those rings hundreds of thousands of times per second from opposite directions. We send them into helical orbits through the collider. They're weaving around each other like an aeronautics show. When we're ready for them to collide, we simply tighten the orbit, and bang! We have luminosity."

Jack remembers the term from his physics courses. Since the photon particles that make up light would interfere with the quark particles being observed, protons are instead smashed together in a vacuum and the smaller quark particles that fly apart are observed by the energy they release—in this way, they are illuminated.

Dr. Tesklowski had used a watch and hammer to explain the challenge of studying subatomic particles. We want to know what makes the watch tick, he had said, but the only tools available to us are too big and clumsy to get inside it. But there's other ways to learn what the components of the watch are. He had placed the watch on his lab table, raised the hammer, and smashed the little Timex into pieces. Say hello to particle colliders, our hammer in hand.

Discovery through destruction. Jack thinks back to that red couch of Pauline's, of her wrecking ball against his every tick.

Jack and Mark walk down a long hallway, following the path of the LINAC accelerator, its clunky asymmetrical casings, pipes and wires visible to their right. Jack is thinking too hard about putting one foot in front of the other. During a college astronomy course, his class was taken to the planetarium for a presentation on mapping the stars—constellations and declinations, light years and parsecs, the degrees of minutes and seconds in long distance measurements by the naked eye. When the room turned to blackness and the daubs of light speckled the domed ceiling, that confined space turned into the infinity of the universe. In the illusion, the ground fell away, he lost his center, and the awe-filled exhilaration made him forget his chair. After, the room lights dropped a rotunda on him like a cage; his equilibrium was still drifting within the endless universe and he had to grasp chair backs to stay upright as he walked out.

Next to this long and bulk-headed sarcophagus of vacuum, he senses some of that awe and disorientation. He is penitent, as if meeting his maker. Is it real, this thrum of energy, more palpable than audible, that soaks into him, seems to vibrate every cell of his body? Each step he loses a little weight.

He looks to the offices on his left, does so as when a child he would lock on to a tree or bench as he spun dizzily on the merry-go-round. Door after door with tall narrow windows beside them revealing tiny spaces with just enough room for a desk and chair. Nameplates protrude from the doorframes, like the professors' offices from college. One of them is stamped, "Dr. Bennings."

The clerical mundaneness of these glorified cubicles next to, as Mark put it, 'the toys of God', tugs on Jack's tether, brings him closer to the ground. Maybe that's why they are put here—to keep the scientists dispassionate and officious, instead of on their knees before the collider and the nothingness it maintains.

Further down, Mark stops at the window to a large room with a dozen computer stations manned by scruffy techs in street clothes. A long LED marquee scrolls data: "…Stack 9.32 at .01 mA/h…Main injector status 29…Recycler 94.93 E10…" Monitors along the walls display seemingly random scatterings of red, blue and green lines, the paths of quarks that are the debris of proton collisions. Gentle curves of lines like the one that trails across the image of the scan in his pocket.

"The LED board feeds us the latest status of the collider—collision rates, proton counts. All collision data is recorded and studied here…"

Mark explains the equipment, the processes, the standard operations, but Jack is drifting. All of this is pretense. He didn't come here to learn the details of Mark's day-to-day. He tingles and hovers with feverous warmth, an impatient wonder to the mysteries of the collider against the mundaneness of beige walls and bored technicians watching data scroll across a green screen.

A heavyset man scruffed with beard and a skinny younger man with pointed nose and cow-licked hair amble up to Mark and interrupt him with questions. Jack moves closer to the exoskeleton of collider. The rapid-fire techno babble of Mark and the young techs turns indistinguishable against the growing resonance of the accelerator. They are like the monitor readouts, the data on the screen—a measure of an event already past. The sounds of electromagnetic energy around and through him is a bellowing thought directed right at him. This is the now, the drone of the present, carrying particles that live a lifetime within the fractions of a second before destruction inside the corridors of nothingness. The cycle of life. Mark, the scientists, Liz, his mother and father, Pauline—everyone. Brief illuminations of chance collisions.

"Hey!" Mark is waving a hand in front of his face. "Ground control to Major Tom?"

Jack blinks, the hum distant, outside of him. He gives a thumbs up. "Commencing countdown. Engines on."

Mark slaps a hand on his back with a chuckle and they return to Wilson Hall and up the elevator to the fifteenth floor observation lounge—two large rooms conjoined at either end by hallways. Here, comfortable couches line the walls and a scaled topographic model of Fermilab sits upon a large table. Huge windows offer an impressive view of the complex, the rings, and the landscape. In the far distance, Jack can see the Hancock tower fingering the horizon some forty miles away.

"It's really something," Jack says as he slips the CT scan out of his pocket and twists it in his hands.

"And it's not just a quantum laboratory, you know. Fermi has over six thousand acres, most of it wildlife reserves. Wetlands, prairie, and woodlands. You'll find Bison, deer and geese here, and hundreds of species of flora and fauna. Natural studies are happening all the time." Mark sits down on a couch by the window. "And that's the grand tour, pal. Of the main facilities, at least."

"Very cool, Mark. Glad I could see it."

"My pleasure. A good excuse to get out of work for a bit." Mark's eyes fall to the film. "So, is that the big mystery that brings you here?"

"What? Oh. Yeah, you could say that." He holds it up. "Just

something I wanted to get your opinion about."

"So, what is it? You've got me curious."

"Here. Take a look at it and see if anything on there seems familiar to you."

Mark takes the curled film from Jack and looks over it, casually at first, then with more intense scrutiny. "Whatever it is, it doesn't seem complete."

"It's not. It's only a partial data read."

"Looks like some kind of medical scan." He traces the partial imagery of Jack's skull on the film. "Is this some kind of head x-ray or something?"

"Something like that."

Mark's finger follows the arcing hairline that streaks away from the white blob at the center of the printout just before the end of the incomplete image. "What's this?"

"That's what I'd like you to tell me."

Mark draws the film closer, his concentration tightens. "Huh. Kind of reminds me of a particle trail."

Jack's breath catches. "It does, doesn't it."

Mark looks up at Jack in a way that sparks memories of their late night talks in the apartment. "So what is this, Jack?"

Alarms trigger in Jack's mind. How much can he say without telling Mark too much? Mark isn't like Pauline; he doesn't have any tolerance for wild ideas and mysteries. Mark exists in a logical, rational, predictable world. "It's a CT Scan. It stopped scanning after some kind of data overrun error."

"Is this a scan of *your* head?"

Jack nods.

Mark takes in a thick, deliberate breath. "So, I still don't get it. What are you wondering about that a medical doctor couldn't answer for you?"

Jack points to the curious line. "I just found this streak odd. I thought the same thing you did. It looks like a particle trail."

"Well, yeah, it *looks* like one, but it isn't." Sharp and adamant.

"Why do you say that?"

Mark hands the film back. "Come on. You're talking about a CT Scanner, Jack. Luminosity is achieved through the bombardment and absorption of photons into tissue and bone. They have zero mass and zero charge. The only energy they acquire is through their wavelength. The most that can happen is that an occasional low-mass atom will shed an electron when absorbing a photon, but that's it. No collision events, no way."

He refuses to accept it so easily. There has to be something more to this. "Okay, fine. But what if something else was operating here? Some force outside of the scan, some event outside of the photons themselves, but perhaps triggered by them?"

"From what possible source, Jack? I mean, seriously. You only have two things—the scanner, and the organic matter being scanned."

Against his control, Jack begins to fluster. "Don't limit yourself to that. Just try to think for a second. What *else*, provoked by x-ray radiation, could cause a collision?"

Mark stands up. "Jack, Jack. Settle down. What the hell is this all about? Maybe if you told me what you were looking for, I might be able to come at this from another angle."

The pressure of the moment is like a lurch of rapid acceleration. Each second of silence without a response makes him seem more suspicious. "I don't know, Mark. I just thought I might be on to something here. Something worth investigating." Christ, that sounds lame.

"What, you mean like some kind of scientific discovery?" They way Mark looks at him, he might as well be saying that quantum particles are fairy superballs.

Jack retracts the film behind his back. "Well, I don't know. Maybe. I mean, what if a collision actually did occur under these conditions? Wouldn't that be a worthwhile discovery?"

Mark's angled gaze is skeptical. "I don't know. Maybe, but—"

"And the error that overloaded the scanner. Don't you think that at least implies something like a collision could have happened?"

Mark gives that stubborn PhD shake of the head. "Anything

could cause an error like that."

Jack turns away. This is getting nowhere.

Mark's voice becomes irritatingly conciliatory. "Jack, I get what you're saying, but that little streak is probably just part of the error, or a hair, or a scratch. Anything."

Jack faces Mark again. "Okay, okay. Probably so. But, I came all this way. Can't you just play the hypothetical for fun here?"

Mark sneers. "Oh man, you know I hate 'what-if's.' That's the theorist's game."

"I know. But…humor me."

"All right." He sighs and gives a grin. "You know, you always manage to drag me into this garbage."

He returns the grin. "Well, come on, I have to make up for eight years of leaving you alone."

Mark sits back down again and folds his hands across his stomach. "Okay. So, we'd need to approach this in reverse. Let's say we have a collision that is detected by X-ray. First of all, you have no sufficient acceleration mechanism at work, so you'd need some kind of attractive force—one with enough mass to accelerate a particle to incredible velocity at short distance. But that kind of force would be off the charts. A black hole, maybe. And that kind of force couldn't be so localized or selective. It would draw everything in. It would be irresistible." Mark's expression sours. "Which doesn't matter because radiation couldn't create that kind of force anyway. Unless…" Mark's voice tapers and he looks reluctant to speak.

"Unless what?"

"I suppose, maybe, a particle of antimatter might provoke that kind of event."

A fluttering in his stomach. "Antimatter?" Why had he never thought of that before? When matter and antimatter come into contact with each other, it results in the immediate and complete annihilation of those particles.

Jesus.

"Yeah, but listen," Mark says. "Only extremely high levels of radiation can generate antimatter, and you wouldn't be here talking to me now if that was the case."

"What about another source for the antimatter, then?"

Mark's face crumples at that question. "No. See, antimatter is rare...virtually non-existent on the planet. It takes us a long time to create just a few particles of it here, using radiation levels way, way beyond a CT Scanner. So what other source for this antimatter could there be?"

Jack knows exactly where. But he holds back, even though the urge to explore this deeper, to find the solution, is an insurmountable pressure making it difficult not to blurt out everything. "You would know that better than me."

Mark grunts. "Well, it's not like your brain is generating antimatter."

Jack's hands tremble. He feels so close, so unbelievably close to the answer. "But, theoretically—"

"God I hate that word."

"—If antimatter was involved, this could explain the appearance of a particle trail?"

The last time he saw Mark this uneasy was when he asked Liz out after too many beers on a long ago summer night and Liz had suggested using a pocket protector in a very unique and uncomfortable way. "It's highly doubtful."

"But possible?"

"Only by the strictest definition, but...maybe." Mark gives Jack an apologetic grin. "I hate to tell you, buddy, but all you have there is the meaningless artifact of a computer error." He stands back up and throws Jack a wink. "I wouldn't start spending that Nobel Prize money just yet."

He hardly feels present in the room anymore. "Yeah. I suppose. Thought I had something...probably nothing."

He gets the Mark Bennings shoulder slap. "Hey, you never know, right? Come on, I'll buy you lunch at the café, then I can drive you around the site. You'll like it. You can pet a Bison."

Part Seven
THE DEADLINE

-3

The moment has thickened. A sludge of viscid seconds.

He eats lunch with Mark. Idle talk about what isn't now, a past that seems more like what might have been. After, they drive around the Fermilab complex. Mark points to a building, a crop of land, but Jack's gaze keeps wandering to the expanse of sky and land leading to that terminal horizon.

He doesn't want to go to Mark's home, to see Dr. Benning's house and watch him kiss his wife and child, prattle over the past, and wonder where the time has gone. But the beer he drinks with Mark after dinner in the basement family room thins his condensed mood while Mark is a ramble of random subjects.

They stay up late. Mark unfolds the bed from the sleeper sofa, and Jack lays there most of the night, unable to stop thinking. He just wants to get home, be on familiar ground, but it seems so far away. He needs to know that he can actually get home, that it's really there waiting.

After breakfast on Saturday morning, Mark offers to drive Jack back to the Skokie depot for his 11am bus ride home. Mark obviously wants to talk. All Jack wants to do is sleep.

"So, how is Liz doing?"

He was wondering when Mark would bring her up. Though never admitted, Mark had always been turned inside out by Liz. Seems to be the way with guys like Mark. They like women who could beat the shit out of them—talk hard, live hard.

"Still Liz."

"Yeah," Mark says, and there seems to be a lot of thought about that. "You know, I don't think she liked me very much."

Zoned out on the road, lines ticking by, Jack smiles small. "No. Not really."

Mark nods, looks back at the road, processing the data and recompiling. "And Lenny's still hanging around, huh?"

"Still hanging out with Liz. Still friends."

"God. All I'll say is, I'm glad my doctorate wasn't dependent upon proving the validity of that relationship."

"Maybe Liz and Len are definitive proof that the universe doesn't make sense."

Mark laughs. "I'm a physicist, Jack. It has to make sense or I'm out of a job."

Aren't we all? He tears his eyes off the road and puts them right on Mark. "Does it, though?"

"What do you mean?"

"You've taken it all apart. Turned over all the pieces. Have you ever seen anything that makes you think maybe there's something behind it all?"

"What, you mean like…intelligent design?"

"Sure."

Head turns, blinker chimes, and Mark passes a Toyota obeying the speed limit. "I call foul. You can't start a deep discussion on a hangover morning. It's just wrong."

"I'm curious."

"I've always been kind of a Deist, myself. Works well with my profession. I see God as some crazy-haired Einstein type working out all the formulas and theorems, laying down the laws, then pushing the 'go' button and letting it all roll, you know? Not much for the finger-snapping, babysitting theories, myself."

"So existence is like some kind of experiment then?"

"Experiment, or invention. I suppose it depends on how you look at God. Experiment would suggest curiosity, invention would imply purpose."

"If it was all experiment, that would mean having to accept possibility of failure."

"Getting kind of bleak there, aren't you, Jack?"

"What if God is Nothing?"

Mark takes his eyes from the road long enough to look puzzled. "What do you mean?"

"What if God is Nothingness?"

Head shaking. "No such thing. It can't exist."

"Nothingness can't exist." There is something pretty ironic about that.

"Nope. The Heisenberg Principle and vacuum fluctuation make it an impossible state. Hell, Jack, even the philosophers have abandoned the concept of nothingness."

"But, God has to be outside of existence, right? Beyond natural law and order. What else can there be beyond existence but absolute nothingness? Maybe nature doesn't abhor a vacuum, it is compelled to a vacuum...drawn irresistibly to it. That's where the pressure of a vacuum comes from, right? The compulsion of matter to fill the void? What if God is the grand unification? The one force that motivates all others?"

Mark's laugh is cautious. "Whatever you're smoking, I think you should share."

"Look at eastern spiritual meditation. They don't pray a laundry list to God, they empty their minds. The *Om*. Maybe they're just trying to experience that nothingness—get closer to God."

"Hey. Jack. I'm a scientist. God and faith, I can't rationalize that. I can only feel it. You're talking about something that can't be measured or detected. Something that, by the laws of physics, can't even exist. But even if absolute nothingness were a possibility, how can you qualify something that you can't experience? Why would you even want to?"

Jack sinks further into the chair, lays his head back, lids slipping down just shy of closed. "I don't know."

The ride is quieter after that, a sampling of mundane comments from Mark between pockets of silent discomfort.

When they pull into the bus depot's parking lot, Jack pushes through his fog of exhaustion to thank Mark for everything.

"Don't mention it, Jack. Don't forget about me, now. Keep in touch."

"Sure."

Concern and hesitation, Mark looking like he's trying to figure something out. "Even if you just want to talk, Jack. You know?"

His nod back to Mark is sluggish, his grin a failure.

Jack waves a heavy hand to the hatchback of Mark's Volkswagen. Luggage in hand, Jack steps into the station and eventually finds himself seated in the row of chairs just left of where Pauline had stood in her drooping blue sweater and long skirt, holding that sign in her hands.

He looks over at the pay phones against the wall. Maybe…

No. Not now. Everything has changed.

He allows his eyelids to fall, the world blinks away to blackness, and he's comfortable here. No troubles, no worries. No Jack.

It's not home anymore. He can't sense himself within these walls. There's no way to release anything into this space. Maybe there's just nothing left to give. This apartment is abandoned, deserted.

He discards his luggage at the entryway and walks past the phone stand. The answering machine flashes at him. Three messages. He hits play and starts to slip out of his coat as Liz's voice plays back.

"Jack. Call me back on my cell. Mom's in the hospital. I'm heading there now."

"Jack, where are you? I called your work number but couldn't get to your voice mail. Mom's here at St. Mary's. Room 204. She's not doing so good. Call me or get down here, huh?"

"Check your fucking messages, boyo. It's two o'clock on Saturday. You need to get your ass to St. Mary's."

Liz's voice is monotone and rumpled with strain, and Jack is punching his arm back through his jacket and glaring at the clock. Seven-thirty. Shit. Keys, where are…shit.

Jack bolts out the door.

He can't see her. He tries. He forces images of Tuesday's dinner, of her mixing meatloaf, sitting at the table, rocking in her chair, but these wisps of memory don't equate to the tubes and wires that drape and curl to this frail old woman who is slowly fading, slipping away from this moment in time. He can't see his mother at all.

Hospital rooms. He hates them. Sounds don't mix here. Dispassionate voices snoop from the corridor, the respirator chugs out choppy mechanical breath, the beep of the heart monitor pokes holes in the paper-dry air. And still, under all of this, a raspy silence scratches somewhere deep down out of reach.

He takes soft, careful steps to the side of the bed. She's not awake, and there should be peace in sleep, but he sees the struggle that squeezes her eyes, draws in her cheeks. Clockwork heaves of breath, lungs pushed against her chest. This is how his father lived his final days—the inert kick and quiet scream of decay.

He reaches out and touches her hand, not sure why he should be so unsettled to do so, like touching the past. Her skin is tepid, the temperature of air.

Mother, my Mother.

She's awake, she's looking at him, and her eyes moan.

"I'm here, Mom." Barely spoken, a thought cast upon the drifting now.

He has her for only a moment, and then her gaze disseminates around and beyond him and her eyelids fall. He releases her hand, draws away.

He saw it, just before her eyes closed, hunched down in the depth of her vapid stare. Nothing. Void. It looked right at him, said his name. It called his name.

There's a swell in the silence. Below him, behind him. He turns and he is not alone. A woman in white. A doctor. She looks at him expectantly, as if waiting for an answer. He fights to find his voice. "I'm...sorry. Did you say something?"

"I said, you must be Jack."

"Yes."

The woman approaches, hand out, lab coat billowing behind her slender frame. "I'm Dr. Evans."

The squeeze of her thin hand brings the ground up to meet him. "How is she? What happened?"

She takes her hand back to straighten the glasses that rest on a tall, delicate nose and tuck under neatly disheveled blonde hair. "Your mother was brought here by ambulance on Friday after she called emergency complaining of difficulties breathing. We put her on oxygen and gave her corticosteroids and expectorants to try to ease her symptoms and stabilize her. Late this morning, her condition deteriorated into a nosocomial pneumonia. We've been administering antibiotics and placed her on respiratory assistance."

"Will she be all right?"

Her answer is gentle and soft. "The next twenty-four to forty-eight hours will be critical. Her age and condition make her situation more...precarious."

Muscles to rubber, his body sags. "You're saying she's going to die." The words feel bigger than his mouth can allow.

"No. I'm just being completely truthful with you. But that doesn't mean there's no reason to hope, to pray, to do whatever you need right now to cling to that chance, because it's still there and worth holding out for. Don't give up on her yet." Her smile holds all the hope and warmth that Jack cannot find within him. "And I can promise you that we're doing absolutely everything in our power to help her."

Jack nods and Dr. Evans leaves him alone with the hush of breath and steady beep of the heart monitor that is now his mother. He wonders where Liz is. Her jacket lies across the chair beside the bed. Maybe out for a smoke, or in the cafeteria getting something to eat. He should probably wait here for her.

He looks at his mother, plugged into the hospital bed. Something twists inside of him, and he rushes from the room into the corridor. Maybe he'll just go find Liz. Find Liz.

Down the hallway, he sees her turn the corner and head toward him, Len close behind.

"Jack! Where the hell have you been?" It's a whispered shout as her feet quicken her approach. Liz's hair is forced into place, her eyes unusually round, and her jeans and t-shirt call no attention to herself. This Liz is far too unassuming, an after-effect, the floating spot before light-dazed eyes.

Len flops his arm in a lazy wave. "Sorry about your mom."

Jack nods to Len and looks at Liz. "I just talked with the doctor. It doesn't sound good."

Liz ploughs a hand through her black drift of hair. "It's not. She got the crazy idea to start packing Friday afternoon. Overdid it. I've spent this whole weekend here watching her get worse. Gasping and coughing. Just couldn't breathe, you know? At one point, she said she wanted to die. In a way, the pneumonia's been a relief. At least now she's mostly out. And when she is awake, she's too far gone to know what's happening anyway." Her head shakes, eyes rove. "You guys do me a favor, huh? I ever get like that, just yank the fucking plug."

Len places an awkward hand on Liz's shoulder. "Hey. Ease up, Liz. Everything'll be okay. Your mom'll pull through this. She's a fighter, huh?" A grin squirms onto his pale, bony face. "You gotta get it from somewhere, right?"

Each day to die a little more.

Len looks back at Jack, holding a half-smile in suspension. "You all right, cap'n?"

Jack jerks his unfocused gaze to Len, uncertain if he had spoken that liquid thought out loud.

Liz takes a step closer and lays a hand on his arm. "Hey, you're not looking too good. You feeling okay, Jack?"

It's like trying to part a fog with his hands. He's so tired. "I haven't been sleeping too good."

"Yeah, well, take it easy there, boyo. I've had enough of this hospital shit in the past month to last me a long time." Her hand takes its time pulling away from his arm. "Oh, I called everyone, by the way. Chris, Tony, Ben. I pawned off calling all the relatives onto Chris. She wanted to come back, but that's just nuts. I mean, all that way, and then…"

Liz keeps talking, but that silence is gushing up, rushing past him, drowning out her words. He can't ground himself anymore. His father is dead. His mother is dying. Once she's gone, the umbilical will be severed, and he'll be left adrift on this moment. No source. No origin. *Head of a Man.*

"Are you, Jack?" Liz looks at him, waiting for an answer. Everyone is looking at him, waiting for an answer.

"What?"

"Going to work on Monday?"

Jack shakes his head. Why would he? "I have to get out of here."

Liz flashes surprise, then her eyes slant with anger. "What are you talking about? You just got here."

"Yeah."

Her hands jam into her hips. "Are you serious? You're just going to leave me here?"

Len acts like he wants to say something, but instead just moves closer to Liz, fingers wiggling at his side.

"Everything's going to be all right, Liz. I promise. I'll set everything right." He heads down the corridor, Liz and Len's heavy stares left behind him.

He can't handle the thought of it all happening again. He can't watch his mother suffer the way his father did. It's not going to happen. He can make sure that doesn't happen.

Spectators. That's what it all comes down to. Spectators to the decay and death of life. Go to work. Watch Greg die a little while Rick beats him down. See Sam die another day as she punches her clock. Come home to witness Liz beat her wings and fan her flames, and Len dry up to Liz's draught.

Die as three cents are saved on generic oatmeal. Die to the canned laughter of the TV sitcom. What feels like life is simply the suspense of death.

How long has he questioned it, wished for a concrete answer as to whether or not it was real, and now, after all this time, he realizes the dread obviousness of the Shrug, the single straight path where it leads. All his skepticism before was laden in denial. He has always believed, he has always known, but never willing to take responsibility for it.

God—the universe—whatever it is that this little blister of reality sits on, has given this power to him. We're not meant to be here. Existence is just a fluke, and all the pain and suffering and death is nature's way of trying to correct it. Maybe God does exist in nothingness. Maybe that's why it feels so right to be there. The Divinity of Emptiness.

Jack knows who he is now. He is the final, painless solution.

He lies on his bed, squeezed between sleep and consciousness. His head feels swollen, inflated, tugging at his body. So, this is it, then? Does he just do it now? He can feel the Shrug more clearly than ever. It's weaving into his every thought.

But it's not so easy to do, this absolute action, this complete negation. It would be one thing to just wink himself out of existence, but to make this decision for everyone? For Liz, for Pauline? No chance to take it back?

No. He can't just do it. He needs a day or two. Something like this doesn't just happen on a whim. He has to set a date, a time, and work toward it. Absolutely.

So, when? When is the best day to end existence? Is a Monday an appropriate day for the world to come to an end? No, no. Nothing is appropriate for a Monday. It probably makes no difference to the Universe, but he just can't stomach the thought.

Wait. Of course. His birthday. It's only three days from now. His thirtieth birthday. It somehow seems just right, like it has been planned out from the beginning. It's perfection.

Fine, then. The deadline is set.

On Tuesday, the second of November, at exactly 2:17am, existence will cease to be.

Consciousness creeps slowly, but not completely. He opens his eyes as tired as he was when he closed them last night. He turns and looks at the red, jittery numbers on his clock. Almost eight. Eleven hours of sleep, yet it doesn't feel like he's gotten any sleep at all.

He drags himself from bed in a slump and lurches to the kitchen. The coffee in the pot is five days old, but he pours it into a cup and warms it in the microwave. No desire to bother with making a new pot.

The microwave beeps a minute later and he walks his coffee over to the computer and turns it on. He thinks about checking in on the website, seeing where the vote stands, but doesn't. There's no vote. Never has been. Jack made the web site for all the wrong reasons. He missed the point.

When he checks his emails, there is a slew, and he scans them briefly, looking for familiar names. He sees one from Pauline, and he frets for a time, hovering over it with the mouse. He shouldn't read it. He shouldn't have anything to do with her. She was just a dream, a diversion. In less than two days time, she won't even exist.

Something about this makes Jack shift in his chair with a jerk.

It's not his decision, damn it. It's already been made. Out of his hands.

But something about Pauline not existing seems strangely wrong, somehow contradictory, like declaring the day quiet while a siren blares past.

Jack rubs his temples, trying to knead away a swelling ache. It doesn't matter. It just doesn't matter.

He clicks on her email.

FROM: *Iamsurfacing@illinoiscable.com*
TO: *jack@shouldlendtheworld.com*
SUBJECT: So this is it, then?

Mr. Jack,

Are you still reeling from our meeting? Are you still puzzling over every word, every moment, as if some answer hides there for you to find? Maybe I disappointed you. I can't help but think that, you know. I saw it in the way you said goodbye to me on Friday, like you were accepting a gift you planned to return the first chance you got. Well that's fine. Maybe it's more than fine. Maybe it's for the best. Maybe I couldnt really afford the present in the first place.

Theres no hard feelings, no regrets, just so you know. I don't want you feeling any guilt about this, about me, about you. Things happen and they dont happen thats life.

I just hope you don't cast aside our time together, bury it away forever like so many other regrets. I worry that you will and that makes me very sad. I'm going to hold strong to this fleeting encounter, remember it, and cherish it, this tender prick of a needle.

I still don't know why you even came here to see me. Why did you? Maybe just to further complicate my life? I din't need that, in case you didn't notice. Mayb eyou were just looking for a couple words from me that I never gave you. I should have, I should have told you and I didn't. But I can tell you now, its never too late, is it?

Everything will be all right Jack. Everythings going to be fine.

Do you believe that? Can you?

I suppose I'd have to believe that to say it. But maybe I can get way with writing it.

are you thinking about it right now, jack? Are you thinking about your little thought as you read this? Are you thinking about ending it all, turning everything to nothing?

I wonder if you already have, and you just don't know it yet.

I don't think you're really so speacial with this power of yours. You think other people can't do it? You think your the only one?

I'm doing it right now, Jack. I'm doing it right now.

-2

Stuck in a knot of time. That's how it feels as he looks out the window of the Greyhound bus as the familiar landscape passes by. The scenery hasn't changed, but it's smaller, more distant and dull—just like him on this rumbling trip.

The bus is carrying a decent load this time around, probably two-thirds full. Jack can't figure out why so many people would be traveling by bus on a Sunday morning, but it's not like he's ever been able to figure out the patterns of human beings. Why should it be different now?

There had been plenty of seats available, yet the little red-haired girl sitting next to him now had bounded down the aisle and leapt into the seat next to his like there was no other option, little sneakered feet swinging with a marathon of energy. The woman with the young girl had dragged behind, her gaunt cheeks shadowed with weariness cast by swollen eyes. She looks uncomfortable now, a rigid slump across the aisle, as her hand inches through her thin hair and she stares ahead, ignorant of or oblivious to every call of attention from the little girl. A small golden-haired doll dances in a pink dress on the armrest beside Jack, compelled by the clutch of youth.

He can't get comfortable in his seat. It's forcing him to be too upright and stiff. His hand skitters about for the reclining mechanism and he yanks it and pushes back. The seat reclines a full four inches, just far enough to make him ache for how much further he'd like it to go.

He shouldn't be making this trip. It's ridiculous and illogical. It simply won't matter in little less than two day's time.

But that email shook him. She's in trouble, and it's his fault.

He never wanted to hurt her. Didn't realize he had. He wants to make sure she knows that. He wants to see her one last time. Tell her that everything will be all right. Say goodbye. He thought about telling her he was coming, but decided not to. She might refuse him, or delay him. There is no longer that kind of time to spare.

He should just do it now. He's being weak and pathetic and meanwhile his mother suffers in a hospital room. How many others out there are suffering at this moment? Is that what the Shrug is all about? Some kind of universal euthanasia? Or is it simply a cold, mathematical equation and he's the variable that makes both sides of the equal sign balance?

He scrabbles once more for the reclining lever and shoves back against the chair. Again. And again. Give just a little more, damn it.

A throat clears loudly behind him.

What the fuck? Why him? Why in the fucking hell was this thing put in his head? He could be one of these other sorry saps, unaware of the knowledge that in thirty-five hours they were going to just stop being. They get the gift of ignorance. No pain. No worry. No deathbed regrets. But he gets the goddamn weight of the world—the entire universe—on his shoulders.

"Mister." The little girl with the doughy cheeks and rose petal lips is staring at him with eyes that are way too big, way too trusting. "You're crunching Lisa."

Jack can't make out what she's saying, can't get away from that fawn-eyed gaze, until he notices the tug against his hand that grips her curly-haired doll on their shared arm rest. He lets go and Lisa is yanked to the pouting girl's chest. She soothes the doll with gentle strokes of her hair. Beyond her, the woman—blank-eyed, drop-shouldered, running a hand through her hair in slow, methodical strokes.

Jack curls up against the window, face presses against glass, and he shudders from dry, quiet sobs.

"Well, look who's here. It's Action Jack." Jazz doesn't smile. She grips a pair of tongs at her side from behind the counter of Capos and Cantos, slapping them against her thigh. "Going to press your luck with a ham on rye?"

The clink of coffee cups and rush of running water from the kitchen jabs at his ears. He winces to the wet slop of chewing behind him as a seated man finishes his sandwich. "Do you know where Pauline is? She's not home."

"How do you know she's not there?" She shears the words with snipping tongue.

"I knocked. No one answered."

"Maybe she just doesn't want to."

Jack lets her eyes sear him for a few seconds. He wonders just what the conversation was like between her and Pauline as they drove back from Fermilab. "Is she at work?"

Jazz picks up fresh-baked scones from a tray with the tongs and begins placing them in the display case. "Maybe she is, yeah. How should I know?"

"I need to see her."

"You think so, huh? Do you think she needs to see you?"

"I don't know."

She drops the last scone in, closes the case, and tosses the tongs with a clatter onto the tray. "Listen. I don't really know you…maybe just enough to be kinda creeped out by you. Definitely enough to see that you're messing her up. I don't know, something about you and something about her that, put together…." She shakes her head and wipes her hands on her apron. "…not a good idea."

"Where's the library?"

She snatches the filter bin from the coffee machine and dumps the grounds into the garbage. He's pretty certain she's not going to tell him. That's fine. Easy enough to find the library without her. He turns to walk out.

"Jack. Wait."

He looks back at her. Her lips press as her eyes keep to the garbage can. "She's not at the library. She's someplace else."

He's never visited his father's grave. Never wanted to. His mother has brought it up to him several times with gentle, maternal manipulation. "I think I'll visit your father after church." It's obvious what she would want him to say, but instead he'd tell her he was busy. Next time. He's been telling himself he'd go with her in a month, on the one-year anniversary of his father's death. But that will never happen now.

"Take a right up here," Jack tells the cab driver as the taxi coasts down the black tar road of St. Paul's Cemetery.

The lawn is preened and meticulous, still green, unnaturally green, and the marble headstones stand in even rows of macabre order. The sun is out, but its an anemic autumn light that casts shadows not heat, and the cold breeze ruffles the flowers placed by the graves, spilling the occasional vase of abandoned carnations, lilies, and roses. Jack looks for Pauline.

He has no idea why she's here. Is she paying her respects? To whom? She isn't originally from Skokie, she told him that, and she never mentioned having any family here. A friend, maybe? Jazz had been no help other than to confirm that she would be here. "Head down the main road. Take the first right before the main building. You'll find her."

"How long will she be there?"

"She'll be there."

The bald cab driver hasn't spoken the entire ride, has hardly moved his head. That's good. Jack has no casual conversation in him. It's all he can do just to keep a desperate clutch on the tethers of his dirigible thoughts.

The cab follows the ribbon of road as it makes a clean, gentle loop around the filed and labeled dead, and there's no Pauline to be found. He's beginning to think that Jazz has played a trick on him. Then, some hundred feet away, he sees a figure standing still amid the crop of stones, a billowing mane of dark hair and long, rippling skirt.

"Stop. I'll get out here." The cab comes to rocking halt and Jack climbs out. "Wait for me. I won't be long."

It's too hard to tell from the distance if Pauline has noticed him, but if she has, she isn't reacting. He steps off the road, onto the grass, into the sharp prick of wind, toward her.

She's facing away and remains so his entire approach. He can't free his eyes of her. Here, now, is the intimacy he never felt before, quiet and personal and vulnerable. The honest slope of shoulders, the surrendering slouch of back. Resignation splays her stance. Five feet from her, he stands silent and still, no desire to speak, no need to.

"You're still here." Her voice is naked and pure.

"Back, actually." He takes a step closer. "I can't stay long. My mom's in the hospital."

"I'm sorry to hear that."

He tries to see whose tombstone she stands before, but she is blocking his view, and he won't move, can't move, because anything sudden could ruin this huddled rabbit moment. "I needed to see you."

Her head cocks ever so slightly. "Needed?"

"Wanted."

A nod that suggests a smile. "Okay."

He doesn't know how to do this. Not even sure *what* to do. He opens his mouth, waits to hear what will come out. "I'm sorry."

"What was that?"

"I said, I'm sorry. Sorry about how I left. Sorry if I hurt you. Just...sorry."

"Did you get my email?"

"Yes."

"Then you know there's no reason to apologize."

"I think there is."

"Perhaps I just don't want it."

"Fair enough. As long as you know it's been offered."

"Duly noted."

He's had eight hours to prepare for this, and in the span of one minute, he's already ruined it, lost her. He can think of nothing more to say. He stuffs his hands in his pockets, stands rigid, one more stone among stones.

Pauline finally turns to him and he sees the ruined, raw face of that email; red, puffy eyes, running nose, pasty face. "I'd like you to meet someone, Jack." She steps to the side and he sees the small, modest marker set flush to the ground. The carved name on the stone almost speaks aloud into the wind—Kaiya Pauline Swanson. The dates below it are horrific in their repetition. 1995-1995.

Somehow, hazed in the foggy gray of his thinking, things begin to make sense. The third riddle. The tattoo. The mystery of Pauline.

"This is my daughter, Jack."

The cold marble epitaph chills his eyes: *Were you to live, Could you forgive.*

His lungs empty. "I'm so sorry, Pauline."

A sucking sob twists her face. "Oh, no. That apology is *not* yours to give." She rears back with a stiff inhale, wipes at her nose, and relaxes with an even breath and defiant smile. "When I found out I was pregnant, I thought my world was ending. I still had two years of college ahead of me. The father was a shit who I had already decided to have nothing more to do with. I was panicked about facing my parents. This just did *not* happen to their children, would not happen. And, I wasn't exactly prime mother materi-al…a drunk, struggling with every aspect of me…who I was, what I believed, if I even cared about anything. How could I ever care for a child? I could offer the baby up for adoption, but how would I hide it from my parents? I would've been seven months by Christ-mas holiday. But I kept telling myself, there's no choice, there's no option. It happened. Deal with it." She sniffs and wipes at her eyes. "All my friends kept pushing me. Get rid of it. You can't have it. Don't ruin your life. And…and I got more and more scared. Every time I visited my parents…trying to hide it for just a little longer."

He's not here. Her voice is miles of distance between them. These words aren't for him.

"Three months pregnant, and I tried to look ahead, but I couldn't—couldn't see how I was going to face my father, how I would ever be able to get through this. So…I decided to just wipe it out, erase it, like it never happened. And then never look back. I made the appointments, shrugged off their counseling, and the date was set.

"I don't even know where I was when I walked into that clinic that day." She points to her head. "I wasn't here." Her hand drops to her chest. "I definitely wasn't here. It was all a blur.

"I remember crying, losing my sense of time. I told them I didn't want to go through with it, that it was a mistake. How funny and sad and pathetic that what seems so obvious after the fact can be so absent when you're about to make the most terrible mis-take…most terrible mistake…

"They told me that it was already done, that everything would be fine. Everything is fine now, just relax. I…was *not* fine. I was so terribly not fine. When it finally sank into me that it was done, I knew what I had to do. And I would not leave there until it was done. I told them that I wanted the baby. I wanted it kept for burial rites. I was going to lay my baby to rest." She squints and gives a bitter grin. "They really didn't like that. 'No, miss, I'm sorry. We don't do that. We've already disposed of the aborted matter. Let us give you a sedative.'" Her eyes charge and spark. "I made it clear to them that a sedative simply *would not do*."

Jack takes a step closer to her. He could reach out to her. He's close enough.

"In the end, I called my pastor back home, he talked to the clinic, and they decided to save themselves the trouble and honor my wishes." She stiffens and smiles wider against the tears that catch on the curl of lip before falling. "That's when I found out I had a daughter. A daughter." She brushes at her eyes again, drops her head to the gravestone. "I named her Kaiya. Three days later, my family came up for the funeral. It was the last time I saw my parents."

"They didn't forgive you." Jack's voice is rough and wind-burnt.

"Not at first, no. My father wouldn't even look me in the eye during the funeral. I only found out later when I called the funeral home that he had paid for everything. After a few months, my mom started calling. I...I just couldn't, though. Couldn't talk to her. Many things were buried that day, Jack."

He moves his hand toward her, wanting to comfort her, needing to touch her, wanting just one more time to be with her. She bridges the distance with her outstretched hand. He folds his hand around the cold skin of hers. "I...I had no idea...I wish I knew what I could say to—"

"Nothing you can say, Jack. But there *are* things I'll be saying to Kaiya for the rest of my life." She zips open her jacket with her free hand and draws up her sweater. The tattoo is stark against her pale skin. "I got this so that I would never spend a day without facing it. The mark of my mistake."

"But, two-forty-three? I—I still don't..."

She nods. "I was going to put the date of her birth and death there, but if I marked that point in time, then every day I would only move further away from it, from her. Time will not stop for regret." She motions her head to the grave. "This is lot two-hundred-forty-three, section C. Two-forty-three anchors me, Jack. It is the center to my life. I may move away from it, but I can always return to this exact point." .

It's staggering—what she must have faced—what she is still facing. To have made that choice willingly is unfathomable. "Why, Pauline? To put yourself through all of that…your parents…why?"

She takes his other hand and peers into him, hard, those chestnut eyes pushing against the back of his head. "Because. No action can be taken without consequences. No decision can be made without facing its repercussions. Do you understand? It's important that you understand that, Jack."

He pulls his hands away, buries them back in his pockets, and looks across the expanse of the cemetery. His mother flits through his jumbled mind and he worries that he left too soon, or maybe too late. "I should really get going."

"Why are you here, Jack? Why did you come all this way? Just to tell me you're sorry?"

"Wouldn't that be enough?"

"A telephone works pretty good for that."

"I wasn't sure you'd want to talk to me."

She rolls her head. "Oh, goodness, Jack. Who are you trying to sell this story to, me or you?"

Jack sighs. Here is the Pauline he knows so well, the one who knows him so well. "Why should I try to figure it out when you obviously already know the answer?" He turns away from her, uncomfortable with his comment, frustrated by Pauline always being right.

She steps in front of him again. "Look at me, Jack."

He does, and it's like trying to stand on smooth ice.

"I saw how you looked at me in that parking lot. You were never going to see me again. You headed home with whatever you got from your friend and that was it. Now you tell me that your mother's in the hospital, but you ride back three hundred miles on a bus to tell me you're sorry?" The shake of her head tries to deny a realization widening her eyes. "You're at quest's end, aren't you? You've made a decision."

He slips on her interrogating eyes and tries to find a place for his hands that suddenly aren't comfortable anywhere.

"Haven't you."

"Doesn't matter, does it? You don't believe me anyway. Don't worry about it. Everything's going to be okay." He starts to walk. He needs to get away from her. He didn't come here to talk about this.

She rushes up behind him, shadowing him. "But it *does* matter! *You* believe it, Jack. It's real in your head. You're living it every day, every minute."

"I'm not going to talk about this." He makes his legs move faster.

"Don't do it. Please. Don't commit to something that you won't be able to live with."

"If it's what I think it is, I won't have to live with it. If it's not, then I won't do anything and everything will be fine."

He feels her firm grip on his arm and gives in to her pull. "No, Jack. *You* won't be fine. You'll put yourself in a place you'll never be able to leave."

There's no point to this. She doesn't understand. He starts walking again. "Never is a very short concept for me right now."

She calls out to him from behind. "Jack! Don't do it to yourself! You'll be all alone there! *I know!*"

There's no way she'll hear him, she's too far from him now, but he has to say it. It's why he really came here, right? So he does. Just for him. He says it as his foot lands upon the hard black tar of the road in front of the taxi.

"Goodbye, Pauline."

-1

The First Rule: *Never end the world based on a personal condition or emotion.*

The Second Rule: *Never end the world based on the actions of, or the personal feelings for, an individual.*

The Third Rule: *Never end the world only to prove that you can.*

Legs dangle over the rocky edge of the hillside of Mount Simon, above the concrete skin of downtown. The vein of the Terrapin River circulates in the distance, fleshy flatlands stubbled with trees round the horizon. From here, as clouds blush pink to the emerging sun and the last stars slip behind the day, Jack keeps vigil at the bedside of the world.

He looks west and sees St. Mark's Hospital far in the distance, where he should be; where he can't seem to be. He turns south and his eyes follow the red burn of taillights through the sleeping retail district to the south end of town where Liz is three hours from finishing her graveyard shift at The Copy Place. Some fifty miles down that road, Sam and Greg are just waking up to start another week of meetings, deadlines, and circular progress on tired ideas. Further south, far beyond his vision, Pauline probably still sleeps, hours away from slipping the bound pages of some old story on a shelf in a dark corner of the library. He looks down at it all.

Twenty hours and counting.

He still feels rooted in the last fugue, that quagmire of emptiness, and his limbs feel as sluggish as his head. It had come last night, right after listening to the petulant message from Liz saying that, if he cared at all, their mom was showing signs of stabilizing, but not out of the woods yet. After, he burrowed into his bed and faded—but not the Shrug. It still hasn't left him, not really. He can't distinguish himself from it any longer.

Five hours of semi-sleep hang on him like heavy, thick clothing that still smell like the fresh dirt of his father's garden from his dream. He's bothered by Pauline's presence in the vision. He's forced to remember her final words to him after that garden turned to cemetery and the rains began to fall—"You're all alone, Jack."

To drown her out, he does what he's been doing since the bus ride back—he goes over the rules in his head once more. They are his neat little checklist, tempered and honed against the emotion of his youth, the melodrama of his teens, and the responsibilities of his adulthood. His guidebook. His perfect little mantra.

But he changes the rules now. Inverts them. He wants to open them up, turn them over, spill out the pieces that make them tick. They must work both ways, like an equation—identical values on both sides.

Never deny the Shrug based on a personal condition or emotion.

Never deny the Shrug based on the actions of, or the personal feelings for, an individual.

Never deny the Shrug only to prove that you can.

He cinches his arms tighter in front of him. The rules, reflected like this, should mean the same thing, come to the same conclusion, yet they seem more like a sinister behest.

Behind him, to the north, the grave of his over-lived father. Before him, far south of here, the grave of Pauline's unlived daughter. Two opposing weights on a scale, and somehow he is supposed to balance them?

Were you to live, could you forgive.

Will these words be chiseled into the stone marker of the world, to the memorial of existence?

No. There will be no stone, no remembrance. No sin to be bound to. No action. No consequence.

No tomorrow.

Alone on the solitary hillside, he leans into the empty space over the world, vertigo makes the ground below seem to rise and fall as a labored breath, and he wants very badly to hold his mother's hand one last time.

Fifteen hours and counting, snuffing out a cigarette on the stoop just as Len arrives to pick him up. Len. Always late. Always reliable. Jack drags feet to the big blue beast of car and the passenger door opens with a whine and pop of metal. "Hop in, Cap'n."

Jack shoves aside the pile of fast food bags and soda cans as he climbs in. "Thanks for the ride to the hospital."

"Not a problem. Gotta go to work anyhow. It's on the way. Wagon took a shitter, huh?"

"Kind of."

"That why you're not at work?"

"Something like that."

Len rolls out a wired-jaw chuckle. "Good ol' Jack, always laying it down with the details."

The car air is like deep-fried cigarettes and he's warm despite being outside in the cold for a quarter hour as he waited for Len. He rolls the window down halfway and puts his face under the opening. Lids slump over his eyes and his head bobs on the crest of consciousness.

"Freaking out about your mom, huh? Don't worry about her. She's doing good, now. She's gonna make it, man. Got a good feeling about that."

"Sure."

"Say, you okay? I mean, you really look like hell, man."

It's like he's floating outside the car, and Len is far away. "What a charmer."

"I'm serious. No offense, but you've been kind of out of it. You sure all your pistons are firing?"

It's like pulling magnets apart to get his eyes open again. "Len. Have you ever just wished that you never met her?"

"Huh?"

"Liz. You ever wish you never even knew her? You know, I mean, since you two never worked out."

Len kicks a grin into the corner of his cheek. "Who says we won't, chum?"

Jack stares at him.

Len's throat sputters. "Yeah, right. Well, I don't know. I guess. Sometimes." A black marble eye thins in thought. "Plenty of times. But hey, we still have fun together. We can still be friends…most of the time. Besides, if I wished away everything that went wrong in my life, I'd still be a little bald pissed dude whining over that whole womb thing not working out. You know?"

Jack nods slow and even, then closes his eyes again and drifts on the wave of motion beneath him.

The respirator is gone, a clear oxygen tube is in its place, tucked below his mother's Bohemian nose. Her chest rises and falls, almost restful—just the hint of a rattle at the extremities of her breathing. Dr. Evans told him that her respiratory and heart rates are normalizing and her systolic pressure is approaching safe margins. She's been wakeful and alert for extended periods. As long as the antibiotics continue to work, she should be fine—for now.

There's no avoiding the fact, however, that his mother's emphysema is a degenerative condition. She will never get better.

He sits beside her, his hand over hers.

He could take all her future and past pains away. She would never have to suffer, regret, fear. No one would, ever again.

And this should comfort him, firm his resolve. It should.

His whole life has been building to this moment, this one decision. And the question is no longer if he should do it. That has been decided. The Shrug will happen. He can feel this. It will happen soon. Can he even try to fight it? Can he resist the Shrug? And if so, how?

No. He knows how. There's only one way to stop it. Regardless of his decision, the deadline still stands.

My God. It really has to be this way, doesn't it?

His fingers rasp against the bristle of beard shading his cheek. He can't remember when he shaved last. "Jesus. Jesus, Jesus, Jesus." He slides his hand off his mother's as he stands—too quickly. His head fizzes over and he stands still until it passes. His body shifts to walk, but his feet are planted. He gulps a breath, holds it, and puffs it out. "Shit." He thinks again that he might walk, body jerks as if to do so, then he sits back down.

Yeah. It really has to be this way. Two possible choices. Which only leaves the decision—does he deny the Shrug or not?

He looks back at his resting mother. "How about it, Mom? Yes? Or no?" He lowers his head and knots his fingers into his hair.

The bed sheets rustle and barely the breath of a voice speaks.

He looks up, sees her open eyes, and leans in to her. "What's that, Mom?"

She grins weakly. "I said 'yes.'"

His laugh is parched. "You should be careful, you know, saying 'yes' when you don't know the question."

"I'm a risk-taker." She manages to pull off a cocky nonchalance, even with that tube up her nose. Then she sputters with a bubbling hack. "Raise my head, would you?"

Jack looks for the controls and holds down the up-arrow button. The bed's motor whirs and elevates her head. "Is that good?"

"Hmm. Yes. Thank you."

"How are you feeling?"

"Better. Tired. Throat's dry."

He stands and pours water from the pitcher on her bedside stand into the straw-topped mug and brings it to her lips. She sips deep twice and nods.

"You don't look so good." Her voice drags. "You need to take better care of yourself."

He sets the plastic mug down. "Oh, this from someone who answers 'yes' to questions she doesn't know."

"Right now, 'yes' seems a better answer to everything."

"'No' is safer."

Her hand flutters dismissively. "'No' is for when you know exactly what the question is."

"Um…Okay." His grin feels lopsided.

She exhales a thin sigh. "Oh dear. I raised a son afraid to say 'yes.'" She clicks her tongue and rolls her head against her pillow.

"Well, there's such a long time packed into those yes's. No's are nice and short…none of that baggage."

She groans. "Boy. Now you sound like your sister. I'd worry about all the wonderful things I might say 'no' to."

Jack turns to the window. An ambulance with perilous strobes of light pulls in under the emergency entrance awning—EMTs hustle to the back of the truck as doctor and nurse fast-step from the hospital doors, the flash of red and blue splashing against their white lab coats. Life just keeps happening. "I'm sorry I wasn't here yesterday. I should have been."

"It would've been nice." Painfully indifferent. Shame is a blister to the burn of a mother's love.

He turns to face her. "I know, I know, I'm…something's just…" He grinds his palms against his thighs. "I'm having a hard time with this."

Her brow eases back and color comes to her cheeks. "I know you are." She digs her elbows in and pushes back, scooting and shifting. She grunts, coughs, and gives up her fight, face slack with exhaustion. "Oh, this bed is so uncomfortable." She sucks in a quick breath, like trying to force the air into her lungs.

He turns back to her. "You shouldn't be pushing yourself. You need to save your strength."

"Just…let me enjoy this."

He stuffs her pillows down further behind her back. "Enjoy what?"

"Talking to you, Jack. Mother and son. And you have to listen. I'm playing this sympathy card to the hilt."

He smiles. "Okay."

"I remember when Walt died. That night. Everyone was crying. Liz cried. Never seen Liz cry since she was eleven. Then I saw you, and you were just…shut off. Like someone flicked a switch on you."

Everyone was weeping. A family of crying, holding, regretting. They had him call the funeral home—said he was the only one in control. The only one who could do it. He had never felt so alone.

"Are you ever going to turn yourself back on? It's time, you know. You can't just turn it all off and expect it to go away. Only you go away. That's no good."

Wrong switch, Mom. Wrong damn switch. "I'm not the one to worry about right now."

"I'm not so sure." She holds her gaze, burrowing in like only she can. "But listen. Everything's going to be fine. God seems to want me around a little longer. I figure I'll oblige Him."

"Glad to hear it."

"And since none of this involves a yes or no question, something tells me there's more bothering you."

"Stop it now."

"Something to do with work?"

"No."

"If you talked about it, maybe I could help."

He tenses. "It's just a decision I have to make. Don't worry about it."

"So much like your father. Have to take on the world single-handedly."

He drops back down into the chair. "Yeah, but Dad always knew what he was doing."

"Who says?"

Jack coughs out an abrupt laugh. "Dad did."

"Well, your father had been around longer, been through his tough times, made his mistakes. Lot of life to learn from. But he was never sure of anything."

"He acted like it."

"Resolute isn't the same thing as being sure. Just means he took a side and stuck to it. That's what you did back then."

"It's hard to be resolute when there seems to be nothing but consequences no matter what you decide."

"Welcome to life, Jack. Listen. Stop worrying about right and wrong. Just worry about what decisions you can live with. Right and wrong will work themselves out."

Jack nods, and for a moment, he loses his mom, the chair, the room. He's overcome by something, and for the life of him, he doesn't know what it is. But it feels solid and certain. "I love you, Mom."

Her eyes glisten. "I love you, too." Her hands smooth out the blankets and regroup in a huddle over her chest. "So what's this all about? What are we talking about?"

He looks at her, and he'd laugh if not for fear of crying. "Nothing, Mom. Nothing."

.

0

He takes them three at a time.

The first nine go down easy. Nine more and he's finding it hard to swallow. After that, his gag reflex really kicks in and he needs twice as much water to flush them down. The pills swish and knock against teeth and he has to corral them with his tongue, taste the bitterness of powder as the coatings dissolve.

Finished, he tosses the empty plastic bottle at the sink. It clanks and spins and settles against the drain cover.

Balance.

He looks at the clock. 11:15. How long will it take? He doesn't know. He only took them a few times for his headaches the first few days after the accident. The Darvocet usually started to work on him in about twenty minutes. He's probably rushing the deadline, but that's fine. He's always been early. Early to everything. At least it should be painless—a dreamy, darkening fog to just fade away in, like his own personal Shrug. How appropriate.

He walks to the printer and takes the three letters from the tray—to Liz, to his mother, and to Pauline. He carries them back to his desk by the three envelopes. Liz and his mom's letter say pretty much the same thing. He folds them twice and slips them into their envelopes and seals them. He holds on to Pauline's and looks it over one last time.

Pauline-

Somehow it seems so much more appropriate to email you this letter, but unfortunately, I can't take the chance that you might read it right away.

I just wanted to tell you that I'm glad I met you. If things had been different, I would have liked to see you again. Maybe I could have somehow persuaded you to let yourself go, to lift this punishment you've sentenced yourself to. If you're looking for atonement, there are other ways of finding it. Besides, I'd hate to think I've saved the world just so you can keep your punishment going. I still don't know what's right or wrong, what any of this is all about, but somehow I don't think that's a part of it.

I thought the Shrug was a way to bring things to balance. End the suffering, end the chaos of life. I got it wrong. The Shrug will only tip the scales. All this, right here and now, is the balance. That constant shifting back and forth, that's just life. One small little spot where we stand and teeter between the extremes. It's not existence that needs to be undone to maintain balance, it's me.

The Shrug will happen if I don't do this. I know you'll never believe me, but I know. I have to stop it. This is the only way.

Ironic, isn't it, that I should just start to understand what life has to offer only when I know that I can't have it, and you've known all along, but refuse to live it? Maybe, even though you wouldn't give it to yourself, you'll accept it from someone else. So I'm giving it to you. A gift.

Don't waste it, Pauline.

Jack

He folds it up, slips it into the stamped and addressed envelope, and seals it. Out the door, he slides them through the outgoing mail slot of the metal postal box on the stoop, then goes back inside. It's all done. There's nothing more to do but wait. He should get to bed. He has a feeling that once it hits, it's going to hit hard and fast.

He walks over to the computer, checks emails one last time. Just spam. Someone somewhere thinks his penis is small. This is what gets to share a place with the last thoughts in his head. A fucking penis enlargement email.

He reaches out for the mouse to shut his computer down, and his breathing quickens, his heart pounds into his throat, his hand trembles and squeezes. The plastic shell of the mouse cracks. He yanks hard, snapping the cord free of the computer, and flings the mouse across the room to shatter against the kitchen wall. His eyes see everything in a pulsing coppery monochrome. His hands jitter and flex for something to be in them, to twist, to snap, to tear. He's clutching at the monitor, heaving it up until the cable snaps taut, and he throws it against the wall with a loud clamorous bang, plaster chipping and flaking. The monitor crashes back down onto the desk, on its side. It sparks and fizzles to a singular point of light on its black screen. He grabs the keyboard, smashes it against the upended monitor. Consonants and vowels and numbers explode into the air around him. The heel of his foot finds the CPU and knocks it over. He hears a loud, persistent racket—an annoying, guttural sound. It's him, his own wailing voice. It feels good. He yells more, an orgasm of rage. He lunges across the room, throws books off shelves, topples the TV to the floor with a shove, whips drawers out of his desk. He can't see anymore, just a blur through a stream of tears.

He staggers to stillness. The room is quiet. Just his gulping gasps of breath as his head swirls. He stands amid the ruin of the room and wipes at his eyes. "Bastards. I lived. For one fucking moment, I lived." He doubles over, hands to his knees, sucking air, and weeps soft laughter.

Now, he can finally sleep.

Part Eight
THE WALKABOUT

1

"Jack, get your butt up. You'll be late for church. Come on."
His father was a brawny silhouette in the doorframe. Most of his
relationship with his dad lately was kept to this kind of border skir-
mish saber rattling.

Jack lifted his groggy head from his pillow. "Come on. Just
this once, can't I miss? I didn't get done with work until after
midnight."

"That didn't mean you needed to stay up until three in the
morning playing your video games."

He groaned and dropped his head back down into the bliss of
fluffy pillow flesh. "Give me a break."

"Now. Get up."

He hurled the covers from the bed. "I'm up!" Legs swung
over the side, hands smacked the mattress and he shoved himself
upright into a slump. "Man. Couldn't sleep in on Saturday because
I had to shovel the stupid driveway, can't sleep in today because of
church...not fair."

"You got it tough there, kid. Real tough."

Amended rule number twenty-three: *Ending the world because your father is a dick may qualify.* "I'm an atheist, all right?" Blurted out, as fast to say as it was to regret. He wasn't one. At least, he didn't think so.

His dad turned on the light. Jack flinched and winced from the glare. No doubt the old man really enjoyed that. Through squinting, sleep-puffed eyes, he looked at his father, dressed in his Sunday finest—fat paisley tie, short sleeve button-up powder blue shirt tucked tightly around a confident gut, navy blue dress slacks. Everyone else wore pants; his dad wore 'slacks.'

"Don't let me *ever* catch you saying something like that to your mother."

"Dragging me into some stupid building to listen to sermons isn't going to make any kind of difference."

"You're living under our roof. Until otherwise, you step to our beat."

Jack turned and pulled open a dresser drawer, grabbed a pair of jeans. "Whatever."

"Yeah, *whatever.*" Tremulous anger ending in the sneer that always looked like he was going to lunge forward, haul back with that loop-muscled arm and drive a fist into him. The threat was there in the hint of teeth and those ball-bearing eyes. But it never happened. He had never raised a violent hand against Jack.

His dad should have walked out then. That was the exit look, the "I'm done with you" grimace. But he crossed the border, stepped into the room and sat down on the crumpled pile of discarded sheets at the corner of the bed. "Listen—"

"I'm up, I'm going, okay?"

"*Listen*, goddamn it." The growl like poured gravel. "Jesus, kid. You manage to find every one of my nerves."

Shit. There it was, dripping down his jowls. Another speech. He shouldn't be surprised. He hadn't gotten one for nearly a month now. Jack dropped down onto the other side of the bed and glared at the dusty-brown carpeting.

"I don't care what you believe or don't believe."

"I was joking. I'm not an atheist." Jack tried to sound conciliatory, but that rarely worked lately. Always too much snap with the tongue, too much pressure of teeth on his lower lip.

"I'm just saying, you're sixteen years old. You're going to think what you want. Nothing we do is going to make a damn bit of difference with what you believe. Hell, Jack, it's not like I believe any of it."

Jack's muscles locked and he stared at his father.

His dad looked almost as surprised as Jack felt. "What, you really didn't know?"

A stupid shake of the head.

Those big shoulders shrugged. "I never have, Jack. Jesus, I thought you…well. Now you know."

All those years, watching his father's head bowed over his meat and potatoes as they all muttered Grace at dinner, cuffing the back of Jack's head when Jack wasn't paying attention during the homily, flipping burgers and turning brats at church picnics while he laughed at something with Father Karrigan. Jack couldn't get his mind around it.

But it was all so obvious, wasn't it? The truth had been there, all along, and he had never seen it as anything other than the way it was. He felt like such a fool.

Every Sunday, as the ushers moved with penitent step down the aisle, touching each pew to allow passage to communion, and his father would tuck in his knees. Jack and Liz and his mom would walk past him, normal as can be. And his father would sit, eyes ahead. Resolute.

Had Jack ever even questioned it? Had he ever asked his parents why? He couldn't remember anymore. It just *was*.

"I did it for your mother. I promised her before we were even engaged. It was important to her. So, if I could deal with it for all this time, you can put up with it for another couple years."

Jack gave a slow nod. "Yeah. I get it." He looked at his father, not seeing anyone different, yet everything felt different.

His dad gave him a hard look. "So, were you just giving me a bunch of bullshit, or do you really not believe anymore?"

"I don't know." His pat answer—it riled his dad to no end—but it was really the truth. Jack had been going through the motions of believing for so long, and lately it just wasn't adding up—not with this weird thought in his head that could wipe everything out like it never was.

"Maybe it's about time you did know."

"Why?" And why the hell was his dad suddenly so interested? He's never given two craps about what Jack thought as long as he mowed the lawn before a rain and shoveled the driveway before the car could make tracks.

"You've got to believe in something, Jack. Every man needs a compass to follow. Otherwise you're lost."

"You just told me you don't believe. I don't get it."

"Well, Father Karrigan might tell you that there's only one thing to believe, but there's more. I've got the mirror, Jack. If I can look at that guy looking back at me in the eye, then I'm on the right track. And I'll always be able to stare down that S.O.B. as long as I'm providing for my family…making sure all of you get all the opportunities I never got. Get me?"

That cold burn of scrutiny was full on Jack now, and he squirmed as he tried to keep eye contact. His dad pulled a crumpled, folded piece of paper from his pocket. As he opened it, Jack recognized the scribblings and his gut lurched.

"I don't know what the hell this is, but I'm guessing whoever would be thinking this garbage can't look in that mirror." He dropped the paper onto the bed. Line after line—numbered, edited, amended, crossed out—of Jack's handwriting. Each line started with the same words. "Never end the world unless…."

Jack's throat was dry and his words rasped. "You're digging in my trash?"

"God damn right." Staccato words said through a thin grin threat over square jaw.

Jack picked up the list. "This is nothing. I was just fooling

271

around."

"That kind of stuff isn't right. What am I supposed to think about that? Huh?"

Jack whipped his head away and stood up, crumpling the paper in his hands. "God. Don't make such a big deal about it."

"Don't you walk your ass away from me. What's going on with you, Jack? You hibernate in this room. Your grades stink. Detention. Bad attitude. Now this kind of shit. You've got no direction, no focus. You're just not productive. We've already got one Liz in the family; we don't need another. Is that where you want to be? No direction, no future? One day, you're going to be neck deep in life, and you'll realize that all this crap you're moping around with isn't getting you anywhere. Then what? It's going to be too late, kid."

Jack shrugged.

"Don't do that, damn it. Don't give me that shoulder shrug of yours. Be a man, for chrissake. You want to tell me to go to hell? Then do it. Don't just sit there and roll your shoulders at me like I'm nothing. I'm trying to tell you something important. I deserve more respect than that."

Jack did his duty. He stood there and listened. Obligation over.

His father stood up. "You get me?"

Jack gave him a succinct nod and his father walked out of his room, back across that border.

His father didn't understand. Couldn't understand. He hadn't been flipping his father off with that shrug, or avoiding the responsibility of making a decision. Jack was only acknowledging the impotence of the advice. His shrug was, if anything, an acceptance—both of the logic and the futility of his father's words. If his dad could do what Jack was fairly certain he could, he would learn to appreciate a shrug.

Jack squeezed the wadded-up list in his fist, chucked it into the trash, and got ready for church.

"Tell me what you're thinking about."

The buttery, androgynous voice of Dr. Illindale brought Jack's attention back to the present. The doctor sat in his burgundy leather chair with his knit, neutral-toned sweater and narrow-crossed legs that ended in brown suede loafers. Everything about his pinched, ovoid face was as passive as his voice.

"I was just thinking about how a father tends to speak to the future."

Dr. Illindale grinned. "That's very poetic. You have quite a perspective on things, Jack." He scribbled onto a legal pad with his gold pen. "Do you care to elaborate on that at all?"

"Remembering something my father told me once that I didn't listen to at the time. It's suddenly coming through loud and clear." Jack shook his head clear of the memory. "I'm sorry. You had asked me something before?"

"I asked what your plans are now."

A crystal cube sat balanced on one of its points on the Queen Ann coffee table in front of him. It caught a spark of sunlight from the frosted window of the office and spilled a rainbow streak onto the cherry wood grain. He picked it up and turned it over in his hands, felt the blunted end and bottom-heavy weight that allowed it to apparently defy gravity. "I don't really know. I suppose I need to get my life back to normal."

"Do you feel that any part of your life before was actually 'normal'?"

"Well, I guess it was normal to me...at the time."

Dr. Illindale nodded his bald head. "That would mean the life you are about to experience will be extraordinary then, right?"

Jack set the crystal cube back down on the table. Illindale was dangling the psychological carrot again. "Maybe. What are you trying to say?"

"Well, I suppose I'm just concerned that you are talking about returning to somewhere you've never been, and in a manner that assumes you know how to get there."

"It's where I want to be. Now that the Shrug is out of my

head, I can do that."

Illindale leaned back, tip of the pen going to his bottom lip. For the doctor, this was a wild gesticulation. "So you think the Shrug is some isolated piece of thought that can just be extracted from your psyche? Like uninstalling software?"

Leather belched under Jack as he shifted in his chair. "Well, that's what the medication is for, isn't it? It's been over two weeks now, and it seems to be working."

Jack had become intimate with Illindale's head bob in the three sessions he's had with the psychiatrist. This nod said that, apparently, Jack liked carrots more than he thought, because he had followed it right into Illindale's snare.

"Jack, the temporal lobe epilepsy is simply short-circuiting certain specific cognitive signals in your brain. So many neurons that aren't doing what they should be doing. The Levetiracetam you are taking is a central nervous system depressant used to suppress those seizures. But it is *you*, Jack, who has been interpreting those signals as The Shrug. It is you who has adapted your entire life around the knowledge that you could end existence. You think the Shrug is just some tiny isolated signal in your head? Based on your rules, your web site, your recent decision to quit your job, and to end your own life, I'm compelled to say that the Shrug has been your entire operating system."

Jack looked out the window to the cold, brown day, frowned at the spindly naked trees, and wished he could be any anywhere else.

Dr. Illindale leaned forward, guided by the hundred-dollar-an-hour sympathy of blue eyes. "Jack, if this wasn't our last session, I wouldn't be pushing this issue. But we don't have that luxury."

"I'm just here because Dr. Haizuki strongly suggested it, but there's no way I could afford you long-term. Not with my health insurance cancelled."

"I understand that. I'm just trying to impress upon you the fact that the medication will not remove the Shrug from your life. That is going to be up to you."

The bottle of pills had ended his life. Neighbors calling the police made no difference. His stomach pumped in the emergency room of St. Mary's didn't matter. He died. And he took the Shrug with him. That life, that universe he existed in, was over. No. He didn't need to resolve the Shrug from his life. He had done that already. Now, he needed to resolve his life from the Shrug.

Maybe he should be telling this to Illindale. Maybe that is what Illindale wanted to hear. But Jack didn't want to share it. For some reason it felt right not to share it. He needed to keep it for himself, not express it, explain it, or qualify it. It just was. So instead he'd keep his answers simple, his words brief, and just get through this session. "I think I'm going to be fine."

"And how are you going to be sure of that?"

"I can't. But wanting it—thinking it—seems like the best chance I got."

2

Liz drove him to his check-up with Dr. Haizuki. She'd been carting him all over town—doctor, store, shrink—and running errands for their mom when she wasn't helping him. Jack still wasn't driving—might never drive again. The Levetiracetam greatly reduced his chances of seizures, but would never stop them completely. Dr. Illindale was right—the Shrug might be gone, but not the specter of it.

Jack still felt like he was trying to stand still after a fast, tight spin. He was no more capable of grasping this new reality than when he had first awoke in the hospital to Liz and his mom staring down at him with that slap of shock and dismay on their faces.

There was no question the Shrug was gone. He had no sense of it, only its absence. He should have been comforted by that, but he only felt incomplete. How could that emptiness have occupied so significant a space in him only to leave such a different hole?

He continued to think about the Shrug as if it *had* existed. Maybe he'd never stop believing that it had been real. Maybe it *was* real. Did that even matter? Not too much. It was out of his life. He just had to figure out what was left.

There were memories now. They crackled and sparked like static. Four years old and curled up in the summer shade around the big oak tree in the front yard, smelling bleached-clean linen that hung on the line and billowed like sails in the breeze. The hot odor of whiskey and wood as his father sanded down a nightstand leg at the kitchen table, ash from the cigarette in his mouth crumbling over his chest. Burnt chicken smoking up the kitchen to a haze as his mom sobbed and his dad swelled purple with rage and lunged at Liz after she called their mom a fucking bitch when told to stay for dinner instead of going out with her friends. So many of them, all flashes of intense memory, then dark, lingering negatives.

And he was touching things a lot, poking and feeling everything around him— the hard, deep-grain top of the desk in his living room, the spiny prickles of the arborvitaes on either side of the stoop, the grit of brick as he ran his hand over the outside wall of his apartment building. He said his name out loud, too, alone in the bathroom or while fixing dinner, kind of in the way he used to walk across the dark utility room of the basement when he was a kid and say over and over again, "No such things as ghosts, no such thing as ghosts."

When he had first got in the car, Liz asked him how he was doing. Everyone was asking him that. "How are you doing, Jack?" He always answered "fine" or "better" or "hanging in there" because that's what the answer was supposed to be. That's what was expected, what they wanted to hear. Nobody wanted to know that sometimes his heart just started beating itself to death and, for a split a second, he'd realize that he absolutely couldn't be here and now. No one wanted to hear that he would walk to the nearby strip mall and wander the aisles of the Bed and Bath Emporium, the Well-Dressed Gent and other shops just so he could be around people. He didn't want anyone to know that, for some reason, he preferred to sleep with a light on now.

How was he doing?

He was caught somewhere between the intake and exhale of a startled breath.

But those small anxieties were preferable to the flash fire rage that had scorched him for the first few days in the hospital—a mute hate for Doctor Haizuki, for Liz and Len, for his mother. Hate for anyone who was part of that horrible, impossible news. He had barely spoken in those first days of recovery.

His hatred had quickly burned out. He had loathed himself for much longer. Seethed with revulsion for the defective, damaged Jack Cross.

He had tried to talk to Pauline, to see her again, but his calls and emails had gone unanswered. She didn't have an answering machine so he couldn't leave a message, and he didn't know if she was receiving his emails. She had called once, the day after he had been brought to the hospital—still stuck in a limbo between the one life he had ended forever and the one he had yet to seize. She had left a message. "From the flames of one life comes the glow of another. Live well, Jack."

He had finally broken down two days ago and called Capos and Cantos to talk with Jazz. When he asked where Pauline was, Jazz's answer had landed heavy in his stomach.

"She's gone."

"What do you mean, gone?"

"I mean gone. Pack slung over her back, suitcase in hand, apartment vacated. Left all her shit behind, too."

"Where?" Why?

"She didn't tell me. Just told me it was time to move on. Said she needed to go on walkabout, and no one could follow. You have this effect on everyone, Jack? Jesus."

He hadn't realized how desperately he needed to see her until it was no longer an option. He had come to believe that his recovery would be through her. What now?

Liz zipped her Impala into the hospital lot and landed crooked between an SUV and a compact. She was quiet. Had been ever since the incident. Conversationally efficient. Jack didn't like it, but he supposed he understood. He was a stranger now.

"This shouldn't take long," he said.

"No problem." She grabbed her keys and fingered her hair in the rear view mirror. "Christ, if this hospital was a bar, I'd have a mug with my name on it by now." Her head shook. "Talk about life taking a real shit on this past month."

"Sorry. Been pretty rough on you, huh?"

"Jesus, Jack. Stop apologizing. I'm not blaming anybody. Just saying I'm going to check myself into the psyche ward if one more person ends up in the hospital."

He grinned. "You'd like it there. Dr. Illindale is really nice."

She flushed, something Jack didn't know she could do. "Hey, I didn't…" Her lips pursed and she dug for a cigarette from the pack in her lap. "Forget it."

"Liz, don't worry about it." But he did, of course. No one seemed to look at him the same. His belief in the Shrug wasn't discussed, and questions were only a tender touch by careful conversation.

Liz sat and sucked on her cigarette, said nothing for a bit, and looked in the rear view mirror again. The heavy eyeliner and lipstick hid it, the short black burst of hair denied it, but she was snuffed out—a tangled line of smoke from a smothered flame. "Well, we should get you in there."

"You did fifteen over the speed limit the whole way here. We're early. No rush." He wanted to talk. He wanted to work out whatever needed to be worked out. Tell her he was still Jack, still her brother, that things could be like they were. Or did he actually want her to tell *him* that?

"What the hell do you want to do, sit in the car?"

"At least you can finish your smoke." He felt the nip of a craving himself. He hadn't had a cigarette for a long time, didn't want one. Time to quit. But his brain kept firing off the impulse to reach for one and light up like it was the most natural thing to do. Logical. It pissed him off and he ignored it.

Liz held her cigarette up for inspection. "I can finish this thing by the time we get to the doors."

He braced himself and looked right at her. "Hey, is everything all right?"

She eyed him as if he were digging in her underwear drawers. Jack knew the look well enough to heed the warning. So much for trying to talk. "Just asking. Forget it. Let's go."

They didn't sit in the waiting room long before his name was called and a nurse led him into the scanning room where the huge ring and flat bed of the CT Scanner loomed. He knew the routine by now, but going through the scan still made his breath and heart quicken.

When the scan was finished, he rejoined Liz and they waited until they were taken to an examination room and met by Dr. Haizuki—round, bronzed face warm with greetings.

"I hope your mother is much improved?"

Jack sat down in the chair by the plain, square metal desk. "She is. Still taking it easy, but she's doing much better."

Liz stood in the corner of the room, leaning against the wall. "She's toking up on this big, steamy pipe five times a day."

Dr. Hyzuki nodded. "Ah. A nebulizer."

Liz shrugged. "Yeah, well. Looks like a bong to me."

The doctor smiled. "If your mother becomes prone to giggling and excessive snacking, you perhaps should be concerned." He turned to the desk and gestured to the monitor where Jack's CT scans were displayed. "Now, let us take a look at things."

There it was, his head, split open like a melon crust stuffed with a cauliflower mass. Somewhere in that bisected gray matter, a small delta of synapses supposedly misfired neurons and became the impetus for the Rules, for his elaborate theories and principles—all the order and logic he had built up against the apparent lunacy of the Shrug.

Haizuki pointed at the top of the screen. "I am feeling very good about what this shows to us. The contra-coup injury we discussed—when the brain was bounced forward after the impact of the fall and abraded by the front of the skull—it's healing well. The contusion is showing no signs of scarring. Also, the post-traumatic brain swelling has responded well to the steroid and diuretic treatments. Since one or both of these conditions were responsible for agitating your seizures, you should not have to worry about that being a further problem. You are a lucky man."

"I guess I am."

Dr. Haizuki wagged a chubby finger at him. "And if you had held to your word and kept your appointment for the EEG, perhaps we would have discovered the temporal epilepsy sooner and you would not have gone through all that...unpleasantness." He smiled.

Jack glanced at Liz. She stood there, eyes to her shirt, picking at a small crusty stain. He looked back at Haizuki. "Sorry about that, Doc. But something tells me it wouldn't have made much difference to me at the time."

"And the medication?" the doctor asked. "Any side-effects from the Levetiracetam?"

"Not really. Some dizziness now and again. Sometimes I feel a little weak, but all that's been pretty rare."

"When was your last seizure?"

That word was repulsive—an ugly, foreign growth on his body. "Only once since I started taking the pills. Very minor. Lasted a few seconds."

Haizuki nodded and scribbled on his clipboard. "As normally they should be. These longer episodes you say you experienced were quite unusual. Perhaps they had a somnolent effect, causing a sleep cycle out of the seizure, but there is no way to be sure without monitoring an episode. It's of no regard, though. I am confident you will not experience them again."

"Glad to hear that," Jack said. "I just want to get this all behind me."

Haizuki set his clipboard down on the desk and leaned against it, hands braced on either side of the edge. "You had your last appointment with Dr. Illindale?"

"Yesterday afternoon."

"I hope you have found help with him."

"Sure. He's worried about me, though."

The doctor crossed his arms. "Is he?"

Jack nodded. "He doesn't seem to think it's going to be so easy for me to just pick up and get on with things." He looked down to his hands that fiddled with the zipper on his coat. "I'll be fine, though."

"Yes?" Haizuki's inflection bounced from certainty.

Jack looked back up and gave Dr. Haizuki a smile. "No worries."

The doctor kept his eyes on Jack for a silent moment before he reached out and turned the monitor dark with a flick of a switch. "Well, I of course can only speak with confidence on your physiological health, and of that I am very optimistic. But, I have to say, I am still amazed by your story, Mr. Cross. It is quite astounding."

Jack leaned back and huffed. "Because my brain was short-circuiting and I had some crazy idea that I could think everything away? Yeah. Astoundingly *insane* is the best way to say it." He snuck a look at Liz—still quiet, still squeezed in the corner, looking disinterested but indirectly focused.

Dr. Haizuki clasped his hands behind his back. "Oh, now. Not insane. But it was real to you. Yes. You faced a tremendous challenge, and overcame it."

"No I didn't. If not for the police, and for you, I wouldn't be here."

"You misunderstand me, Mr. Cross. I mean to say that you overcame this negative decision, this Shrug as you call it, despite the tremendous attraction you said it exerted upon you. You did it the only way you knew how, at your own expense, in the belief that you were saving everyone and everything."

Liz snorted from the corner. "Jack Cross, superhero."

The room was getting warm, and Jack couldn't sit still or find a comfortable place for his eyes. "You're making fun of me now."

"Not at all. Mr. Cross. Most of us go through our lives hoping that, before our time is done, we will have taken some significant action, a validation of life—to feel we have faced the test and made the right decision. In a most terrible and wonderful way, you were given that opportunity, and I think you passed. Dr. Illindale may worry for you, but I do not."

Jack saw the soft edges of sincerity rounding the doctor's smile and widening his eyes. He had no response to give other than to stand and face him squarely.

Haizuki put out his hand. "You are a remarkable person, Mr. Cross, and despite the insufferable infuriation you caused me, I am very glad to know you."

Jack stared at the offered hand and the doctor's smiling face for a long time before he finally, happily, shook it.

3

"You've been pretty quiet, you know," he said as they neared the end of the drive back to his place. Barely a word had been spoken. He'd had enough. He might piss her off, but he was going to find out what was wrong.

Her head turned to him, but eyes were locked in place on the road. "What are you talking about?"

He looked out the passenger window, watched the strip mall off the highway pass by. "I don't know. Seems like something's been bugging you."

"Don't try to read me, Jack. You suck at it."

"Hey, no big deal. You just haven't been saying a lot ever since...well, ever since I was in the hospital."

"Oh. Wow. Huh. You mean ever since my little brother tried to kill himself because he believed he could blow up the fricking world?"

"Not 'blow up' the world, just...undo it."

She flopped one hand up off the steering wheel and slapped it down on her thigh. "Oh, yeah. Sorry. Jesus, do you know just how fucked up that is?"

Jack ran a hand across the cracked and torn leather upholstery and nodded. "I think I have a pretty good idea."

Her loose hand snatched the steering wheel and she concentrated ahead of her. "All this shit has been happening. Dad. Mom. Len. You. It's like I've got my hands around the collar of somebody who's kicking my ass. Everything lately is making me feel like I've got to change, and *I don't want to*."

"Yeah. Things feel pretty different."

Her attention was back on the rear view mirror. "Forty isn't that far away, you know? Can you believe that?" She sighed. "Can't be eighteen forever, can I?"

He grinned. "Not for lack of trying. So, what are you telling me? You're going legit? Skirt and blouse and briefcase, home from the eight-to-five to husband and kids, soccer practices, and weekends at the cabin?"

She bared her teeth with a sneering smile. "Not one damn chance of that. But I think maybe I need to shake things up a bit."

"What do you have in mind?"

She turned the wheel left, through a yellow light, onto his road. "Frig wants to go to California."

"Really."

The Impala drifted to the curbside, lurched once from her heavy brake foot and fast kill of the engine. She faced him with blunt eyes that blinked once. "He wants me to join him."

It felt like bombshell news, but somehow didn't hit him that way.

"He wants to get in with a band that has a chance, in an area that will give him a chance. He knows a guy down there with connections."

"And you've known Frig how long now? A month?"

"Six weeks. But that's not the thing." She swiveled and threw a leg up and under her on the big seat. "Frig and I work out, we don't work out. Doesn't matter. But I'll be out of this craphole town, someplace where things are happening. Maybe I'll try paint-ing again. And hey, I'll be closer to Mom when she moves. I won't leave right now. In a couple of months, maybe."

Everyone was abandoning this ship in irons. Now he would be the only one left. And why should he be? He didn't have the fate of the world on his shoulders any more. He was just Jack—whoever that was.

Her fine-lined eyebrows rose. "Well? Aren't you going to say anything?"

He wanted to say many things. "Don't leave me alone here" and "Take me with you" were top on his list. But something else suddenly felt more right. He snatched his fedora from beside him on the seat, donned it, and whipped his body around to meet Liz's impatience. "Come with me to Dad's grave."

One year ago, there had already been snow on the ground. Not a clean, sparkling cotton cover, but a wet, gray sludge. Muddy ruts and yellowed grass showed through slushy gashes and splotches on the ground. Trees littered that mess with their remaining crum-pled leaves of dun. The Wisconsin northlands were boot scrapes on an old mat, and Jack had watched his father be lowered into the ground to the whine of the winch.

One year ago, he had shed no tears. The cold, late November wind had blown through him to rattle the sticks of winter foliage.

This was not that year. No snow has fallen. The grass still gri-maced with green. Jack Cross wept at his father's grave.

He stood, Liz in the background, and remembered what he couldn't, or wouldn't, remember until this moment. The sturdy security of his father's mass when, as a child, he would fall asleep against that firm round gut, his father's big hands moving in small circles on his back on the old recliner downstairs. He saw the hard-love look roosting above stern jowls when his father had pulled the hammer from Jack's small hand choking the handle too high and told him to lever his blows and let the head of the hammer do the work.

No overwhelming sadness or regret that heaved Jack's chest. His sobs were groping hands in a dark room, and now the bump against something solid, identifiable, and there was location. Orientation.

He startled from the arm that slipped stiffly around his shoulders. He looked down at the short, black fingernails and alabaster skin of Liz's hand dangling by his chin and he wiped his face with his coat sleeve.

She offered him a slanted grin. "Don't worry, little brother. Let 'er rip."

His father's gravestone. Squared-off granite with rough, chiseled edges—big but plain—block letters spelling out his name: Walter Lee Cross. No epitaph. He had always said he made his point in life. So he had. Jack gave it a good long look as he leaned into Liz and snuck an arm around her waist.

Liz gave a rough squeeze. "Good idea you had, boyo. Woulda never thought so, but good idea."

He studied her, not sure if she was being sarcastic. "Yeah?"

She seemed to think about it, then gave him a quick once-through nod. "Yeah. I think I needed this, too."

He questioned her dry and stolid composure. "How so?"

"Well, guess I needed to tell the old man off one last time. Get it out of my system. I've done that. Got in one last 'fuck you' and he couldn't say a damn thing back to me. Just had to lie there and take it. Now maybe one day I can miss him a little."

Jack sniffed loudly. His face felt stuffed and hot with snot. "That's…. that's real touching, Liz."

"Yeah, well, that's as good as it'll get, but better than it was. But the real reason why I'm glad we came—I…well, it's kinda cool. I got to be here for you, be your big sister. Never really been that, have I?"

He really wanted to tell her she had, but the time for lies were done. "You were what I needed at the time, Liz, but I think I'm ready for a big sister."

"What you needed at the time? I'm not so sure about that. Not after everything that's happened." She withdrew from him, head down, wrapping and unwrapping the string of her hooded sweatshirt around her finger. "Why didn't you ever tell me, Jack?"

"What?"

"Why didn't you ever talk to me about what you were going through?"

The way she stared made him take a small step back and remember that night he had gone over to play the game at her place after the accident; Liz without the armor of indifference. "Is that what's been bothering you?"

Her glossy eyes answered before she drew a protracted breath to speak. "I guess it has. I thought we were closer than that. I thought we shared everything with each other."

He couldn't figure it out. Was this a different Liz, or had he gotten her wrong all this time? "Liz...don't take it personal. I mean, I didn't tell *anyone*. How could I?"

"You told that Pauline about it, though, didn't you?"

He had mentioned Pauline to Liz after she had asked about the message delivered by the nurse. But he had never mentioned telling Pauline about the Shrug. "Yeah. I did."

Her nod had all the aspects of a sharp shake of the head. "That really sucks, Jack. You know, I've always said that friendship is defined by who you run to when the shit flies. Maybe I could have helped you. Maybe I could have just been an ear for you."

"Listen, I wanted to tell you, all right? But you wouldn't have believed me."

"No shit, Sherlock. But I still could have been there for you. It's just, it's really shitty that I was on the outside all this time and never knew it."

He moved closer and leaned down to stare up at her downcast eyes. "Hey. I'm sorry, okay? But you have to realize, it meant a lot to me that you didn't think any less of me. I didn't want to risk that. I didn't want you seeing me like some kind of basket case with crazy thoughts."

Her left eyebrow peeked as she tilted her head back up to him with a grin. "Stupid. Like I didn't think that already."

He smiled back, shaking his head. "Right. Are we okay, then?"

She nodded, grinned. "Buy me a six pack and everything'll be cool."

He chuckled. "So, did you tell Len about moving to California yet? This is going to kill him."

She scoffed. "You think so, huh? I told him. He's actually encouraging me to go. Offered to pack my bags."

"Really." Maybe Len was being facetious, or maybe he welcomed the opportunity to kick an addiction he hadn't been able to shake on his own. Either way, good for Len. "We'll still get together, though, huh? In the game?"

"Absolutely."

He liked that thought, this idea that despite all the change in this world, some reality existed that was still constant. He could still be Orson the Sorcerer, still know what needed to be done and what magic to use to do it.

"So what about you, Jack? What's the plan?"

He stepped forward and brushed away the leaves that gathered in front of their father's gravestone. "What could you possibly mean? I'm jobless, loveless. Almost everyone I know is packing up and moving on. Why should I be planning anything? My life's perfect."

Liz laughed a little, a wistful roll that struck Jack as a sad sound to hear in this place.

"Well, I know what I probably *should* do." He bobbed his head to their father's plot. "I know what he would want me to do. But that's not going to happen. Not yet, at least."

She frowned. "You're losing me."

"You ever hear of a walkabout?"

"Outback psychiatry, mate. 'Course I have."

He straightened his back and broadened his stance. "When I get back to the apartment, I'm packing up and heading out."

"What? Now? Where?"

"I'm going to find her, Liz." Had he known all along? The plan seemed sudden, yet so definite and clear.

"Her? You mean Pauline?"

It was worth it just for her expression. Jack wanted to remember that face forever. A small but completely satisfying turn of the tables. "Yeah." His confident smile felt really good.

Her scowl and curl of lip definitely gave the impression she didn't like the idea. "But you have no idea where to look. She could be anywhere. Jack, that's...crazy."

"Maybe. But somehow it feels like the first sane thing I've ever done. I have some ideas of where to start. And, if I don't look too hard, I just might find her."

Liz turned quiet, ponderous, exchanging glances between him and some point down and to the side of her. "I'd tell you to get your head examined, but that's fricking pointless. What about money? What about your apartment?"

"I'll deal with all that when I have to. But I have to do this, Liz."

"She sounds like a pretty weird chick, Jack. You sure she's worth it?"

"That's what I plan to find out."

"Wow." The hand she ran down her face seemed to wad up the uncertainty into her fist. "How long are you going to be gone?"

"As long as I need to be. As long as I can be."

She thrust her finger at his chest. "You keep in touch, here me? Buy a goddamn cell phone. Never understood why you don't have one."

"I will. You'll hear from me, don't worry."

"Mom is going to flip out about this, you know."

"I'll break it to her gently. Sorry to leave you holding the bag with her."

She waved an unconcerned hand. "Nah. It's all good. Mom and I are actually kind of bonding. You know, in that bitchy, whiny kind of way." A shiver scuttled down her body and she zipped up her sweatshirt, frowning at the gravestones around her. "Okay,

Jack. This whole cemetery thing is really starting to bum me out. Can we get out of here?"

He turned back to his father's gravestone, the mental shutter going off, brandishing the image. He wouldn't be back. He knew that. This wasn't the ground to drive a stake into and fetter himself. It was just the canvas for a season, somewhere for time to pass over. He straightened his fedora until it felt snug on his head.

The cold wind had stopped, leaving just the crisp chill under the gray day. The first snowflake fell on his cheek. Maybe it wasn't the first; maybe one had fallen somewhere else to land on another's chapped skin, but it was the first for him, and he felt a distinction in being able to declare it so, and keep it as his own.

Jack shrugged and said, "Yeah, I'm done here."

ACKNOWLEDGMENTS

An extensive amount of time was spent between 2004 and 2007 doing some of the most eclectic research of my life for this novel--philosophy, religion, physics, medicine, literature. Below is a listing of just a fraction of the sources I used.

But I would be leaving a huge hole in the exploratory background of this novel were I not to mention the amazing day spent at Fermilab touring their facilities and grounds. It was one of many singular moments as I worked on this novel.

During this time, I also spent countless hours sinking deeply into an online site called Nothingness Theory, dedicated to the idea of and concepts surrounding nothingness (referenced below). I found the material presented by Corey D. Kaup, the author of this theory, to be deeply engrossing and intriguing. It was this forum that pointed me in the direction of both Freud's work and Tillich's work. I am forever grateful to Corey for his thoughtful and thought-provoking work. I tried so hard to bring him and his and work directly into the novel, but instead his ideas and theories subtly permeate this entire novel in ways that I cannot adequately convey.

"Advances in the Treatment of Epilepsy", Benbadis, Selim R. M.D. and William O Tatum IV, D.O., University of South Florida College of Medicine, Tampa, Florida, aafp.org, July 1, 2001

Beyond the Pleasure Principle, the Standard Edition, Sigmund Freud, translated and edited by James Strachey, W. W. Norton & Company, Inc. 1961 (essay originally published in 1920)

The God Particle - If the Universe Is the Answer, What is the Question? Lederman, Leon M., with Dick Teresi, Houghton Mifflin Harcourt, 1993

Nothingness Theory, the connection between the evolution of the universe and human thought, Kaup, Corey D., www.nothingnesstheory.com, Kaup Communications – all rights reserved, 1989 – 2014

Surfacing, Atwood, Margaret, Copyright 1972, O. W. Toad, Ltd. First Anchor Books edition, 1998

Systematic Theology, Volume One, Reason and Revelation, Being and God, Tillich, Paul, The University of Chicago Press, 1951

"Traumatic Posterior Fossa Hematomas", Dirim, Berna Vidinli, with Nezahat Erdogan, Fazil Gelal and Engin Uluc, Turkish Society of Radiology, 2005

ABOUT JAMES L. PETERS

Has James Peters ever worked in the marketing department of a large furniture company? Has he ever roleplayed in online fantasy games? Was he indeed the youngest of five from a large family? And if he answered, "Yes," to any or all of these questions, then what else could possibly be true? How does this forever stretch and strain the seams of reality that try to hold the fabric of your sanity together for you? Just what might he be thinking at this very moment?

Quite possibly, he is acknowledging the blessings of a wonderful wife and family, boardgames with his great group of friends, and his fortune of being a lifelong citizen of Wisconsin in the U. S. of A.

Made in the USA
Monee, IL
21 September 2022

13450411R00166